PRAISE FOR
Buzz Off

"If you're wondering how beekeeping and mysteries go together, then pick up Hannah Reed's *Buzz Off* and see what all the excitement is about. Reed has come up with a great setting, rich characters, and such a genuine protagonist in Story Fischer that you'll be sorry the book is over when you turn the last page. Start reading and you won't want to put it down. Trust me, you'll be saying 'buzz off' to anybody who dares interrupt!" —Julie Hyzy, award-winning author of
Grace Under Pressure

"Action, adventure, a touch of romance, and a cast of delightful characters fill Hannah Reed's debut novel. *Buzz Off* is one honey of a tale."
—Lorna Barrett, *New York Times* bestselling
author of the Booktown Mysteries

"The death of a beekeeper makes for an absolute honey of a read in this engaging and well-written mystery. Story Fischer is a sharp and resilient amateur sleuth, and Hannah Reed sweeps us into her world with skillful and loving detail." —Cleo Coyle, national bestselling author of
the Coffeehouse Mysteries

"A sparkling debut . . . Delicious."
—*Genre Go Round Reviews*

"Will appeal to readers who like Joanne Fluke and other cozy writers for recipes, the small-town setting, and a sense of community." —*Library Journal*

"A rollicking good time. The colorful family members and townspeople provide plenty of relationship drama and entertainment. The mystery is well plotted and this series promises to keep readers buzzing."

—*Romantic Times* (4 stars)

"Everyone is simply going to go buzz-erk over the marvelously quirky cast of characters in this fabulously funny new series . . . Hannah Reed has a deliciously spicy, adorable sense of humor that had me howling with unabashed glee. You couldn't get as many colorful characters if you poured them from a box of Froot Loops. *Buzz Off* has just the right blend of mystery, romance, and humor that will charm anyone's socks off. If this fantastic whodunnit doesn't buzz to the top of your list, I'm simply gonna have to sic Grams on you . . . and she doesn't mess around. Quill says: If you are in need of a quirky, light, incredibly humorous cozy, look no more. Hannah Reed has whopped 'n chopped and stirred up a formula for a mystery that will line up an audience who will beg for more!"

—*Feathered Quill Book Reviews*

"In her debut book, *Buzz Off*, author Hannah Reed combines an intriguing whodunnit with a lively, action-filled story to create one sweet cozy mystery! . . . *Buzz Off* is a charming beginning of what promises to be a fun series! . . . A yummy treat for fans of cozy mysteries."　　　—*Fresh Fiction*

"Highly entertaining."　　　　　　—Associated Content

Berkley Prime Crime titles by Hannah Reed

BUZZ OFF
MIND YOUR OWN BEESWAX

Mind Your Own Beeswax

Hannah Reed

BERKLEY PRIME CRIME, NEW YORK

THE BERKLEY PUBLISHING GROUP
Published by the Penguin Group
Penguin Group (USA) Inc.
375 Hudson Street, New York, New York 10014, USA
Penguin Group (Canada), 90 Eglinton Avenue East, Suite 700, Toronto, Ontario M4P 2Y3, Canada
(a division of Pearson Penguin Canada Inc.)
Penguin Books Ltd., 80 Strand, London WC2R 0RL, England
Penguin Books Ireland, 25 St. Stephen's Green, Dublin 2, Ireland (a division of Penguin Books Ltd.)
Penguin Group (Australia), 250 Camberwell Road, Camberwell, Victoria 3124, Australia
(a division of Pearson Australia Group Pty. Ltd.)
Penguin Books India Pvt. Ltd., 11 Community Centre, Panchsheel Park, New Delhi—110 017, India
Penguin Group (NZ), 67 Apollo Drive, Rosedale, Auckland 0632, New Zealand
(a division of Pearson New Zealand Ltd.)
Penguin Books (South Africa) (Pty.) Ltd., 24 Sturdee Avenue, Rosebank, Johannesburg 2196,
South Africa

Penguin Books Ltd., Registered Offices: 80 Strand, London WC2R 0RL, England

This is a work of fiction. Names, characters, places, and incidents either are the product of the author's imagination or are used fictitiously, and any resemblance to actual persons, living or dead, business establishments, events, or locales is entirely coincidental. The publisher does not have any control over and does not assume any responsibility for author or third-party websites or their content.

PUBLISHER'S NOTE: The recipes contained in this book are to be followed exactly as written. The publisher is not responsible for your specific health or allergy needs that may require medical supervision. The publisher is not responsible for any adverse reactions to the recipes contained in this book.

MIND YOUR OWN BEESWAX

A Berkley Prime Crime Book / published by arrangement with the author

PRINTING HISTORY
Berkley Prime Crime mass-market edition / May 2011

Copyright © 2011 by Deb Baker.
Cover design by Judith Lagerman.
Cover illustration by Trish Cramblet.
Interior text design by Kristin del Rosario.

ISBN: 978-0-425-24159-2

BERKLEY® PRIME CRIME
Berkley Prime Crime Books are published by The Berkley Publishing Group,
a division of Penguin Group (USA) Inc.,
375 Hudson Street, New York, New York 10014.
BERKLEY® PRIME CRIME and the PRIME CRIME logo are trademarks of Penguin Group (USA) Inc.

PRINTED IN THE UNITED STATES OF AMERICA

10 9 8 7 6 5 4 3 2 1

Acknowledgments

Special thanks to:

- Friend and writer Anne Godden-Segard, who can always bring me out of writer's block with witty comments and clever concepts of her own.

- Shannon Jamieson Vazquez—I couldn't do it without her guidance.

- Martha Gatchel and Heidi Cox for their fabulous recipe contributions.

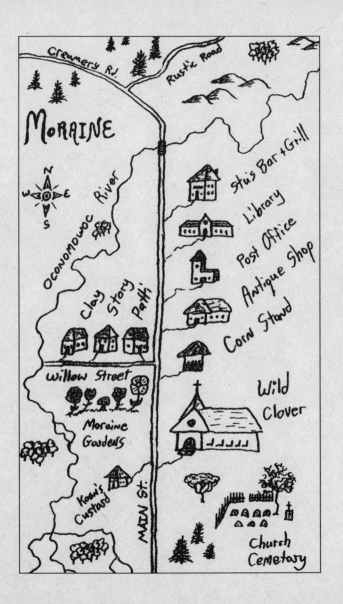

One

I missed the clues leading up to my honeybees' finely orchestrated plan to abandon me. They took off right before noon on a sunny May day, rising as one large buzzing ball with the queen in the center, where she would be protected by the entire honeybee community—workers, housekeepers, nurses, guards, and drones. Drones, that is, if all those females had even bothered taking any of the boys along.

In honeybee colonies, girls rule.

I took off in hot pursuit. Or as hot as I could wearing a pair of metallic-purple flip-flops. Not the greatest footwear for a chase, but the bees hadn't bothered to give me any advance warning.

The black circular mass of bees headed for the Oconomowoc River, then veered to the right before reaching its bank. Lucky for me, since I wouldn't have been able to follow if they'd crossed over to the other side of our small town of Moraine's spring rain–swollen river. Next they headed down a deer trail, taking the path of least resistance with me flopping along behind, trying to keep up. But it was useless. I couldn't help noticing that I was losing ground quickly, the distance between me and them widening by leaps and bounds. Or rather by trips and stumbles on my part.

The swarm flew toward a rustic wooden bridge that spanned the river, compliments of the state of Wisconsin's commitment to increasing and improving its hiking trails.

My escapees didn't take the bridge, but kept going due north.

Another sharp turn, like they knew exactly where they were going—which they most likely did thanks to bee scouts who would have been out searching for new digs while I was puttering among the hives, thinking everything was just swell, totally oblivious to this particular group's impending departure.

Honeybees swarm when they outgrow their communal homes, the same way we do when we start our families and realize at some point that we need more space. I was supposed to be able to read the signs of a colony getting ready to swarm, but I'm new at this game and learning everything the hard way. Which according to my mother was my standard mode of operation anyway.

I did know this much for sure:

- They would have left part of the colony behind, mostly the weaker ones.

- The renegade queen would have stopped laying eggs and would have slimmed down so she could make the flight.

- From the size of this swarm, I guessed that several thousand of them had absconded with whatever food sources they could carry in those handy little built-in pouches of theirs.

- Most of the boys would still be lounging around the old hive, since they were basically good for only one thing, and they tended to be more of a burden than they were worth.

- A newly hatched queen would be in the "wings" ready to take over for those left behind.

- She would be a virgin, but not for long. Then she would begin repopulating what was left of her colony.

My name is Story Fischer, christened Melissa at birth and called Missy until friends and family gave me my more colorful moniker based loosely on my ability to fabricate convincing tales. For the record, I never told outright blatant lies. They were more like enhanced embellishments. But I *had* walked a fine line between fact and fiction.

I like to think I've outgrown that trait.

At thirty-four years old, I'm trying more for dignified and classy, since I'm a recent divorcée with a ticking clock. But who's paying attention to age and time? I say to myself often, sometimes sarcastically, other times with more of a moan.

Thank God I was alone at the moment, because I lost my grasp on that dignified and classy thing. It was impossible to watch the rough ground I was running along *and* keep an eye on the honeybees in the air at the same time. I tripped over an obstacle, which turned out to be a fallen branch, and took a header, landing flat out, face-first, before raising up in what a yoga student would call the cobra pose. The swarm of bees crossed the Oconomowoc River. Then they vanished from sight.

Jeez!

From what I gathered after studying volumes of informational resources I collected and referenced often, my bees would find a place to hang out in foliage until worker bees prepared the perfect spot, most likely in the hollow of a tree. Before that happened, I had to find and corral them back to the beeyard, but this time into a larger, roomier home. They belonged in my backyard where I raised honeybees and bottled honey products with my own custom label, "Queen Bee Honey."

This swarm of honeybees didn't know it, but their chances of surviving in the wild without my help ranged from zero to none. Something bad would get them for sure—mites, diseases, predators, starvation, hosts of dangers awaited them if they didn't come to their senses. As usual, I had to do their major survival thinking for them. In return, they supplied all kinds of honey products and a decent profit. What a great partnership. Usually, anyway. When they behaved themselves.

I didn't have any more time to invest in my jailbreaking bees, though, because I was due back at my store, The Wild Clover. I had taken only a few minutes to walk the two blocks to my house to grab lunch when the traitorous flight occurred. Just my luck, the bees would have to cause trouble on Saturday, my busiest day. The Wild Clover happened to be the only grocery store in Moraine, Wisconsin, and a successful one at that. It specializes in local products and produce as well as more common staples that bring in regular customers. One-stop shopping was my ongoing goal.

My store's shelves were well stocked with Wisconsin-made brats and sausages, fresh-picked rhubarb, watercress, fiddlehead ferns, maple syrup, my honey products, coffees, wines, cheeses, and Danish kringles—Wisconsin's exclusive, wonderful pastries composed of flaky dough rolled out thin, filled with fruit and nuts, baked, and frosted. Delicious.

I got to my feet, wearing only one of the flip-flops, found the other, shuffled into it, and assessed the damage to my body and spirit. None really, if you didn't count being outsmarted by flying insects.

"You have dirt on the side of your face," my cousin and part-time helper Carrie Ann Retzlaff said when I walked in the door of The Wild Clover. "And stuff in your hair, like branches. That was some long lunch. What happened? You look like you've been rolling around in the hay."

She plucked a twig from my hair and gave me a smirky, knowing grin. Carrie Ann was referring to the recent hand-holding I'd been doing with Hunter Wallace. He'd been my boyfriend in high school, then not my boyfriend for lots of years. Now? Well, maybe again. As usual, I was in a major state of relationship confusion, a condition I'd displayed most of my dating/married/divorced life.

My cousin grinned. "Come on, share. What kept you so long and who sent you back looking like this?"

"Nothing happened," I said. "At least nothing worth talking about and certainly not anything hot and sexy." I hurried to the back storage room, which also served as my office and break room. There, I put myself back together before returning to the checkout counter to take over for Carrie Ann.

My cousin was thin as a honey stick, with spiky yellow hair and an equally thorny drinking problem that came and went at random intervals. Currently, it was gone. I could tell by her work attendance. She was actually showing up on time and doing her job without botching most of it. When dealing with an alcoholic employee who happens to also be a family member—and at times more a charity case than anything else—small steps that everybody else takes for granted are monster accomplishments.

Because of Carrie Ann's drinking, she'd lost her hus-band, Gunnar, and her two children. But recently Gunnar had noticed her progress and her continued improvement, and he was letting her see the kids every other Sunday as long as she was sober and supervised. We were all keeping our fingers crossed that this time she would make it the whole nine yards for one last, game-winning touchdown.

By *we* I meant pretty much everybody in town, since our community was too small not to notice things like my cousin's ongoing battle with booze. But my immediate family was especially watchful. That included my sister, Holly, who owned half of The Wild Clover thanks to a financial bailout during my divorce, my grandmother— aka Grams—and me. My mother, who couldn't charm a starving dog with a meaty bone, doesn't believe people can change for the better. Worse, yes. Better, no way. Her philosophy shows in the wrinkles in her forehead and the sour expression on her face. The lines around Mom's mouth are permanently turned down. Holly says that only happened after our father had a massive heart attack five years ago and died before the paramedics arrived. I say they've always been there.

My sister tends to border on delusionally optimistic.

"Holly called in." Carrie Ann thought to tell me this after I'd already looked down several aisles without finding my sister. "She'll be late again."

Figures. Working shifts with Holly was always dicey. But I still had the twins, Brent and Trent, who took as many hours at the store as their college classes allowed. I could see Trent stocking a new shipment of Wisconsin artisan cheeses at the far end of aisle three and Brent was helping a customer select a Door County wine.

I used my cell phone to call Holly. No answer.

"I was hoping you could stay," I said to Carrie Ann, thinking of the honeybees I'd lost and how I had to reclaim them before their collective brain signaled a move to parts unknown. They tended to operate like robots taking commands from some cloaked mother ship we mere humans couldn't see.

"Sorry," my cousin said, slinging a purse over her shoulder, a sure sign she was leaving no matter what I said or how hard I begged. "I have a meeting."

Which is what she said every time she wanted to get out of additional work or responsibility. That woman had more AA meetings than breaks during her short shifts at The Wild Clover, and that was saying a lot.

"Okay," I said, resigned, since anything that kept my cousin focused on sobriety had to come first. "See you tomorrow. Or is tomorrow one of your Sundays with the kids?" I hadn't checked the schedule, which I should stay more on top of. Holly took care of that bothersome chore, but since all real responsibility fell to me I needed to have my fingers on the store's pulse more than anybody else.

"No, this isn't my weekend to see them," Carrie Ann said. "I wish Gunnar would loosen up a bit more."

"He's coming around," I said. "A few months ago, he wouldn't let you see them at all."

Carrie Ann looked forlorn at the moment, but she was a survivor and never let anything get her down for long.

After she left, I looked around the store and sighed with contentment.

The building had been an abandoned church with a "For Sale" sign out front for the longest time. Until I had the idea for a market, bought the building, and gutted the interior, leaving the fine maple floors and stained-glass windows, front, rear, and overhead. After a coat of fresh paint and installing shelving units, coolers, and carefully selected stock, the store opened.

The great thing about working at The Wild Clover on a daily basis was the interesting and diverse relationships I developed with my customers. They took an active interest in me and my life, and I reciprocated. It felt good to know so many people cared.

The bad thing about being a permanent fixture at the store was that, along with the good people—most of them fit into that category—came the few that I wouldn't tolerate if given a choice. Unfortunately, personal selection wasn't an option as a business owner.

I'd known many of my customers my whole life, and it made me feel like I was part of a huge family. Like my dentist, T. J. Schmidt, and his wife, Ali, who came in for groceries.

T. J. Schmidt had it made, according to the pecking rules of our small town. He had been a local kid at a time when Moraine wasn't much to look at, then he had gone off to college, which wasn't a big deal since most of us did. But he'd continued to take advanced studies and actually brought a wallful of certificates back home to put his new skills into practice. Most others who had followed professional paths hadn't returned, probably thinking they'd be wasting their talents in such a small place.

T. J. was a local boy in his heart and he'd be one until he went to his grave.

Of course, most of his incentive to come back had to do with his wife, since they'd been an item throughout high school and beyond, and Ali liked small-town living just as much as he did.

"Did you remember you have an appointment Monday?" T. J. reminded me. He had one of those pudgy ageless faces, with the coloring and complexion of a newborn.

I nodded. "And I bet you'll come find me if I happen to mentally block that painful fact out of my mind."

T. J. laughed because what I said was so true. Nobody got out of cleanings, fillings, and root canals while he was around. "I'll be gentle," he said. "You won't feel a thing. I promise." And with that big fib, he headed down aisle four where I could see him chatting up customers.

"We just stocked fresh rhubarb," I said to Ali, knowing she loved the stuff. And off she went.

The other side of the coin—the bad part of such a public life, far removed from any warm and fuzzy family feeling—the forced-to-tolerate, dark side came strutting in shortly afterward. She was a daily shopper. Wouldn't you know it? That type always is.

"I'm having a horrible time selling your ex-husband's house," Lori Spandle said, wearing a certain look of wide-eyed self-interest that screamed *Insincere Salesperson*. Or maybe I thought that because I knew her phony-baloney side only too well.

"That's too bad," I said with matching concern.

"Nobody wants to live next to a head case."

"Thanks, Lori," I said. My ex's house was next door to mine. "I appreciate the term of endearment. Your kindness knows no bounds."

Lori Spandle, besides being our only real estate agent, had slept with my husband. Not that I should have cared, since we had been separated at the time and no way was I going back to *that* jerk. But Lori was married to the town chairman and shouldn't have been messing around at all. That particular fidelity rule was number one in my personal book of marriage code, conduct my husband hadn't bothered upholding through our entire marriage—something I only found out much later.

Lori was also a year younger than me and had been after every guy I'd ever dated or even considered dating since middle school. With those big boobs, she'd had her share of successes, too.

"You have all kinds of other places to keep those bees," Lori said. "They don't have to be in your backyard where the entire town has to endure the menaces. They're ruining my business."

I couldn't stop the wide grin I felt crossing my face. Wasn't that a shame? "Patti Dwyre doesn't seem to mind my bees," I said, "and she lives right next door to me, too. Neither does Aurora at Moraine Gardens across the street."

"Aurora lives in some kind of alternate reality. She doesn't count."

"Are you here to shop or did you stop by just to complain?"

"Just wanted you to know what kind of problems you're causing for property values in this town." With that she flounced down aisle one to squeeze fruit and eat grapes.

What Lori said was true about me having other options for my beeyard. Grams owned a lot of country acreage, and not too long ago when the town was debating banning my bees, I hid them there for safekeeping. After that issue blew over and my honey business expanded, I moved the hives back into my backyard where I could keep a better eye on them.

Besides, one thing people don't realize is that honey-bees do as well and sometimes better in towns and cities where they have more diverse nectar sources and longer flowering seasons. Especially with Moraine Gardens right across the street from where I lived. All those wonderful native species blooming throughout the season. That was like bee heaven.

For the next half hour I worked the register without even a pause. After that, I had a breather—time to look around The Wild Clover with my usual pride and joy. Sales had been climbing steadily ever since day one, thanks to word of mouth, loyal customers, and my honeybee side business, which most visitors and residents really appreci-ated. Plus, I constantly worked on coming up with new, innovative ideas.

Like the beeswax candle-making class coming up at three o'clock this afternoon in the basement of The Wild Clover, where former church members had at one time congregated for fellowship. I was thrilled to bring my ver-sion of fellowship back to the space.

Weekends in Moraine are busy as long as the weather holds, which is always a new adventure in southern Wis-consin where I live. Today was bright and sunny, although the air was still a little crisp. Our unincorporated town boasted a cozy library, a frozen-custard shop, Stu's Bar and Grill, an antique store, Moraine Gardens, and The Wild Clover, home to Wisconsin-made goodies. The town also sat along a rustic road where tourists could take in some pretty spectacular landscapes—quaint towns, rolling hills, and a boatload of lakes and rivers. Some of our visitors discovered they could put their kayaks in the Oconomowoc River at the dead end by my house and paddle up and down the river. The scenery was all woods, ridges, and marshes.

With monthly library events and weekly arts and crafts at my store, word had gotten around that Moraine was worth the stop. I had almost a full class of eighteen students for the candle-making class. Only two spots left. Yes, today's event promised to be a killer.

A killer event, is what I'd been telling customers all week. Looking back, I really wish I hadn't called it that.

TWO

Ten minutes before the candle-making class was scheduled to begin, Holly still hadn't arrived, which had me grinding my teeth, chewing my nails, and considering ripping out every hair on my head. Or on hers, if I could get a firm grip on it once I tracked her down. I worked hard to have a full staff every Saturday. That meant at least two—better yet three—of us at all times. But today was one of those out-of-control staffing situations that come up constantly for those of us in the service industry. The twins, after witnessing the tense condition I was in, felt badly that they couldn't help me out, but they had a wedding to attend, which was a perfectly good reason not to stay. Even in my desperation, I could see that.

As I was punching keys on my cell phone, trying to contact Holly for the hundredth time—not much of an exaggeration—my sister strolled in the door. I reined in my impulse to attack her with a Momlike tongue-lashing. Genetics, I'm discovering, are hard to overcome.

Holly managed to agitate me more than the twins, who rarely bugged me, or even Carrie Ann, who brought on some serious cases of frustration. Mainly Holly drove me nuts because she was supposed to be my partner, and partly because she was family, which I figured gave me carte blanche in the major annoyance department.

Holly was three years younger than me, making her thirty-one. She had married into big money when she said *I do* to Max Paine. The upside of marrying rich was all the disposable cash she had access to, and her seemingly unlimited generosity in loaning me what I needed to buy out my ex-husband's share of the store and to obtain all the honey-making equipment and supplies to go into the bee business. The downside was that since Max happened to be on the road most of the time making all that dough, Holly chose (okay, maybe it was mostly Mom's idea) to entertain herself by getting involved in the actual everyday workings of The Wild Clover. That loan I'd so gratefully accepted wasn't without permanently attached strings, as I found out too late.

Although if I wanted to be honest, I would have taken the offered loan anyway, but with my eyes wide open, not blindsided.

Regarding her involvement in Queen Bee Honey: Holly was afraid of honeybees and would rather be stomped to death by wild horses than walk into the apiary, where the only risk I could see was a bee sting here and there. Big deal. And she wasn't even allergic! Her bee phobia was a problem I decided to help her get over by engaging her in bee activities every chance I got. And if she never got over it, at least there was the revenge factor for letting Mom talk her into getting involved where she shouldn't.

Besides, anyone who can afford to drive a Jag needs a reality check every once in a while.

"About time," I said when she strolled up to the cash register finally ready to make a condensed contribution of time and effort. I heard a little witchiness in my voice as several candle-making students walked by and descended into the workshop where I'd already set up the supplies we'd need. "Why didn't you answer your cell? I've been calling for hours."

"Dead battery," she said, holding up her cell phone, showing me the black screen.

I glared.

"Didn't you get the MSG?" Holly asked.

Now, for most of us *MSG* would be an Asian food additive, a different kind of salt than the ordinary table variety. In Holly's world where text-speak threatened to take over her vocabulary, it meant something entirely different. *MSG* equaled message. So what she really meant to say was "Didn't you get the message?"

"Carrie Ann said you'd be late," I answered, still really mad. "That's not the point."

"SS (*So Sorry*)," Holly said, dripping with sarcasm, as if I was the one with the problem, as if she hadn't done anything wrong, as if—

I took a deep breath.

I was flustered, a condition brought on easily by most of my family members, excluding Grams, the only one in my family who never had a single mean-spirited thought or word for anybody.

In my haste to start the class on time, I almost lost my footing while hustling down the stairs, causing me to arrive at the bottom with a little too much noisy flair. A real attention-getter when I would have preferred a graceful entrance. A moment of silence ensued as everyone in the room turned and stared. Then I took another calming breath and propelled myself into the midst of a roomful of eager candle-making dippers.

The scoop on beeswax, as I explained to my students, was:

• Beeswax is secreted by honeybees from a gland in their abdomen.

- They use it to make the structural walls of honeycombs, those tiny six-sided cells.

- Honeycomb cells are where the young bees are raised and where honey and pollen are stored.

- A bee must fly 150,000 miles to produce one pound of wax.

- Beeswax is used to make so many things, including soaps, candles, cosmetics, dental wax, a coating for cheeses, and to waterproof leather and wood.

- Beeswax never goes bad, which explains why it has been found throughout history as far back as the days of the pharaohs' tombs.

I had already prepared the beeswax by rendering it—cleaning and draining—and had melted it in slow cookers borrowed from friendly customers, since the church didn't have its own kitchen facility. There were all sizes and shapes of beeswax candles, but for this event I'd decided on tapered candles, those elegant ones we used for special occasions.

We were all set to go.

The great thing about candle making is that it attracts all kinds of people—young, old, male, female. Most of the people at the table were locals, and the others were folks who came my way often enough for me to learn their names and remember their faces.

Stu Trembly, the owner of Stu's Bar and Grill, sat at the end of the table next to his girlfriend, Becky, the expression on his face showing that this wasn't his idea of how to spend a Saturday afternoon, but he was going along and making the best of it. What a guy!

Stanley Peck, sixtyish, good friend, amateur beekeeper, and a widower before his time, sat to the right of Stu and Becky. Stanley had a noticeable limp when he walked, ever since the time he shot himself in the foot while squaring off with temporary field workers who had been tending to his farm. Stanley had lost that round without any of the workers making a single move.

I always hoped he wasn't armed when he visited the store, but I'm pretty sure that was wishful thinking. Stanley had a bit of a temper—displayed only once or twice in my presence—and add to it a concealed, loaded, illegal weapon? Not a good combo.

Next to Stanley sat Milly Hopticourt, The Wild Clover's official newsletter editor and recipe tester. Then there were the weekend shoppers who had signed up earlier today. Finally, unfortunately, there were several kids in the mix.

I say unfortunately, because these kids were Kerrigans and had reputations for their unruliness and lack of anything remotely hinting of discipline or constraint. The Kerrigans had lived in Moraine even longer than my family, and they procreated as though they were trying to repopulate the world after an apocalypse wiped out most of humanity. Many of the kids in the room were Gus's grandchildren. Gus was close to my mom's age, had a total of eight children and his was only one small branch of the Kerrigan clan. Plus all Gus's kids stayed close by, having families of their own. Kerrigans were everywhere. Even though the business owners cringed every time Kerrigans brought their kids to town and had been reacting with that same dread throughout the generations, the children usually grew up to be honest, loyal, and hardworking members of the community.

At least most of them did. Like any big family, there were bound to be a few exceptions.

Ten minutes into my spiel, the kids were getting antsy and leaning over the pots of melting wax whenever they weren't handling every single item on the table. Then two more adults came down the steps, about to fill those last two empty spots at the table and make me the winner of a bet I had going with Carrie Ann that every last seat would be taken.

I immediately recognized one of the latecomers as Rita Kerrigan, Gus's sister-in-law. Rita hadn't aged nearly as well as my own mother even though they were around the same age. She carried a lot of extra weight and it had worked a number on her knees. Just getting down the steps seemed like a major effort for her.

The other woman, who came downstairs right behind Rita, was twig-thin and a stranger to me. She seemed nervous and shy, carefully avoiding meeting my gaze. The last thing I wanted to do was single her out by asking her to introduce herself, since she was obviously uncomfortable. Instead, I smiled warmly and welcomed both of them.

"Let's get started with the actual process," I said, after summarizing what we would do in the next hour. How we would dip our wicks (that got a snicker from Stu's end of the table) into melted wax to begin to create tapered candles, then let them cool a little before dipping again. Each dip into the melted beeswax would add another thin layer of wax to the wick, until slowly but surely candlesticks would form.

The fun began. Or continued, as in the case of the kids, who dripped melted wax everywhere on the table (smart me, I'd put down layers and layers of newspapers) and on the chairs. That was going to be a mess!

The naturally sweet fragrance of honey filled the room.

The woman who joined the group late wasn't doing much other than nervously wrapping her wick around her fingers, so I went over to help her. Although dipping candles was hardly rocket science. Even the youngest kid was into the groove.

"Like this," I said, taking the wick and making the first dip for her, then handing it back. A few drops of wax fell on the newspaper-lined table. "Hold it in the air for a few seconds before dipping it again. Let it cool slightly."

Then I noticed, since I was up closer than before, she was wearing a cheap brown wig that didn't fit quite right, as if it were at least one or two sizes too big. She was older than me, or so I thought, and her wrists were excessively thin, the skin on her hands transparent, with protruding blue veins. When I handed the wick back, her fingers were ice cold to the touch.

And I thought she smelled like death, even over the sweet fragrant honey coming from the melted beeswax. Don't ask me why that idea popped into my mind, because I didn't know what death smelled like, or even that it had a smell. But if it did, this woman emitted it. Not powerful or over-whelming, more subtle and impossible to put into words.

I took a step back and saw Rita Kerrigan glance over, as though she was assessing the woman. When they had come downstairs, I thought they were together; but neither had spoken to the other, so I figured my first impression had been wrong.

Then I got busy with others in the class, enjoying the excitement on my students' faces as the candles they were dipping began to form. Afterward, we strung our creations to dry from a long dowel I'd hung especially for this event.

The emaciated stranger disappeared at some point, leaving behind the candle she'd made.

Something about her seemed vaguely familiar, so when the others left with their candles, I checked the class sign-up sheet lying near the checkout counter. The last two places were still blank. Rita Kerrigan and the unidentified woman hadn't registered.

"Why should they have registered, coming in at the last minute?" Holly said a little snappily when I questioned her. "I was checking out Ali Schmidt's cart full of items; she came back because she ran out of sugar, and they whizzed right by us. GMAB (*Give Me A Break*), will you!"

"Well, did they pay?"

"Um, no. I forgot." Holly didn't have enough respect for

the good old dollar bill most of us worked hard for. But knowing Rita, she'd remember later and pay up. The other student . . . well . . . that one was lost.

"Did they arrive together?" I pressed on.

"How should I know?"

"What's going on with you?" I said. "First you show up hours late for work, then you're crabby and defensive. What happened to my perky, positive sister?"

Holly leaned against the counter. "Max and I had a fight on the phone last night. I'm staying with Mom and Grams."

That explained her bad mood. She had two perfect excuses for being cranky. She'd actually argued with her husband, as amazing as that was since those two always acted like honeymooners. Worse, she'd been overexposed to Mom. Our mother was a lot like the sun—fine in small doses, but stick around too long and you'll get a bad burn.

Mom and Grams live together. Mom moved in with my grandmother when my ex-husband and I agreed to purchase our old family home after my dad died. My ex wasn't my ex then, of course, but the yellow warning light in my brain began flashing at me shortly after we made the move from Milwaukee and he started flirting (and more) with every female in town.

I stopped to think about Holly and Max. Had they ever had an argument before? Not that I was aware of, which always made me wonder about them. Who doesn't argue once in a while?

"What was the fight about?"

"Lots of things."

I studied my sister, noting that she had gained a few pounds. We both had the same build—voluptuous according to Holly, bordering on chunky in my opinion. Holly and I watched every little thing we ate or our hips expanded exponentially. "What's the biggest issue?"

"He's out of town again." Holly did a dramatic eye roll. "What else is new? That's the whole point, he's always gone."

"But if he isn't even home, why are you staying with Mom? Personally, I'd rather walk in front of a speeding train or throw myself into shark-infested water."

Our mother was a demanding control freak who didn't particularly approve of or like me and showed it in not-so-subtle zingers, shots across my bow, which I tried to deflect without firing back. Most of the time, my subterfuge worked.

"IDK (*I Don't Know*)," Holly said to my incredulous question about why she would voluntarily stay with Mom. "I'm sick and tired of being all alone in that great big house, I guess." Holly rubbed her temple. "I still have a few things to do in back."

"I'll close up."

As soon as Holly disappeared, right when I was flipping the closed sign, I saw Grams's Cadillac Fleetwood edge over to the side of the street. The front tire jumped the curb before bouncing back down and settling.

"Speak of the devil," I muttered before opening the door.

Mom got out of the passenger seat and was already griping. "For cripes' sake," she said to Grams. "If you'd let me drive, we wouldn't be running up on sidewalks. You're going to kill somebody one of these days. Wait until your next driver's license renewal. You're never going to pass."

"Hi, sweetie," Grams called when she crawled out of the driver's seat and saw me. "Closing up for the night?" My eighty-year-old grandmother looked dainty, with her trademark daisy in her tight gray bun and a pocket-size camera hanging from her wrist.

"That's the plan," I said. Mom marched past me into the store. I thought about running away, but decided against it. Even when she looked me up and down with her standard sour expression, and I knew what was coming next, I still didn't flinch—at least not outwardly—or change my mind about bolting.

"That's your business attire?" Mom asked. We'd been

down this road before, but apparently she liked the view because we went in that direction often.

"I like how she looks," Grams said. "Snappy."

With that, she took my picture.

"Tomboy jeans, thongs on her feet . . ." Mom couldn't get used to the idea that the definition of *thong* had changed over the years and no longer meant flip-flops. "Disgracefully casual."

I rolled my eyes. I'm pretty sure my grandmother captured it on film.

"Business is going to suffer because of it. Mark my words," Mom crabbed. Like it was any skin off her nose. "And you shouldn't close at five o'clock. That's much too early."

Another road well traveled. I pointed out the same old landmarks again. "We'll stay open longer hours after Memorial Day. Like we always do. Customers know our hours. They don't mind. And business doesn't warrant staying open late on Saturday nights. Case closed."

Like that was going to happen.

"We're going to Larry's Custard Shop for frozen custard," Grams said.

Mom frowned. "Your grandmother intends to eat her dessert before her meal."

Grams grinned. "When you get to my age, you can eat in any order you feel like. Want to come?"

"Thanks, but no. I have a few things to do here yet." Which wasn't true. "You two have fun."

Grams smiled like she really would have fun. How she could stay positive inside Mom's major bubble of pessimism was beyond me.

After they left, Holly came out of the back room.

"We need to work on your outlook," I said. "You better come to my house. Stay with me for a few days."

"Really? Really?" Holly squealed and actually jumped up and down. "GTG (*Got To Go*) get my stuff."

"You need to get over to my place as soon as possible. Hurry." That just slipped out as she ran out the door. Good thing she hadn't been really listening or I would have had to explain the remark and she might have made a U-turn and run for the hills instead.

Because whether she liked it or not, we had a swarm of bees to recover.

Three

"Absolutely no way," Holly said when I told her the plan of attack regarding the capture of my swarming bees. "Buzz off."

We were near the back entrance to my house. I blocked the door so she couldn't get inside and plant herself where I couldn't get her moving again. She'd have to wrestle me to the ground to get in, though she would beat me for sure in hand-to-hand combat. I'd seen her perform some kind of impressive drop-and-hold maneuver on a shoplifter not too long ago. Holly knew the moves, but I counted on my sister to show a little restraint when it came to family members, especially her one and only sibling.

I held a flashlight in case she made any aggressive moves. Not that I planned to actually hit her with it. Just threaten to if she came at me. The flashlight wasn't purely a prop though, more a necessity for beaming in on renegade bees than a defensive weapon.

My backyard, where we were at a standoff, was much

longer than it was wide, with a neighbor on one side and an empty house waiting for a buyer on the other. My ex had lived there until last fall when he finally moved away. Thank God for small miracles. According to Mom, the only upside to our marriage-gone-bad was that we hadn't had children together. I agreed. Because that meant I never, ever (did I say never?) had to see his cheating face again or live through any more humiliating incidents in which he tried to sweet-talk someone from my hometown into bed. How humiliating was that?

I'd been trying to counter residual bitterness with a new positive attitude about life. At the moment, my sister wasn't helping me get to that happy place.

"I can't believe my eyes," Holly said when her gaze fell on the neatly stacked yellow hive boxes out back. "How many beehives do you have now, anyway?"

"Ten or twelve," I lied.

Actually, forty beehives stood between the house and access to the Oconomowoc River, which wound along the back of my property. The rest of my hives numbered another forty or so and were scattered along open farm fields and fruit orchards where local farmers rented hives filled with honeybees from me to pollinate their crops.

Holly was backing away with a wild look in her eyes, not a good sign.

"You don't have to do much at all," I reasoned with her. "Just hold this flashlight when we find them, so I can see what I'm doing if it gets too dark. Which I could remind you wouldn't have been a problem if you hadn't taken so long getting here."

I didn't want to mention that fog was rolling in from the west, creeping up from the low-lying river in swirls like it had become a living and breathing thing. Light wind lifted a few strands of my hair. I pulled my hoodie tighter, noting that the temperature had begun to drop quickly as the sun headed west.

"I'll come with," said a familiar voice out of the cedars separating my property from my neighbor, P. P. Patti Dwyre.

P. P. stood for "Pity-Party," since Patti whined about her life nonstop, weaving her personal misery through the rumors and innuendos she spread like peanut butter about town. I'm sure she knew what we called her behind her back, but that didn't encourage Patti to change her ways.

"I'll come with you," P. P. Patti said again, plowing through the privacy hedge, proving the term *privacy* held little weight in her small world of gossip gathering. "Even though you never help me with anything."

Patti wore binoculars around her neck, a ball cap on her head, and a canvas vest with multiple pockets. She was all ready to start out, which made me suspicious that she'd been listening in to the entire conversation.

"That isn't true," I said. "I helped you set a raccoon trap just last week, didn't I?"

"All I got in it was a skunk and I didn't see you rushing over to help with that! Nobody does, and I'm the most volunteering person in the whole community."

Mainly to feed your gossip addiction, I could have said. "I appreciate your offer to help find my bees," I said instead, throwing a hard look at my sister, who thought she would escape her bee-catching destiny because Patti had stepped up and volunteered. *Ha!* "And three of us will make it even easier," I continued. "Getting the swarm back to the beeyard isn't going to be the hard part. They'll come along as docile as a flock of newborn ducklings following mommy duck."

My sister snorted.

"It's true," I said. "They don't have a hive to defend, which is the only reason they would attack in the first place, and they won't leave their queen, who has to be protected in the middle of the entire clump, so we're safe. The hardest part will be finding them."

"Did you see which way they went?" Patti asked.

I pointed northwest.

"Oh no," Patti said. "Not there."

Just then, we heard a gunshot coming from the general vicinity where I had, only seconds ago, pointed. We had a moment of silence.

Holly was the first to speak. "Is it turkey-hunting season?"

"I don't know," I said. "How does anybody figure it out? Keeping up with all the different hunting seasons is impossible. There's some kind of lottery system involved and different hunting dates depending on the draws. That's all I know."

"It sounded really close," Holly said.

"Turkey season is over," Patti said. "And sound travels. It could have been miles away."

None of us felt too worried.

Hunting was a way of life for many of the residents of Moraine. People didn't hunt within the business and residential districts, but with all the forests and fields surrounding town, hearing a gun go off wasn't any big deal. If we had been in Milwaukee, which was less than forty miles away (and where I had gone to college and started up in my bad marriage), we'd have already been on the ground, crawling for cover. Here, it was part of the daily routine of small-town life.

"We'll be perfectly fine going into the woods," I said. "Rifles aren't allowed around here, only shotguns and they don't have the power and range that rifles do. It isn't like bullets are going to come zinging at us just because we heard a shot."

"Listen to you," Holly said. "Suddenly a weapons expert."

That little tidbit on firearms came courtesy of Hunter Wallace, my maybe boyfriend, who happened to be a cop and therefore up to speed on all that shooting stuff. Some of it, a tiny amount, had rubbed off on me. He'd even taken me target practicing at the police range and said I wasn't too bad, at least when I remembered not to accidentally point my weapon at other people.

Another shot resounded.

I checked the time on my cell phone. Seven. We had at least an hour before dark.

"Did you know sound doesn't travel in outer space?" Patti said.

Holly and I looked at Patti, not sure whether to believe her or not. Like it mattered at the moment.

"We'll need protection if we're going in where I think we are," my neighbor stated. "Flashlights, pepper spray, anybody have a weapon?"

Patti wasn't concerned about the blasts we'd heard, but about something much creepier and more otherworldly than a shot in the distance.

"SC (*Stay Cool*)," Holly said to Patti, moving closer. Holly always was a sucker for drama. She knew exactly where Patti's concern came from, and I could tell she was very close to getting totally involved in our caper. "He never hurt anybody."

"That we know of," Patti said ominously, before throwing in a whine. "I have enough problems with my health conditions and trying to make ends meet in this economy. I can feel my blood pressure going up right this minute and that isn't good—not good at all."

"You're both overreacting," I said. "Lantern Man, if he really exists, is totally harmless." But I felt the hairs on my arms stand at attention. "And to make something perfectly clear," I continued for Patti's benefit, "I didn't start that particular story."

I sounded defensive even to myself, but I'd been accused more than once of being the Lantern Man fiction author, and so I set the record straight every chance I got.

The three of us were talking about strange sightings along a secret tract of land. Nobody other than locals knew the land existed. It consisted of a mix of woods and fields and ran between a state trail on one side and private landowners on the other. We called it The Lost Mile because it had been overlooked when a survey was prepared to divide up surrounding land, an oversight that wasn't that unusual when working with large parcels of farmland. The mistake happened so many years ago nobody could remember when it was finally discovered and nothing had been done to remedy the situation.

The Lost Mile was the equivalent of a city block—a little under a full-mile long—and had been logged at one time. An overgrown road cut right down the middle of it and a young forest of pines and maples flourished on its sides. The Lost Mile also had a history. It had generated some wild stories, mostly because of the teenage parties held along its paths. Hippies squatted there in the sixties and some of the old-timers claim someone had been killed in there when a motorcycle gang discovered it. Although none of them could recall the circumstances or who the victim had been.

Then, sometime during my senior year in high school, Lantern Man arrived. He'd been seen or, rather, his lantern light had been seen, by enough witnesses to make the rest of us sit up and pay attention.

And scary, weird stuff began to happen.

Nobody would think of going in there after dark.

"I've changed my mind about helping you," Patti said abruptly. "I have better things to do than get caught in dark and fog in The Lost Mile. I'm staying home where it's warm and dry."

With that, she disappeared through the cedar hedge.

"Okay then," I said, turning to my sister. "You're the only one still standing."

"I'm not afraid of The Lost Mile, if that's what you think."

We both knew what terrified Holly more than anything: bees. "I can't do this alone," I said. "You have to help."

Which was totally true. If I had even the slimmest chance of getting them back tonight, I needed a partner. And Holly was it.

"Look at the fog," she pointed out. "Patti's right."

"We'll only look for a little while. Besides, I've been thinking about them and I'm pretty sure I know where they went and it isn't anywhere near The Lost Mile. This will be a piece of cake."

Which was a total lie on more than one count, but I needed her help, and she wasn't enlisting on her own.

Holly didn't say yes, but she didn't say no either, and she wasn't backing up to make a run for it. Her lip popped out in the pout she gave when she was about to go along with something she really didn't want to. I could read my sister like the back cover of a children's storybook.

We slipped past the beeyard, walking lightly over the field mix of dandelions and grass that carpeted my backyard. I kept it natural and chemical-free to benefit the honeybees, another sore topic between Mom and me. Holly hugged the hedge line as far from the hives as possible and disappeared behind my honey house, still heading in the right direction.

I loved my honey house, which I had moved from my beekeeping mentor's apiary after he died. I painted it yellow with white trim to match my house. The honey house was the size and shape of an oversized garden shed and contained all the gear and equipment I needed to harvest and process honey from my hives. I could smell its sweetness floating on the damp air.

Holly reappeared on the other side and we fell in step, turning to the right at the Oconomowoc River's bank. Fog rolled thicker now, lying in the low areas, but we would head uphill in a few minutes and visibility would improve.

With a good hour before dark, we had plenty of time to find my bees. They might be able to outrun me on a short sprint, but that heavy blob wouldn't have made any real mileage before settling in a tree for the night.

As we turned onto the same deer trail my bees had followed earlier, I heard crashing behind us. A beam of light swung wildly from side to side. Not a sharp, crisp funnel of light, more blurred and diffused by the haze.

"Lantern Man!" Holly practically screamed, which wasn't a brilliant move if we'd really stumbled across some kind of ghost or creepy creature from another dimension. Not that I believed in those things, but still . . .

"The Lost Mile is still ahead of us," I said. "It's on the other side of the river, which is the only place he's ever been seen." I really, really hoped that were true.

"Quick! Hide!" Holly ignored me and vanished into the thicket alongside the deer path, leaving me to face whatever was charging our way. I considered jumping on Holly's hysteria train and scampering for cover.

Southern Wisconsin doesn't have wolves or bears or moose, so I wasn't worried about an attack from a wild, woman-eating, four-legged creature. Coyotes and foxes were plentiful in our area, but they didn't attack humans. Did they?

Besides, I reasoned, suddenly feeling foolish for my irrational thoughts, animals didn't carry light sources.

Still, I felt my heart rate pick up speed at the thought that I might actually meet up with the infamous Lantern Man.

The light beam was close enough now I could tell it was a flashlight, not a lantern.

And P. P. Patti was right behind it, binoculars and all.

"I thought you didn't want to be in the woods after dark," I said.

"I don't," Patti said, sounding out of breath. She looked around. "So we have to hurry. Something important came up. Where's Holly?"

"In the bushes. You can come out now, Fearless Wonder."

Holly had the decency to look embarrassed, but I wasn't sure if it was because she had left me to fend for myself or because she had revealed a cowardly part of herself residing under all that casual bravado. I'd already known about her cowardliness, exposed the first time we'd worked together with minuscule honeybees, so she wasn't sharing any new flaws.

Holly had burrs stuck in her hair but that was her problem, and I wasn't about to tell her they were there. That's the least I could do to thank her for her teamwork.

"I just got a bulletin over my scanner." I realized Patti's heavy breathing wasn't because she had been traveling fast. It was pure excitement that had her panting.

"You have a scanner? Like a police scanner?" Holly asked. "WTG (*Way To Go*)! Awesome."

Patti nodded, speechless, while she caught her breath.

That little gem—the scanner—explained why Patti always had breaking news before the rest of us did. She had a full arsenal of spying equipment, including a telescope, which seemed to be pointed in every direction at once, including at my windows.

Patti took a deep breath before starting in. "It came through on one of the auxiliary channels. One of the Kerrigans is missing," she said. "The police chief won't do anything about it because it hasn't been twenty-four hours, so the Kerrigans put out their own news bulletin and are organizing a search party as we speak."

"Which one is missing?" I asked, thinking the situation must be serious to get that kind of reaction. I really hoped it wasn't one of the younger ones.

"And missing for how long?" Holly butted in. "It couldn't have been more than a few hours since we had Kerrigans at the store making candles and they didn't seem worried about a missing family member. V (*Very*) weird."

"She went missing right after she left your class, Story."

My heart sank into my stomach. "Not one of the kids." I thought of the little troublemakers, how overly exuberant they'd been. Alive and not missing at all. Then.

"No," Patti shook her head. "Not a kid. So, do you want to keep guessing or should I tell you who?"

"Who?" Holly and I said in unison.

"Lauren Kerrigan," Patti announced.

Holly gave me a sharp glance.

After a brief pause while I took in the name Patti had flung out so casually, I said, "That is the most outrageous thing I've heard in a long time. Is this some kind of joke? Did someone put you up to this?"

"Why? No! Why? Tell me." Patti was what Moraine's locals called an outsider, and despite all her gossiping, she always would be. She hadn't been born and raised in our community, so even though she had latched on to all the town's current drama, tapping into Moraine's main artery with a permanently placed IV, she wasn't part of our past and wasn't privy to old secrets we kept.

And Lauren Kerrigan's name had been tucked away in Moraine's most secret jar where it resided in a dusty corner of our topmost pantry shelf. Out of reach, out of sight, out of mind.

I hadn't heard her name spoken in years.

"It's true," Patti said. "I wouldn't make it up. Can one of you tell me why the big reaction? Who is she?"

"Are you sure she was in my candle-making class?" I asked, ignoring Patti's demand for more info.

She shrugged. "Apparently. At least that's what I heard."

I thought back to the strange woman in my class, the one who'd looked vaguely familiar. But Lauren Kerrigan had been my age; the woman in the basement of The Wild Clover looked much older than her mid-thirties. Was it possible?

A little inner voice whispered an affirmative.

Then Holly said, "Why all the uproar? She's been gone only a few hours. Seems like a knee-jerk reaction to me. Way OTT (*Over The Top*)."

"I'm with you," I said to Holly. And for the first time in memory, I thought Johnny Jay, our police chief, had made a good call. He'd made the right decision to give it twenty-four hours before alerting the troops. Though I'd rather eat road kill than admit Johnny Jay and I agreed on anything.

But Patti wasn't done dispersing information. "She came into town and was staying with her mother on the Q.T.," she said.

I shook my head in bewilderment. Rita Kerrigan was Lauren's mother. Rita had kept her distance from her daughter during the candle-making class. Although now that I thought back, Rita had stayed close by.

"Why didn't Rita say anything?" I wondered aloud.

"Lauren asked her to keep it quiet?" Holly guessed.

"Then why come at all?"

"I have more," Patti said. "When Rita Kerrigan went home from The Wild Clover after the class, she found her nightstand drawer wide open. A gun was missing from inside it and nobody can find Lauren. Something awful might have happened to her."

"Or to someone else," Holly suggested.

Instantly, I thought of the gunshots we'd heard. Just as quickly, I rejected the next thought that popped out of nowhere. That they were connected. A missing gun and a gunshot didn't necessarily have to add up. Did they?

But why had Lauren come back to Moraine?

And where was she right now?

"What if she killed somebody again?" Holly said.

"Killed? Again?" Patti said, practically shouting in excitement.

"Some people," I said, sending Holly a *shut-up* look, "have overactive imaginations."

Four

"Lauren Kerrigan," Patti said, slowly rolling the name on her tongue and crinkling her forehead. Finally, she said, "There's a big story here. I can feel it in my bones. Spill the beans."

Holly and I glanced at each other. My sister's eyes told me she'd defer to me. There was a story, but Patti wasn't going to get much of it from me. The whole thing was too long and complicated, not something that could be explained in a two-sentence blurb. "Another time," I said.

"Oh, come on," Patti said. "I'm trying to get a reporting job with the local newspaper and this could be my ticket."

The Distorter? I said. "You want to work for *The Distorter*?"

The Reporter," Patti corrected me, sounding offended at my own "distortion" of our tiny news rag's name. "I need a big story to get in the door. Joel Riggins works at the paper and he promised to collaborate with me on a big, juicy piece once I find it."

"That kid reporter?" Holly asked. "Isn't he about twelve?"

"He's going off to college. I want the position when it opens. So spill."

"Is that reporter talk?" I asked. "Spill?"

"Come on, you guys!"

"It's nothing. No big deal," Holly said. "She's just one more from the Kerrigan clan."

"I heard you say 'kill again.' You can't fool me."

Just what we needed, Patti broadcasting Holly's careless comment to the entire community.

"EOD," Holly said.

Which meant, *End Of Discussion*.

"EOD?" Patti said. "Can you talk normal English for once? All this EOD, POD, COD stuff. I mean, who understands what you're talking about? Half the time, I'm clueless."

"I don't like to waste breath," Holly retorted.

While Patti and Holly continued to discuss the pros and cons of acronyms, all kinds of memories surfaced in my head.

As if I'd ever forgotten in the first place. The past was hard to get away from. It might disappear for a while but it always comes back in some form. The best a person could do was have a perfectly clean slate all along. But who manages that?

Certainly not me. Or Lauren Kerrigan.

Back in high school, Lauren had been a beautiful teenage girl with a gift for getting any guy she wanted. She knew how to dress to attract attention, had long blond hair and a to-die-for complexion. She was the kind of female that guys loved and girls absolutely didn't.

Lauren became the newest addition to my close group of friends senior year when she started dating T. J. Schmidt only a few weeks before the bottom dropped out of our party barrel. Our future dentist and his longtime girlfriend, Ali, were in the midst of another of their relationship crises, only one of multiple routine breakups, when Lauren seized the opportunity to insert herself into the action. She moved in fast. T. J. hadn't stood a chance.

We were all tight back then, and having Lauren around complicated things. Suddenly our friend Ali was replaced, and the dynamics of the group changed in some inexplicable and very uncomfortable way. I felt the change in us that very first day when she came around on his arm.

Now here we were in the woods looking for my runaway honeybees and all of a sudden we were talking about Lauren Kerrigan.

"What a blast from the past," I muttered to Patti and Holly. Shadows moved and swayed around us, became longer and more sinister. Overhead, the trees seemed to grow taller and denser. Kind of creepy, considering the topic under discussion at the moment.

"Blasts. We all heard gunshots," Patti pointed out, using *blast* in an entirely different context than I had. None of us had moved from our spots on the deer trail. "This is too spooky for me. What if what we heard were shots from Rita's missing gun?"

"Would a handgun have sounded that loud?" Holly asked, looking at me.

"That's a really good question," I said, again thinking back to the shots we heard earlier.

"You knew all about the differences between rifles and shotguns a little while ago," my sister pressed. "GA (*Go Ahead*). Enlighten us. What kind of gun was it?"

"Uh, uh . . . How should I know?" I said, realizing I'd used the extent of my limited weapons knowledge on the town's no-rifle policy.

"Wouldn't a handgun make more of a firecracker sound?" Patti asked.

Holly piped in. "Or a noise like those snap-n-pops we used to throw on the ground when we were kids? Remember? They sounded like caps?"

"We don't know if the shots were fired from close by,"

I said, "or from far away, so all we're doing is wildly guessing."

Too bad Hunter hadn't been with us when we heard them. He would have known.

I looked down the trail and noticed Holly and Patti doing the same. Up ahead, the path we were following would come out into a clearing, marking the southern end of The Lost Mile. Somewhere north of there it had all started for us back then. Or ended for us, if I wanted to go and be all dramatic.

"Tell me what's going on," Patti demanded. "I'll find out from somebody else, and what if they tell me wrong? Don't you want me to get the story straight?"

My nosy neighbor had a very good point.

"Besides," Patti added, "if you can't trust your best friend, who can you trust?"

Oh jeez, not that again! My next-door neighbor was NOT my best friend. At least not from my point of view.

Holly gave me an amused smirk.

I decided to give Patti the bare bones facts since she wasn't going to quit bugging me until I did. "In high school a bunch of us went into The Lost Mile from the other end. Some of us had been drinking."

Holly snorted.

"Okay, all of us were, but some more than others. And bad things happened." That was an understatement. Too much booze and even more bad judgment had ridden shotgun with Lauren Kerrigan when she pealed away from the northern entrance to The Lost Mile. "Lauren took off on her own," I continued, "drove into town, and ran over somebody."

Holly stepped in. "Not just anybody, either. Johnny Jay's dad. Wayne Jay."

"Our Johnny Jay's father?" Patti said. "She killed the police chief's dad? That's horrible. How come this is the first I'm hearing about it?" Patti's eyes actually gleamed with glee, and I had to think the world was filled with gossiping people who thrived on the bad fortunes of others. Please, don't let me ever be one of them!

I vowed to watch myself carefully.

"What happened to Lauren?" Patti wanted to know.

"She went to prison," I said. "And no one saw her again."

There was so much more to the story and it all came rushing back. Lauren had turned eighteen the week before and so had been tried as an adult. Her defense team pushed hard for vehicular manslaughter while driving under the influence, which sounded terrible enough, but Murder One was much worse. They appealed to the jury, imploring them to consider her state of mind, which at the time had been swimming in straight vodka.

Lauren's life was in the hands of twelve jurors. If they came back with a charge of criminal negligence, her sentence would be light. None of us thought that would happen. And we were right.

The jury couldn't do that.

Lauren had three strikes against her from the very beginning.

Bullet point one: She couldn't remember a thing, which wasn't so surprising considering her condition. After striking Wayne Jay, her car skidded into a tree. She got off easier than her dead victim, only suffering a mild concussion and a bad hangover. Maybe if she had been able to recall the night, she might have been able to defend her actions. Or at least offer an explanation.

Two: Another big factor that hadn't helped her case was Wayne Jay's position in the community. At the time of his death, Wayne Jay had been in the same shoes his son went on to fill after his death. Lauren's victim had been the local police chief.

Three, and most important: After hitting Johnny Jay's dad, Lauren had backed up, then ran over him a second time. This was the totally incriminating evidence her attorneys couldn't rationally explain away.

P. P. Patti nudged me. "Wake up." She waved a hand in front of my face. "Calling Story Fischer."

I blinked. "Sorry, I was lost in the past."

"Is there more to tell?" Patti asked.

"That's pretty much it."

"But Holly said she might be back to kill again."

"Ignore me," Holly said. "I say weird things sometimes."

"No kidding," Patti said, shifting her eyes to me. "Can't you give me something I can use that's special? Something to tie things together? I have a hunch this is the breaking story I need to get into the newspaper job as a full-time investigative reporter." Patti grinned. "I like the sound of that—investigative reporter."

"I'll have to think a little," I said to get her off my back. P. P. Patti might get the entire historical scoop from another resident as soon as we retraced our steps and cleared the woods, but she wouldn't get the finer details from me. I didn't want to go there.

"Should we go home and call for help, report what we heard?" Patti asked. "Or should we keep going on this path, in the dark, with Lantern Man running loose and who knows what else?"

"You can go back and report the shot if you want to," I said, fumbling with the flashlight I'd brought along until its beam lit up the ground at my feet, knowing what Chief Johnny Jay would say if I were the one doing the calling. It wouldn't be pleasant. Or printable. "While you're doing that, we'll keep going."

"We?" Holly said.

"You and me. In case you forgot, our original mission was to find and retrieve a swarm of honeybees. Somehow we got sidetracked."

I cut my eyes to Patti.

She was hesitating, trying to make up her mind which way to go, caught between two potentially exciting possibilities: Running home to be the first to report shots fired, which could possibly have been from Rita's missing gun. Or staying with us in case we found something more tangible, equally newsworthy, or even better. I was pretty sure this was a no-brainer for Patti. And I was right. She decided in a flash.

"I'm staying with you two," she said, taking up a position behind Holly as I claimed the lead. Patti had said the same thing in my backyard about coming along, right before she reversed directions and backed out, but this time she seemed to mean it. No way was Patti going to miss an opportunity like this, whatever "this" turned out to be.

Even though we still had time before dark, I was relieved when we crossed the wooden bridge to the other side of the river and into the clearing where The Lost Mile began, leaving the semi-darkness of the trees' canopy behind us for a few final rays of sunshine. We were on higher ground with the fog behind us, but I knew we'd have to deal with it again on the way back.

Not an encouraging prospect. We had to get going.

"What are you doing?" Holly asked when I stopped to scan the tree line.

"Looking for my swarm. They have to be close by."

Holly groaned.

Patti added her two cents. "Who cares about a stupid bunch of bees when we should be investigating a possible shooting incident?"

"Exactly," Holly agreed, just to agree with anything non-bee related.

Patti marched past us without a backward glance, proving that curiosity can outweigh caution under the right conditions.

"Wait for us," Holly called. "We should stick together."

We caught up and followed close behind Patti. She

stopped every few minutes to scan the woods through her binoculars. Then she began moving ahead fast, on a mission to infiltrate the lowly *Distorter* rag sheet, ready to face anything to get her story.

I grabbed my sister's arm.

"What?" Holly said, trying to shake free from my grip.

"You're on your own, Patti," I said, holding my sister back.

"My allergies are starting to kick up," Patti called back. "That happens every time I go into the woods. I'll only go a little farther. If anything happens, I'll yell for you." With that, she disappeared down the path like a bolt of lightening.

Holly wiggled into a contorted position, spun around, and broke my grip. "We have to stay together. What's wrong with you?"

"There they are." I pointed out the clump of bees in a dead white birch about halfway up its bare branches. My original idea had been to locate them, snip off the branch where they clung, and carry them home. I'd have to revise the plan.

They were too far up off the ground to reach.

Holly spotted them and gurgled like a drowning woman.

Five

I tipped my head back and eyed up the situation. The white birch was totally dead with large holes drilled into it that could only have been made by a pileated woodpecker. But the trunk seemed solid enough in spite of all the holes. "We'll have to come back tomorrow morning," I said. "With a ladder."

"We?" Holly whimpered.

"You and me."

"Quit including me in your bee problems. IOH (*I'm Outta Here*)."

I grabbed her again and refused to let go, even when she pulled the same move she'd used on me in the past and wrestled me into a headlock.

"You're the one who wanted a partnership," I croaked through the clench, working to break it, "when all I wanted was a loan and monthly installments."

"I wanted a partnership in the grocery store, not in the bee stuff."

"You don't get to choose. You're either in all the way or you aren't in at all. Let me go!"

Holly released me so abruptly, I lurched forward.

"I hate when you do that," I said. "I'm telling Mom."

"Oh right, Squealy. Like she'd care."

"What are you? Twelve?"

"NC (*No Comment*)," my sister said, starting to laugh. Pretty soon we were both grinning, on good terms again.

"Let's go back to your house," Holly said. "I'm getting cold."

"We better wait for Patti. She won't go far."

"Of course. You can't abandon your *best* friend. But I can."

"I have the flashlight and you aren't getting it." I waved it in front of her, snatching it back when she made a grab for it.

"Should we follow her?" Holly said. "Hasn't she been gone awhile now?"

I slid down the trunk of the tree my bees had chosen, tucking my knees against my chest. "I'm waiting here."

"What about the bees?" Holly looked up.

"What about them?"

"What if they attack?"

"It's not sunny and warm anymore. They're sleeping." Which wasn't exactly true. Most beekeepers, myself included, believed bees didn't sleep at all. But Stanley Peck insisted he could hear his bees snoring. Whatever the case, Holly bought my reassurance and slid down next to me.

"I can't believe Lauren Kerrigan came back to Moraine," I said.

"I never really knew her," Holly said. "I was a freshman that year."

I nodded in understanding.

The three years between Holly and me had seemed like an enormously wide age gap during our teens. We hadn't really gotten to know each other until recently, and now the difference in ages didn't matter one tiny bit. What's three years in the scheme of things? But back then it was huge.

"I remember how long you were grounded," Holly said. "And how the lawyers said you weren't supposed to talk about what happened, even with your friends. And how you had to go to court and testify. What a bummer. Did anybody ever figure out why she ran over Wayne Jay two times?"

I shook my head. "No. She was so drunk when it happened, she was lucky she didn't die from alcohol poisoning."

"What a horrible thing to go through."

"I can't believe that emaciated woman in my candle-making class was Lauren Kerrigan. I wouldn't have recognized her in a million years. Why didn't she identify herself to me?"

"Afraid to, I bet. Maybe she came into the store planning to greet you, or thinking you'd recognize her. When you didn't, she chickened out."

"That makes sense. And Rita didn't want to force the issue."

"Exactly. She was letting Lauren take as much time as she needed to adjust."

"I have so many questions. Bullet point number one: Did she just get out of prison?"

"Probably," Holly guessed.

Sixteen years had gone by since Lauren was dealt a life sentence, which everybody knew wasn't really for life but long enough to count as forever when you're eighteen years old. "Bullet point number two: Why come back now? And three: Where is she right this minute?"

"She didn't have anywhere else to go," Holly said, stating the obvious answer to bullet point number two.

"She got drunker and drunker that night," I said, remembering remarkably well considering how many years had passed. "She started arguing with T. J., saying he didn't care about her enough. Then she ran off. None of us even tried to stop her."

"You can't blame yourself for what she did." Holly

sighed loudly. Feeling more generous toward my sister, I picked a burdock burr from her hair and flicked it away.

"It's getting dark," she said, looking around. "Are we totally insane or just plain stupid?"

"Lantern Man never hurt anybody."

"But he vandalized property."

"That could have been a teenage prank that got out of hand."

Holly shook her head. "No way. He exists. What were you guys doing in The Lost Mile that night, anyway?"

"The only reason we came here was because T. J. and Hunter started talking tough about how we weren't afraid of things that didn't exist, and some of the other kids dared us to walk through."

"How dumb was that to actually go?"

"The dumb part was bringing booze with us. Lauren had her own personal flask of vodka."

"I remember you guys went in right after Lantern Man's first attack."

"It could have been a prank by other kids," I repeated, not really believing it.

"Yeah, right," my sister said.

What had happened was this:

- During my last year in high school, a group of sixth graders had decided to camp in The Lost Mile.

- Late that night, while sitting around a campfire, they spotted a beam of light coming toward them, swinging back and forth as though someone was carrying a lantern.

- As the light came closer, they shouted out, but nobody answered. The light paused, then continued coming.

- They heard snarling like an angry wild animal.

- The kids panicked and ran out of the woods, leaving their gear behind.

- The next day when they went back to their campsite, the camping equipment had been destroyed. And the tent and sleeping bags had been slashed to shreds.

- Whether the destruction was caused by claws or a very sharp knife, nobody every found out.

- There had been reports every year since then, tapering off as The Lost Mile's reputation for malicious hauntings grew and people stopped going in.

"These woods belong to Lantern Man," Holly said, standing up. "And he doesn't tolerate trespassers. Let's go home before he realizes we're here and comes for us."

Just before I made up my mind to abandon Patti to her fate, we heard thrashing in the brush to the north.

"OMG (*Oh My God*)!" Holly shouted, loud enough to wake the dead.

"It's Patti," I whispered, not sure at all. "Quit screaming."

Sure enough, my nosy neighbor came into view just in time to save both of us from totally flipping out, since I'd started feeding on Holly's anxiety and was on the verge.

"I didn't find a thing," P. P. Patti said. "Absolutely nothing. But I'm probably going to break out in a rash from tromping through all this brush. I bet poison ivy is everywhere. One time, I squatted in the woods to tinkle and got it all over my heinie."

"Thanks for sharing that," I said, thinking I'd be howling with laughter at the thought of poison ivy all over Patti's butt if the darkness of the woods wasn't starting to spook me.

"Remember Hetty Cross?" Holly asked me, bringing back more scary memories. "That time she caught us on her property?"

"Where was that?" Patti asked.

"Across that way." Holly pointed up the logging road and a little to the north. "When we were kids, we used to call her the Witch. I could run faster than Story, so I always got away. But she grabbed Story once."

"What did she do to you?" Patti asked me.

"She hauled me off her property by my ear." I could picture the Witch as vividly as if it had happened yesterday. "And warned me never to come back or she'd make stew meat of me."

Holly laughed. Patti cackled.

"Have you ever been pulled by your ear?" I wanted to know. "It really, really hurts. Quit laughing."

"After that," Holly added, "we made sure we avoided the Witch's property lines whenever we played in the woods. She's an awful woman. I can't imagine what her husband has to put up with."

Hetty's husband, Norm, did most of the shopping in their household. He was a regular customer at The Wild Clover, so we were on casual small-talk terms, while I hadn't seen Hetty in the store more than half a dozen times. Which was perfectly fine with me.

An animal howled in the not-so-faraway distance.

"Let's get out of here," Holly said. "While we still can."

"That was just somebody's dog," Patti said.

"I'm right with Holly," I answered back, because very shortly, if we didn't hightail it out of The Lost Mile immediately, my imagination was going to get as wild as Holly's. Between the Witch—who still lived nearby—and Lantern Man, my bravado was slipping away.

We stumbled out of The Lost Mile, crossed the bridge, and retraced our steps. After making our way back through the fog and darkness, we walked to the business end of my short, dead-end street, turned left, and ended up on bar stools at Stu's Bar and Grill.

Right into the middle of major drama.

Six

Saturdays at Stu's are all-you-can-eat chicken wing nights from four o'clock until ten. The place was hopping. Stu made the best wings on the planet and it wasn't just my personal opinion. He's won awards. First he marinates his wings in several different kinds of special secret sauces, then deep fries them until they're golden brown before heaping them onto steaming plates. Tonight he had three different kinds—BBQ wings, honey mustard wings, and toasted sesame wings.

The three of us couldn't decide which kind to share. I'd eat any or all of them, so I wasn't the problem. But Holly and Patti couldn't seem to agree. Finally, I stepped in and ordered for us.

"A sampler plate of all three kinds," I said to Stu. He set three Leinie Honey Weiss beers on the bar in front of us and went to fill our wing order. I shoved the lemon wedge down the neck of the bottle and sipped while studying the action.

The bar was busy for two reasons. First, there were the customers who were there because of chicken-wing night. Stu always drew a big crowd for that event. Customers came early, drank enormous quantities of beer, and stayed at least until the clock struck ten when the all-you-can-eat ended.

Second, and more important, the Kerrigans had turned Stu's Bar and Grill into their unofficial missing-person head-quarter as they organized the hunt for their family member. Kerrigans swarmed the place, equipped with walkie-talkies instead of cell phones, since cell reception could be spotty in our hills and valleys. Lauren's brothers passed out radios to anybody who stepped forward to help with the hunt.

Lauren's mother, Rita, walked by me, looking dazed and barely staying upright on her bad knees. I tagged her shoulder.

"Everything's going to be all right," I said, not sure of that at all, but wanting to give her as much encouragement and hope as possible.

"Oh, Story, I don't know. She had terminal colon cancer," Rita said, which explained Lauren's deflated, aged appearance and the wig on her head. "She got a medical parole from that women's correctional place. They do that when a prisoner is close to the end. I was looking into hospice care for her."

"I'm so sorry," I said. "She did look awfully sick when I saw her."

"You didn't recognize her. She thought you would. I'm sorry I didn't warn you in advance, but she made me promise to let her do it her way."

"We'll have plenty of time later, once she's found."

"I'm afraid she might have done something drastic, like . . ." Rita paused as though she couldn't bear to go on. Even though she didn't finish, she didn't have to. I knew Rita was worried that her daughter had committed suicide. "Coming back to Moraine was a terrible mistake," she continued. "I could see as soon as she got here yesterday that she was having trouble handling the strain."

"The search party will find her soon. Look at all the friends who turned out to help."

"If it isn't already too late." Rita licked her lips and spit out the words she feared the most. "What if she used that gun on herself?"

"I'm sure she wouldn't do that," I said. "There's a logical explanation, I'm sure."

Patti's eyes were wide like dinner plates and she opened her mouth to start blabbing. I knew exactly what she was about to tell Rita. That we'd heard shots and they might have come from the missing weapon. "We heard—" was all she had time to say, because right then I stepped down from the bar stool and stomped on her foot as hard as I could, considering I was wearing flip-flops.

Patti's eyes stayed wide and her mouth made a little round circle. "Owwww," she said, "that hurt. What's wrong with you? You did that on purpose."

I glanced over at Rita, but she'd turned away to talk to someone else, and hadn't noticed our little exchange. I took the opportunity to bark at Patti. "We aren't going to tell Rita about the gunshots. She'll only worry more than she is already, if that's even possible. Promise you won't say a word to her."

"Okay," Patti said, after thinking it over. "You're right."

"But one of us should let Johnny Jay know. And it shouldn't be me."

"I'll call the police chief in a little while and inform him personally. Until then, my lips are sealed with super-glue." Patti slid off the bar stool and wandered off where I couldn't keep an eye and ear on her in case she couldn't find the glue. I noticed Holly had vacated the seat on the other side of me as soon as the wings were gone and was mingling with the other customers.

Just then the room went so quiet you could hear a single

chicken bone drop onto a paper plate. All eyes turned toward the front of the bar.

Our police chief Johnny Jay, decked out in his full uniform, had entered and everybody who hadn't realized beforehand was suddenly struck with a remembrance of the past—that it was Johnny's dad who had been killed by Lauren Kerrigan, struck down and run over by her, not just once, but two times.

And here Johnny was, forced to deal with her as a potential victim because of his position in law enforcement, having to decide when to officially step in and do something about her disappearance and possibly get involved in his own organized search party.

I've known our police chief since kindergarten, and we've gone rounds all the way through high school and beyond. Raptors and rodents would become best friends before Johnny and I learned to tolerate each other. Unfortunately, because of Johnny Jay's position of power, he got to be the hawk most of the time, leaving me to scamper for cover like a mouse.

How was I to know the big bully (aka major jerk) would become the police chief?

But right now, I actually felt sorry for him. Or at least I could sympathize over his loss.

To preserve his public image, Johnny Jay would play it by the book, wait the allotted time according to textbook rules before making a decision on Lauren Kerrigan's alleged disappearance. But on a more personal level, I suspected he wouldn't look too hard for answers. I also wondered if handling this missing-person case was a conflict of interest for Johnny, considering the past. Although it wasn't like the town had the option of replacing him. Johnny Jay was pretty much it in the way of law enforcement.

For all I knew, he was responsible for Lauren's short stay in town. She could be staggering around on the shoulder of the interstate with lumps on her head from Johnny's police baton, and tar and feathers plastered all over her body.

"What's going on here?" Johnny Jay wanted to know. I heard the menace in his tone.

"We're going out to search for Lauren," Gus Kerrigan, her uncle, said. "And you know it."

"Maybe she snuck out of Moraine the same way she came in," Johnny Jay said, really warming up the crowd.

Everybody started talking at once. Some of the comments back and forth got too ugly to repeat. A few of the Kerrigan men looked angry enough to lose self-control and punch the police chief in the face. Especially Terry, Lauren's younger brother, who was the tallest, bulkiest Kerrigan of the bunch. If he managed to dodge Johnny Jay's assortment of weapons and got his hands on him, our police chief would end up ground dog meat.

Some of the Kerrigans, including Robert Kerrigan, another of Lauren's brothers, must have sensed that Terry was going off the deep end of reason, working himself into big trouble, because they moved between the two, blocking Terry's path to Johnny Jay.

Negative vibes bounced through the bar. Several tablefuls of customers scooted out the door.

"We don't need your help," Rita called out to Johnny. "And there's no law against looking for her. Unless you plan on making one up."

At this point, the uninitiated might wonder why the Kerrigans weren't treating Johnny Jay with more respect given the circumstances, but the truth was the police chief had been taking out his hostile feelings on their family since the tragic night he lost his dad. The Kerrigan clan had paid enough bogus tickets to practically fund the new police and fire station, and when Rita's dishwasher caught on fire, help didn't arrive any too fast. The Kerrigan family's patience with Johnny Jay had run thin long ago.

"There's no law against searching for someone," Johnny

admitted, grudgingly. "As long as you don't trespass while you're doing it. But she shouldn't have come back in the first place, stirring up all this trouble."

By *trouble*, I figured he really meant Lauren Kerrigan's appearance, no matter how brief, had stirred up a whole lot of emotions we'd rather have kept buried under the weight of time and distance. At least, that's how I felt. But it was too late now.

"There were gunshots," I heard from the back of the room and groaned inwardly, recognizing Patti's voice. "Two of them."

So much for reining in Patti. Now she was staring at me, waiting for me to back her up.

"They came from the direction of The Lost Mile," I added, ignoring the police chief's glare when he realized who was speaking up. I glared right back.

My confirmation of Patti's statement, which on its own and without collaboration might not have meant quite as much, got everybody's attention.

Rita gave a little scream and her knees almost collapsed. "She went back to where it happened!" Rita bellowed, leaning on her brother Gus for support.

"It didn't happen there," Gus said.

We all knew Johnny Jay's dad hadn't been run down anywhere near The Lost Mile. It had happened right on Main Street almost in front of the Lutheran Church, which was now my grocery store. It had ended for Wayne Jay in the street next to the church cemetery, to be more exact.

"Well, that's where it started." Rita meant the excessive drinking that had led up to the disaster.

Patti spoke up. "Story, Holly, and I walked all of The Lost Mile after we heard the shots, and we didn't find anybody, dead or alive. Isn't that right?"

"That isn't exactly true about walking the whole thing," Holly said, disagreeing with Patti over more than text-speak and chicken wings. "We only went partway."

"I went ahead of you."

"You would have been gone longer if you'd walked the entire way." Holly didn't back down. "Besides, it was getting dark. You could have missed somebody if they were . . ."

Holly bit back the rest of her sentence, but we all filled in the blanks. We might have missed a body if it was dead on the ground off the old logging trail instead of right in the middle of it.

"What did the shots sound like?" Gus wanted to know, fixing his gaze directly on me, as if I'd know. Despite what I'd told Holly and Patti, I certainly wasn't a weapons expert just because I happened to be almost dating a cop.

I gave everybody the palms up and shoulder shrug that meant I was clueless.

"Did they sound like they came from a rifle?" Gus prompted me.

When he saw my blank face, then Patti's, he added more description. "Like a big explosion? Something that would cause you to flinch or cover your ears?"

Holly pushed through to stand by me. "Sort of," she said.

"No way," Patti said.

"I don't know," I added.

"Or like popping sounds?" Gus didn't give up even though all of his witnesses were telling different stories.

"Distance matters," Terry piped up and said to Gus. "You and me, we can tell the difference no matter how far away those shots were fired. But these girls aren't going to know. We're wasting our time."

"They were real kabooms," Patti said. She made an explosion with her mouth that didn't sound anything like what we'd heard.

Rita moaned again. The sound of those shots seemed to be growing faster than the size of the proverbial fish that got away.

I jumped in to ease Rita's mind. "I'm sure we heard shotgun shots."

Johnny Jay inserted himself into the conversation. "What kind of pistol was it, Rita?"

Everybody turned to stare at him like they'd forgotten he was still part of the group.

"She knows guns about as well as these girls," Gus said. "But I can tell you. It was a short-barreled Sig Sauer."

That meant nothing to me but Johnny perked right up. "That's a powerful little weapon. A lot of kick and a bunch of noise. What was Rita doing with something like that?"

"I gave it to her," Terry said, still sounding angry after the police chief's rotten comments about his sister Lauren. "For protection against creeps who like to take matters into their own hands." Implying that he might be talking about Johnny.

"We have to find her," Rita said.

"We'll need volunteers to go into The Lost Mile," Robert Kerrigan said, which earned him a few dropouts from the search party. "Oh, come on," he called to those who started for the door. "We're fanning out in groups. Nothing's going to happen to you." But the ones leaving didn't turn back.

"What about out on the street where it happened?" Gus said. "We need some of you to comb through the cemetery and others to go house to house on the other side of The Lost Mile to find out who fired those shots Story and her friends heard. Terry and I will cover The Lost Mile."

"You're wasting a good Saturday night," Johnny Jay said. "She couldn't handle coming back. It's as simple as that. Lauren Kerrigan has left town for good."

He didn't say, "Good riddance," but we all heard it anyway.

Johnny Jay must have been satisfied to get in the last word because he stalked out after that.

Seven

Most of Stu's customers cleared out soon after, some walking through town to search for Lauren in the vicinity of the tiny white marker pointing out the exact location of Wayne Jay's death. Others left to drive along the perimeter of The Lost Mile canvassing residents, hoping one of them had fired the shots we heard. Gus and Terry, true to their courageous words, went off to search The Lost Mile.

Holly, not exactly the search-and-rescue type, felt she'd done her part—whatever that was—and went back to my house to settle in for the night. Patti joined one of the search parties just in case something big happened to give her the exclusive she needed to qualify as a real reporter.

"Aren't you going along with the masses?" Stu asked me from behind the bar. I looked around to discover I was the only local resident still there. A few tables had customers, but I didn't recognize them.

"No," I said. "There are so many people running around in the dark, they're going to start banging into each other."

"Except Gus and Terry in The Lost Mile. They could use some help."

"Count me out. I was in there earlier. Not only is it too dark to see much, thick fog is moving in. Visibility is going to be zero."

Behind the bar, Stu dipped drink glasses into soapy water. "But it's Saturday night. Why are you all by yourself? Shouldn't you be out with Hunter?"

"It's his weekend to work. Every other one," I explained.

"Well, I really think you need a strong man right about now."

I glanced sharply at Stu because that sounded like some kind of come-on to me, but Stu read my facial expression, laughed casually, and motioned toward the door where I saw Hunter Wallace coming at me.

My pulse rate sped up a notch or two just looking at the man. He had on his black leather Harley jacket, tight jeans, and a gait filled with pure masculine confidence. He came up to my bar stool and wrapped his arms around me from behind, pulling me close.

For the first time since the woods, I felt warm and protected, which, as any woman should know, is a completely false sense of security. No one else can fend off all those things that go bump in the night. But just for a few minutes, I believed it could happen in Hunter's arms.

"Where's Ben?" I asked, hearing the eagerness in my question and realizing, not for the first time, how much I'd changed since I started seeing Hunter again. Ben was Hunter's canine police partner, and until I met him, I'd been afraid of dogs, a fear I hadn't managed to conquer since a vicious dog attack as a kid. After getting to know Ben, though, I discovered I kind of liked the big Belgian Malinois in spite of his four padded paws and intimidating size.

"He's in the truck," Hunter said, giving me one final squeeze before sitting down next to me. "We're here to assist with the search."

"Officially?"

Hunter nodded.

"Johnny Jay's going to love that," I said, grinning at the thought. Our police chief was very territorial about the town of Moraine and its business, but sometimes he was forced to work with the county sheriff's department, which was where Hunter and his canine pal came in.

"Where's Gus Kerrigan?" Hunter asked.

"Out searching."

"He was supposed to meet me here."

"He and Terry are over at The Lost Mile."

"Wish he'd taken the time to let me know that."

"He must have forgotten in all the excitement."

Hunter looked into my eyes, like he could read my mind. "How are you doing with all this?"

"Lots of bad memories floating to the surface. Other than that, I'm fine."

Hunter nodded in understanding. He'd been right there with us and must have his own unpleasant memories.

"Fill me in," he said. "What's happened so far?"

That's what I liked about Hunter. Unlike my ex-husband, he treated me like a thinking human being rather than some kind of toy. I wasn't just eye candy to Hunter.

I had just finished telling him about the gunshots, our adventure through the woods, and the scene at the bar with Johnny Jay, when T. J. Schmidt came in. He walked over to the bar and joined us.

While he ordered a double shot of scotch, I studied him. He looked like his face had been bleached right along with his teeth.

"This certainly is unpleasant," he said. "It's just like Lauren to leave town with her name on everybody's lips and to return the exact same way. She always was nothing but trouble."

That last comment surprised me, since T. J. had been

dating Lauren at the time. But then again, because of that he'd been forced to go through more legal hoops than the rest of us, and had even been accused of buying the booze that led to the tragedy. Eventually he'd been cleared of any responsibility, but still, I guess I could understand why he looked upset right now.

T. J. polished off the scotch in one big gulp and ordered another.

"Where's Ali?" I asked him, thinking he needed his wife right now to keep him fit for work tomorrow morning.

"She left a few hours ago to visit with her sister in Milwaukee. Chris and Ali get together once a month for a girls' night out."

"Lucky her," I said, really wishing I was someplace else, too. After that, we all went quiet in an awkward silence, not knowing what to say. Lauren hadn't been around long enough to actually qualify as part of our group. If anything, she had come between us. Once I gave it more thought, I realized she really had been nothing but trouble.

Then Carrie Ann's ex, Gunnar Retzlaff, walked into the bar. He and my cousin had also been in the woods that night. "I'm looking for Carrie Ann," he said. "Has anybody seen her?"

Nobody had. Which I thought was pretty strange. Carrie Ann usually was in the thick of things. Gunnar looked worried.

He had a dark complexion and always looked like he needed a shave, which instead of looking sloppy, gave him an attractively disheveled look. He was also one of those guys who really listened to a woman when she spoke, unlike most men, who don't seem to listen any longer than they have to. Hunter and Gunnar were cut from the same kind of cloth. They actually absorbed and retained what we said. Too bad Gunnar's relationship with Carrie Ann was so strained.

"She hasn't been in the bar since I came in," I said. "We're talking about Lauren. You know she's back? Or rather was back and now is missing?"

Gunnar nodded. "I heard."

"What if Lauren really killed herself?" I said. "Wouldn't that be terrible?"

"You are the sorriest bunch I've had in here so far tonight," Stu said, looking us over. "And that's saying a lot. It can't be as bad as all that. The search party will find her safe, she'll settle back in, and everybody will get used to the idea of having her around again."

Then I remembered what Holly said about Ali Schmidt being in The Wild Clover when Lauren and Rita came in for the candle-making class.

"Did Ali recognize Lauren when she came into the store?" I asked T. J.

He frowned, puzzled. "What are you talking about?"

"Holly said Ali came because she forgot to buy sugar and was at the register when Lauren arrived. I thought she might have recognized her and mentioned it to you."

"She must not have noticed," T. J. said. "Or believe me, she would have told me. What happened?"

So I had to explain to everyone about Lauren joining the class at the last minute after walking right past Holly and Ali. And about the cancer and chemo and how I didn't recognize her because she'd changed so much.

"She looked ten years older. And way too thin." I glanced at T. J. "I'm not surprised Ali didn't know her when she came through. I was in the same room with her for the entire time and didn't recognize her."

Hunter stood up and gave my arm a gentle squeeze, which meant he was taking off. "Ben and I need to get to work. Time is critical."

"I'll help," T. J. said.

"I'm going through The Lost Mile," Hunter warned him.

"In that case, forget it," T. J. said, putting up his hands like he was warding off evil.

Hunter smiled. "Thought you'd change your mind."

"Why search there?" T. J. wanted to know.

"Story heard shots from that direction. It's as good a place to start as any."

"I still want to find Carrie Ann," Gunnar said. "I'll try to meet up with you later."

"I'll help," I said to Hunter, volunteering against my better judgment, partly because I didn't want him to be alone if he found something awful. And partly because, hey, I had the hots for him. That is to say, whenever I wasn't considering running in the opposite direction. Call me conflicted. Right now I was in hot mode.

He nodded. "Good."

Just then Hunter's cell phone rang and he answered it. "I'm at Stu's. Weren't we supposed to meet here?" he said, while the rest of us were silent, trying to glean as much from the one-sided conversation as we could. But all he said was, "Right, I'll be there in a few minutes."

"Now what?" T. J. asked.

"Gus, Rita, and the rest of them are waiting to get started on the north end of The Lost Mile. Let's go, Story."

With that, he headed for the door. I scurried along behind. I loved a man on a mission, one who valued my opinion right along with the rest of me.

"Keep me posted," T. J. called out, ordering another drink. "I'll be at the bar for a while."

Eight

When Hunter pulled up on the side of the road on the north end of The Lost Mile, a small group of Lauren's immediate family was waiting near their vehicles, which were lined up in an uneven row. Flashlights and headlights cast them in eerie, murky light. We jumped out of his sheriff's SUV. Hunter went around to the back and reappeared with Ben harnessed and leashed at his side, two heavy-duty flashlights in his hand. He handed one to me.

A Belgian Malinois looks a lot like a German shepherd. Ben had short, deep brown fur with black tips, a black face mask, and black ears. He gave me a curt tail wag in greeting, which I would have completely missed if I hadn't been studying the big dog's ways in the last few months as Hunter and I edged closer to an intimate relationship.

I'd seen Ben in action when he responded to Hunter's attack commands, several times while they practiced together and once in real-live action. Not only was Ben an amazing animal, Hunter was really good at teaching police dogs to do their stuff, one of the main reasons he'd been put in charge of the K-9 unit. He loved those animals.

When we joined the anxious group, Rita stepped forward and handed Hunter a plastic bag.

"You didn't touch them?" he asked her.

"No. I did it just like you told me. With gloves."

Hunter opened the bag, exposing a pair of pink pajama bottoms. He offered Ben the opportunity to explore the contents, adding a one-word command, "Smell."

I wanted to ask a bunch of questions, but Hunter was in serious work mode and I was just along for the ride, watching the action from the sidelines. Until now I had had no idea Ben could actually track a missing person so I had a bunch of unspoken questions. This was going to be an interesting adventure.

Ben did some sniff-sniffs with the pjs while Hunter outlined his plan to the Kerrigans. "I want all of you to stay right where you are. Story is coming with me. If we find Lauren or any evidence that she passed this way and my cell doesn't pick up a signal, Story will come out and inform you."

"I'm going, too," Gus said, a firm set to his jaw. "Lauren is part of our family."

Hunter shook his head, just as firmly. "You might confuse Ben." He went on to tell all of us a few facts about tracking dogs:

- Ben's opportunity to follow a trail was reduced to hours, unlike a bloodhound that can still trail a scent weeks later.

- Tracking dogs trail after the odor of skin cells that flake off a body. (Which, ew, I didn't even know that. My body flakes skin all the time?)

- Ben should have Lauren's unique scent from the pair of pajama bottoms she had worn the night before.

• But other family members might have a similar smell, which could throw Ben off. He needed to fully concentrate on trying to follow Lauren's scent. The more similar scents nearby, the harder Ben had to work at his task, and the higher his risk of failure became.

• Therefore, the Kerrigans had to stay behind.

Gus held out a walkie-talkie, resigning himself to a more passive role. "Story, you don't have to go along," he said to me. "Hunter can take this walkie-talkie with him and use it if he needs to."

I grabbed the mobile radio. "I'm going. My scent won't confuse Ben, and I know my way through this area better than most of you." Which was true. I hiked these woods often. But always in the light of day.

Hunter released Ben from his leash and we headed into the darkness of The Lost Mile, surrounded by a cloak of blackness, dependent on the small halos of light from the flashlights. We moved fast and wordlessly. Ben seemed to know exactly how far ahead of us he should stay, operating just beyond our beams. At times his head was down, nose to the ground, at other times he paused to sniff the air.

But we always kept moving forward, so it seemed Ben knew what he was doing.

I thought about the last time Hunter and I had been together in this spot, sixteen years ago, and about how that one night seemed to be defining the present. And about how I'd left Hunter behind at the end of my senior year when I moved to Milwaukee. Not that our relationship had been in the best shape when I left. We'd both been young and immature and had said and done things we shouldn't have.

Ten minutes later, fog began to swirl around us.

"Can we talk?" I asked at one point. "Or will that interfere with Ben's tracking work?"

"He's been trained to ignore distractions. We can talk all we want."

"Do we want?"

"Not yet. I'm listening."

"For what?" But Hunter didn't answer.

Several times after that, I lost sight of Ben, but every time, just when I was sure we'd lost him for good, he would reappear out of the fog like an apparition.

Speaking of apparitions.

"Any recent Lantern Man sightings?" I asked Hunter in a low voice.

"Nothing new," Hunter said keeping his voice low, too. There was something about the dark woods and fingers of fog that brought out our caution reflexes.

"But you checked for reports before you came tonight?" I asked him.

"You bet."

"Not that there would be anything to report, since he managed to scare everybody away a long time ago. Nobody comes in here after dark anymore."

"*We're* here. Shhh." He paused and I could tell he was listening for something.

"What?" I whispered. "What?

"Nothing."

"You're creeping me out."

"Sorry."

This time when we started moving again, I stayed closer to Hunter. He was as alert for trouble as Ben was. I should have felt very safe with those two. I was working hard to achieve that warm, fuzzy feeling, but it was hard to do in this cold, damp place.

The walkie-talkie clutched in my hand crackled, startling me. I almost dropped it. Robert Kerrigan's voice came through loud and clear. If wild things roamed in this part of the woods, they had our exact location by now. "Find anything yet?" Robert's voice boomed.

I fiddled with the controls and answered him, "Nothing."
I looked around as I walked, trying to get my bearings in
such low visibility. "I think we're about halfway through."
Ben came into our circle of light, still working the ground.

"There are more of us gathering here at the road," Robert said. "Lauren wasn't anywhere in town and nobody we
talked with fired those shots you heard. You and Hunter
are our last hope."

Wonderful! That's what I always wanted to be, someone's last hope.

"Any possibility she just drove off?" I said into the radio.

"She didn't have a car. And none of ours are missing."

"Oh," I said. "Okay. Roger. Over and out."

Hunter chuckled quietly beside me. "Very professional,"
he said with a teasing tone. "So who's Roger? Does that
mean I have more competition? I thought I drove them all
away for good."

"I'm a hot babe," I reminded him in case he hadn't noticed.
Keeping a man on his toes was a full-time job for a woman. I
glanced around. "Where's Ben?"

"Around here somewhere."

I glanced around again, thinking Ben had been gone
longer than usual. Then I heard him bark. Hunter tensed
beside me.

When Ben barked again, Hunter moved off the old logging road. I followed, recognizing the decaying white birch
with the woodpecker holes. My bee tree! Hunter headed
for it, then past it. I could see the dark outline of my bees
even in the fog, although it seemed thinner here. The black
blob of bees stood out against the cloud cover.

When I drew my eyes back to earth, Hunter was squat-
ting next to a large heap on the ground. Ben was quietly
standing guard.

"Stay back," Hunter called to me, rising and swinging his light away, sweeping the beam high over a clump
of trees, so I couldn't get a good look at what was on the

ground. "Don't use the radio," he said. "This place will be mobbed with people if you do." He came over to me. "Here. Hold both flashlights and keep at least one focused on me."

He studied my bee tree.

"My swarm," I offered, noting that all the activity on the ground hadn't fazed the bees at all. The chill and darkness had them tucked in close to each other, virtually immobile.

Hunter moved on to another tree, a maple with lower branches.

I avoided looking at where Ben stood, and instead my eyes and the light beams followed Hunter as he began to climb the maple. He swung effortlessly up from branch to branch. What on earth was he doing? Then I realized he was climbing up the tree to find a cell signal. He needed to make a phone call. Yet Hunter had told me not to notify the search party. Why not?

I found my voice.

"Is that Lauren?" I asked, continuing to shine the light on him as he'd asked me to do. "Is she dead?" If it was Lauren, I figured she must be dead, since Hunter hadn't bothered to attempt CPR.

But Hunter was intent on other things and he didn't seem to hear me ask if the body belonged to our high school classmate.

A moment later, one more branch up, he found what he needed. Cell coverage.

"Chief Jay," he said with more professional courtesy than Johnny Jay had heard all night, or deserved. I groaned inwardly at the thought of having to answer questions from our police chief.

I tried to listen to the one-sided conversation, but my head was spinning. I had started out with Hunter on a lark, never expecting to actually find Lauren, and all I could think of was how sad this all was that she had finally been freed from prison, only to end her life with a bullet.

How lonely and distraught she must have been to take

such drastic measures. What should have been a new beginning, a new start, was a final tortured farewell, especially for the family left behind. Briefly, I felt bitter toward her for the pain she continued to inflict on Rita and the rest of the Kerrigans. T. J. was so right. She'd been nothing but trouble.

Hunter gave Johnny our location and warned him about the search party congregating out on the road north of The Lost Mile. He recommended plenty of backup.

Then he started down, jumping to the ground from the lowest branch of the tree.

That's when I first discovered the dead body we found wasn't Lauren Kerrigan.

It was Hetty Cross, the Witch.

Nine

Hetty Cross had been one of my neighbors, loosely speaking. When I lived in Milwaukee, my neighbors lived right next to me, so close I could look through their windows and tell what they were watching on TV. We didn't even have to know each other's names—and most of the time we didn't—to be considered neighbors.

P. P. Patti and I were obviously neighbors since she lived right next to me. She could pry into my private life, probably knowing exactly what I did inside my home thanks to her telescopic lenses. Even in the city, Patti would be considered abnormal.

Here in Moraine, neighbors weren't defined by meters, feet, or yards. Hetty Cross and her husband Norm lived at least half a mile away from me. But because of the river, lost land, fields, and government-owned trails standing between us, no other houses or residents existed there.

So in the scheme of things, we were neighbors.

Not that Hetty had a single neighborly bone in her body.

She wasn't known for her friendliness, which was her prerogative. No one held it against her. That was the beauty of a place like this. If you wanted solitude, you could have as much as you could stand.

Apparently, Hetty had ended up with a lot more desolate alone time than she'd bargained for. The Witch was dead. The same one who had yanked me across her property line by my ear when I was a kid.

Good thing I had a strong stomach, because even with that going for me, my insides were doing flip-flops for a variety of reasons. One, I wasn't particularly used to death (other than honeybees, because they had short lives and so many predators). Two, I knew this dead person personally. Three, she was lying right there almost in front of me and as hard as I tried not to look, my eyes had a mind of their own and took in every bit of the scene.

And then there was number four, which had been confirmed a little later when the powers-that-be (aka Johnny Jay and Hunter) requested the presence of Gus and Terry Kerrigan. A certain weapon was lying on the ground on the other side of Hetty's lifeless body and needed to be identified. Gus and Terry reluctantly did so.

"Are you absolutely sure?" Johnny Jay asked them.

"It's a short-barreled Sig Sauer," Gus said. "And it looks just like the one Rita owns."

"That's all we can tell you," Terry said, letting the chip on his shoulder show in every single move he made.

"That'll do it," Johnny Jay said, pleased with how the case seemed to be progressing along.

So unless things changed later, it appeared that Hetty had been shot and killed with the handgun from Rita Kerrigan's nightstand drawer.

Letting my vivid imagination run rampant, that meant Holly, Patty, and I could have been in this exact spot earlier in the evening right with the killer. He—or she, as the case might be—could have been hiding behind a tree watching and waiting for us to move away. And Hetty could have been lying right next to me while I sat on the ground leaning against the trunk where my bees landed for the night.

I felt chills. Hunter noticed, removed his black leather jacket, and wrapped it around my shoulders. "Not that kind of cold," I muttered.

"I know, but it's the best I can do."

Lauren Kerrigan was still missing just like before, but suddenly her rating on the importance scale rose dramatically, earning her the full attention of a much wider group of concerned individuals.

Suddenly, Johnny Jay really, really cared about where she was. It didn't take him long to put out an all-points bulletin. After that he skirted the tree with my bees, giving it a wide berth like everyone else was doing, and turned his full attention my way.

"Missy Fischer," Johnny Jay said, still calling me by my schoolgirl name, knowing it bugged me. "You're telling me that you and your sister just happened to be in this exact location mere hours before you just happened to find this body."

I stared at the emergency crew, at the stretcher, at the body bag on it, wishing I hadn't had to divulge that particular bit of information. But a team was dusting for fingerprints. What if they pulled my fingerprints from the tree, if that was even possible? My fingerprints and my sister's had to be all over the place.

Better to get the truth out in the open right from the start rather than give Johnny Jay more ammunition later on. In spite of Mom's gloomy assessments, I really *was* learning from past mistakes.

"Ask my sister or Patti Dwyre, Johnny Jay," I said, realizing way too late that my prints weren't on file and I might have possibly slipped under his radar. "They will confirm what I told you."

"Of course, they will," Johnny sneered. "And I'm Police Chief Jay to you. Don't call me Johnny again."

Okay, I thought, mentally coming up with some choice new names that suited him better.

Hunter stood off to the side, talking to a group of county deputies, leaving me alone in the clutches of the police chief. The town residents were divided as to why Johnny hated me so much. One side believed it was because I had turned him down years ago when he had asked me to prom, when I chose to go with Hunter instead. Jeez. Wouldn't anybody? I thought that explanation was lame, because who held a grudge like that over years and years?

The other side of the fence insisted it was because of the time Johnny was tormenting a younger kid and I'd hauled off and decked the bully with my backpack, which happened to be loaded down with heavy books. Johnny went face first in the snow right in front of everybody. He lost some fearful respect that day and spent a long time earning it back.

Whatever the reason, the negative feelings he had for me were mutual. I didn't hesitate to reciprocate, although I often wished the man hadn't grown up to be in a position of authority over me.

I was in his sights, that was for sure. "And you're telling me you didn't see Lauren Kerrigan shoot and kill Hetty Cross in cold blood?" he said for what seemed like the hundredth time. But this time Terry Kerrigan and some of the others were in earshot. Terry didn't look happy. Neither did Robert. They scowled at the police chief.

Johnny went on, still badgering me. "You say you heard shots. You were right here where it happened. You saw something or you did something, or you know something, and I'll take you in and throw you in a cell if you don't start talking. *Now!*"

"What's going on?" Hunter said, finally strolling over, but still taking his sweet time.

"This is nothing to you, Wallace," Johnny said to him.

"Afraid it is. This is county land," Hunter replied, while

I admired his coolness under pressure. The man was easy, relaxed, and confident. "Gives me jurisdiction."

"Like hell it does," Johnny shot back. "This is town land."

The two testosterone heavies were probably as confused as everybody else over The Lost Mile's jurisdiction and who owned which parts of it. Did the town own this stretch? Or the county? Or one of the landowners? Before the mess would be officially sorted out, if it ever could, these two were in what was referred to as a particular type of manly contest to see whose stream was longer.

At least Johnny Jay's attention wasn't focused on me anymore.

I considered slinking away.

Ben stood off to the side, leashed to a tree. I walked over and kneeled down beside him. Petting his sleek coat earned me a gentle kiss. "We should get away," I said to him. "While the getting's good."

A skirmish broke out. At first I thought Johnny Jay and Hunter were duking it out over territory, but it turned out Terry Kerrigan was making another attempt to get at our police chief. "You dumb-ass pig," he said, directing the slur at Johnny while others struggled to hold him back. Terry was always good at giving lots of advance notice when his hackles were up. I suspected he was more noise than anything else. Someday the others weren't going to jump in to stop him and we'd all get to see how tough he really was.

"You bumbling idiot!" he shouted again. "You better stop accusing Lauren until you know the facts. This is slander." Terry spit on the ground. "You have no business bad-mouthing her."

"Get him out of here," Johnny Jay said to the other Kerrigans, "or I'll take him in." A group of relatives hauled Terry off. "And take her with you, too," Johnny said, pointing at me. "She's just in the way."

Finally! I'd been released from the scene, although

Johnny's poor attitude made me consider staying just to see how much more I could annoy him.

"I'll call you later," Hunter said, following me a short distance so we could have some privacy. "Lauren has been here, no question about that. Ben had her scent earlier. We're going to keep following her trail."

He took my hand and I gave his a gentle squeeze. He squeezed back. "Good luck," I said, before hustling down the logging road to catch up with the others, relieved to be away from the crime scene.

I had a list of questions as long as The Lost Mile and I tossed them around in my brain as the group of us walked toward the north entrance. It was the opposite direction from my house, but no way was I walking the other way alone. I would catch a ride home from somebody.

My thoughts were these:

• I'd heard two shots earlier. Were they the same ones that killed Hetty?

• Had Hetty been shot twice? Or had the shooter missed the first time? Or had Hetty shot at someone herself?

• If Lauren shot Hetty with Rita's gun, why did she do it? Had Lauren gone into The Lost Mile to kill herself? What if Hetty had been trying to stop Lauren and the gun had gone off accidentally?

• And finally, would Ben be able to track down Lauren?

By morning at least one of my questions was answered. Ben had completed his mission—he'd found Lauren Kerrigan.

Dead.

Ten

Sunday morning's dawn brought sunshine, but with a lingering springtime nip to the air. Bright and early, Stanley Peck knocked on my door, right as I was pondering the most effective way to launch my sister out of bed. She'd locked the door to the spare bedroom and told me in both text-speech and normal-person-dialogue to take a flying leap off a high bridge.

"I'm telling Mom to take you back," I shouted through the door before letting Stanley in.

"I heard about your bees swarming," Stanley said. "And I'm here to help you get them back." I sort of could tell that, because Stanley was in full head-to-toe bee gear: a zippered full white suit, wide-mesh netted veil, boots, and elbow-length canvas gloves.

He wasn't taking any chances.

"I love you to death," I said, zipping up my hoodie and slamming loudly out the back door for Holly's benefit. Then we located an aluminum ladder, a small hedge clipper, and the right sized cardboard box for the job at hand.

Stanley walked beside me carrying the ladder. His limp was more pronounced this morning, reminding me not only of his self-inflicted shooting accident but also of yesterday's shots. I really wanted Hetty's death to be an unfortunate accident.

"Not much farther," I said to encourage Stanley when he paused to rest his leg.

"Your bees are going to get active soon," he said, something I was well aware of. Once the day warmed up, they would be on their way.

Last night's fog had dissipated and the Oconomowoc River flowed along fast and strong, still swollen from all the spring rain we'd had. Not a cloud in the sky. If not for recent events, this moment would be perfect.

While we walked, I thought of Hunter and Ben. Hunter hadn't called like he said he would, but it was still barely dawn and they might have worked late into the night. Right now, Hunter was probably catching up on his sleep, preparing to go a few more rounds with Johnny Jay. He'd better bring along more county cops to support his efforts, because Johnny Jay had a bull's brain and the same mentality. But Hunter had grown up with Johnny, too. He'd figure out something.

"Are you still feeding your bees?" Stanley asked. He was new to beekeeping (even newer than I was), having only started last year when he dated a woman who had a few hobby hives of her own. That's how the obsession began for most of us. We met someone who kept bees and suddenly we were hooked.

Stanley had a million questions every time I saw him.

Honeybees survive on the honey they store up before winter arrives, but by spring their supplies are dwindling, especially during a cold and rainy spring like the one we'd had so far. A smart beekeeper helps them out over the

winter by not being greedy, and leaving enough honey for
them to get through the season on their own. But sometimes we misjudge, so then honeybees need supplemental
feedings of a sugar syrup mixture.

"Nope," I said in reply to Stanley's feeding question. "I
left them enough honey."

"I didn't. They ran out. I've been feeding them sugar
syrup for a while now."

"Keep feeding them until the days are warmer and they
have more pollen sources to draw from."

"They have dandelions."

"Still, keep helping them a little longer."

"A shame about Hetty Cross," Stanley said, bringing
up her name for the first time. It didn't take long for news
to travel through Moraine. A forest fire fueled by gasoline
would be slower.

"It really is," I agreed.

Then I stopped abruptly and looked around. Things had
changed.

The tree I was looking for was still the same dead one.
I recognized it by the woodpecker holes drilled all over
it. And my honeybees were still on the same high branch,
waiting for the sun to rise higher and the temperature to get
warmer before taking off again.

But other things had changed.

For one, the tree trunk now acted as an anchor for yellow crime tape staking out an area on the other side of the
tree, framing the spot where Hetty's body had been found.

For two, Tim Hartman, one of Johnny Jay's police officers, sat on a folding chair, standing guard. Or rather, sitting guard. Tim was the oldest cop on the force.

"Hey, Story," he said. "Who's that with you in the Hal-
loween costume?"

"It's Stanley," I said. "We're on a bee rescue mission."

"You're entering a restricted area. Whoa up."

"We aren't going any farther anyway," I said, setting

the empty cardboard box on the ground and patting the tree. "Stanley, you can lean the ladder against this tree right here."

Tim stood up. "Now, wait a minute. Don't you see the tape?"

"Sure I do, but it's on the other side. I'm going up this side of the tree. See my bees?" I motioned upward. Tim followed with his eyes.

"Bees? If I'd known bees were up there I wouldn't be sitting so close." Tim quickly folded up his chair and backed up with it under his arm.

"They're harmless. But it's really important that I go up and get them."

Tim looked doubtful. "I don't know about that."

"If I don't get them now, they'll leave and I won't be able to follow them. I promise. I'll stay on this side, get up and down before you can blink both eyes, and be gone, out of your hair for good."

Which was really an insensitive comment once I thought about it, because Tim didn't have much hair for anything to get caught in. But he didn't seem to take it the wrong way.

"Nobody needs to know," Stanley said, throwing a little espionage into his voice. I wondered if Stanley was carrying a weapon this morning. Illegal, of course, but that's Stanley. One of these days, he'd answer to the law, but not because of me. As long as Stanley and I stayed on the same side, he could carry grenades for all I cared.

"I don't see any harm in it, I guess," Tim said, reluctantly. "We've pretty much picked over this area. In fact, I was wondering if the police chief forgot I was still over here."

"All right then." I dropped my faux rhinestone studded flip-flops at the foot of the ladder and put on a pair of leather gloves. With the hedge clippers tucked in the belt I had worn for this special occasion, I grabbed the cardboard box and started climbing. Once I got to the tree's big vee, I ran out of rungs and had to leave the ladder behind. I kept climbing up another twelve feet or so, clutching smaller branches to help with my ascent.

I'd climbed trees as a kid, going to the very top of the highest and swaying back and forth. But this time, in my thirties and not as graceful as I used to be, which wasn't saying all that much, the height seemed . . . well . . . way too high. And looking down made me feel light-headed, which wasn't the best scenario considering where I was. The box was hampering my movement. I felt wimpy and simpy like Pity-Party Patti, so I quickly pulled myself together with a silent pep talk and kept going.

A little higher and I stopped, eye level with my swarm of bees. They crawled all over each other, more active than I expected given the chill in the air. They eyed me back as I carefully readjusted myself, trying hard not to look down.

Stanley was right behind me, not quite as high, but close enough to hold the box in his gloved hands while I snipped away at the branch where the swarm clung. Good thing it wasn't much of a branch or I would have had to do some sawing and they might not have stuck around for that.

With one gloved hand I snipped, with the other I grabbed the branch, holding it firmly above the swarm. Once the cut was clean through, I bent down and gently placed the branch, swarm and all, inside the cardboard box Stanley held out. At least half the bees flew up in the air, but the other half remained clumped together to protect the queen.

"Don't I need to trap them inside this box?" Stanley said, fumbling with the box's flaps while the air darkened with buzzing insects.

"No, leave it open. They'll stay right with you and the ones that flew off will come back."

"You have bees all over you," Stanley announced. He had a lot of bees on himself, too, only Stanley was protected and I wasn't. Something in my personality made me do foolish, impulsive things, like not wear full protection when performing dangerous high-wire stunts like this one.

But I like to think my bees are used to me and trust me. Which is why they crawled around only on my hoodie and arms, checking things out. Not a single one stung me. As it turned out, looking at the masses of bees covering us, it was a good thing Holly had locked her door against me and Stanley had taken her place. He could handle this. My sister would have had an old-fashioned conniption fit and we would never have gotten the bees safely into a box.

"Don't worry about them," I said to Stanley, noticing that he wasn't.

From the ground, I heard, "Good Lord. Heaven help us. Are you two okay? Gad!"

"It's okay, Tim," I called out. "If you're uncomfortable just stay back. But they aren't going to sting us. They don't have a hive to protect. Right now they are perfectly tame. Docile cute little things, aren't they?"

"I'm out of here," Tim said, dropping his folded chair to the ground and hurrying off.

Stanley and I began our descent, finding out quickly that climbing down the tree was harder than going up, especially with the baggage we carried. And Stanley's wide-brimmed veil kept catching on branches.

"I've got them safe and sound," he said, finally reaching the ladder and making it the rest of the way, clutching the box filled with honeybees.

I leaned against the trunk, still pretty high up in the tree. My eyes wandered to the taped area where Hetty's body had been. Now that most of the bees were below me, either inside the box or following Stanley as if he were the Pied Piper, I could hear more than buzzing. Voices. Coming from the west.

Well, why not? Sunday morning was a great time for a long walk along the Oconomowoc River where hikers liked to follow the national scenic area called the Ice Age Trail. Since Moraine's segment of the Ice Age Trail happened to sit right under a migratory flyway, spring was the perfect time to bird watch along it.

Except I thought I recognized one of the voices as our police chief's. I had to get out of here fast.

"What are you waiting for?" Stanley said from below. "Let's go."

I'm not sure what happened next, but when I went to put my feet on the top of the ladder, it must have shifted because I remember feeling like it had moved underneath me. I tried to grab for something. Anything. Then I felt myself pitching forward.

When I hit the ground, I actually managed to land crouched, with my feet flat on the ground like a female ninja. Then my legs crumpled and I went over sideways.

"Are you okay?" Stanley said. I could hear the concern in his voice.

I stayed where I was, taking a mental inventory of all my moving parts.

"I think so," I said, spitting out a mouthful of decomposed leaves.

Then I heard another voice, a familiar one. "You better think again, Missy Fischer, because you aren't going to be okay when I get done with you."

Johnny Jay towered over me. I sat up and realized I was now on the wrong side of the crime-scene tape.

"You're under arrest," Johnny Jay said to me.

"Oh, come on, Chief," Stanley said, sounding slightly riled. "It was an accident. She fell."

"And you get that box of bees out of here before I arrest you, too."

Johnny wasn't alone. Some of his officers were backing away while bees hovered over Stanley or crawled around on him. Part of me wanted to see Johnny Jay try to get at Stanley through all those honeybees.

"Go on, Stanley," I said, rising slowly, shaking off leaves

and dirt, and noticing none of the bees had stayed on my clothing for the crash landing. The last thing I wanted was for Stanley to get arrested. Or searched, given his probably concealed weapon. "You know how to introduce them to a hive, right?"

Stanley nodded, so I told him which hive in my beeyard was empty and waiting for the bees to occupy it.

"And get my sister up and over to The Wild Clover to open up. I think Johnny might be serious about arresting me."

"That's Police Chief Jay to you," Johnny said. "Show disrespect one more time and I'll throw the book at you."

I didn't know cops actually said that. But our police chief must watch a lot of crime dramas on television.

Stanley hurried off.

"You contaminated a crime scene," the police chief said.

"You were finished here anyway," I fired back.

"I'm about to read you your rights, so shut up."

"Oh please."

Johnny Jay used his fat fingers to tick off all my violations. "I've got your fingerprints all over the place, you were at the scene of the crime and it isn't clear exactly what time that was, you came back this morning and contaminated the area again, and for all I know you had something to do with Lauren Kerrigan's death, too."

That was the very first I'd heard Lauren wasn't missing anymore.

"You found her?" I said. "She's dead?"

Johnny Jay began reading me my rights.

Eleven

While I waited for Johnny to get around to booking me, I listened in to cops talking shop. They didn't seem to notice me scrunched down in the corner, trying to look as inconspicuous as possible. Just maybe, Johnny Jay would forget I was there and the right door would open and I'd be gone.

From the bits and pieces of overheard conversations, I pieced together a few facts:

- After I'd gone home, Hunter, with Ben's help, had found Lauren Kerrigan during the night.

- She had been shot with the same handgun that killed Hetty Cross. Rita's gun. The one missing from her nightstand and found next to Hetty's body.

- Both women had been shot in their torsos. I couldn't help imagining my insides seeping out onto the ground while I breathed my last few tortured breaths. It wasn't a pleasant experience, even in my imagination.

There were differences between the two women's last moments, though. Hetty had dropped down on the ground as soon as she was shot and didn't move from where she fell. But Lauren hadn't died right away. She'd managed to crawl deeper into the woods, away from the logging road. Lauren must have been in shock (who wouldn't be?) because she would have had a better chance if she had stayed on the logging road. Unless the person who shot her was still nearby and she was trying to hide.

I still didn't know if the shots that killed them were the same ones we'd heard, but I'd bet Grams's farm on it. Since no one had come forward about firing those shots, they had to be the ones that killed Hetty and Lauren.

My skin crawled to think how casual Holly and Patti and I had been when we heard those shots go off, standing around shooting the breeze while two women were dying in the woods less than a mile away.

Johnny Jay finally found time for me before I could plan an escape route, and he put me through the paces— fingerprints, mug shot, treating me like a dirt bag—all attended to by him personally. I had to wonder if that was his standard mode of operation. Did he really do the bookings himself usually? I bet not.

I must be a special case.

"So, Missy Fischer," he said. "Are you ready to talk? I have a special room reserved just for you. We could have a little chat."

"I want a lawyer," I said. "I have nothing to say to you."

With a gloating look on his face, the police chief took me down a hall and locked me in a jail cell.

"Too bad we can't set bail until tomorrow morning," he said. "Let me know when you decide to start talking."

The last place I wanted to spend Sunday night was in this place. But I'd never tell Johnny Jay a single thing. Not that he'd listen anyway. "Don't I get a phone call even?"

I shouted after him, but he ignored me. "I want my cell phone back!"

A door slammed.

I was alone, feeling like a caged animal.

My only chance was Stanley. He'd do the right thing. Get my sister on the case. Patti might help. Someone would call Hunter. Grams would gather all the old-timers and threaten a riot.

Right?

Hours and hours seemed to go by before I heard human sounds. Sally Maylor, another police officer and a loyal store customer, unlocked my jail cell.

"You're free," she said.

In fact, all the charges that Johnny Jay had manufactured were dropped by the time I walked out into the midday sunshine. Compliments, I soon learned, of a hunk of a man with the sexiest body and the brightest smile in the world. Was I ever happy to see him!

"Hetty died on county land," Hunter explained, driving me back into town to drop me at The Wild Clover. "Johnny didn't have the authority to arrest you."

"He thinks I had something to do with Lauren's death."

Hunter snorted. "Johnny Jay can't hold you for questioning when we don't have all the facts. Especially since there's a chance, slight, but still a chance, that Lauren shot Hetty, then turned the gun on herself. That would pretty much close the case."

"I didn't do anything to get arrested over," I said.

"Jay claims you contaminated the crime scene. How did you manage that? And what were you doing there in the first place?"

So I told him about my swarm and falling out of the tree.

"I can imagine the whole scene," Hunter said, a big goofy grin on his face, like he was really enjoying himself.

"You need grace lessons. Ever since I've known you, you've been a klutz."

"That is so untrue," I lied.

"Let's take dancing lessons together. That might improve your coordination and we could have some fun at the same time."

"Maybe later," I hedged. "I'm really busy with the store and my bees right now." Not that I wouldn't really enjoy spending time in Hunter's arms, but I had two left feet when it came to dancing, and that whole refusing to follow thing applied to other aspects of life as well. Something about my body always wanted to lead.

Hunter pulled up in front of The Wild Clover and double-parked. Judging by the number of cars pulling in and out of parking spaces and customers going in and out of the store, we were doing some good business. When tragedy struck, my store became a hub of activity, a meeting and commiserating place. And current events certainly qualified as tragedy, with two deaths at once.

I turned to Hunter. "You're not convinced Lauren killed herself after murdering Hetty, are you?"

"Some important characteristics of suicide aren't there," Hunter said.

"Like what?" I made the mistake of asking.

"Lauren didn't leave a note. She didn't contact anyone in advance, either. She didn't shoot herself in one of the typical places like in her head, the shot wasn't angled up, the shot went right through her clothes when most suicides will lift up their clothes first . . ."

Well, that certainly was more than I needed to know. "So you're thinking both were murdered?"

"Johnny Jay is determined to wrap up the case fast. I say we're going to investigate all possibilities. He wasn't too happy with my department or me. Getting the guy to cooperate hasn't been easy."

Who happened to be my sort of boyfriend Hunter, who had a past of his own, but had straightened out and hadn't touched a drop for years and years.

"Thanks. You're sweet for understanding. I'll call him after work." Carrie Ann broke her grasp on me. "I don't know what got into me. Not that I wished her dead or anything, but I never liked Lauren Kerrigan from the very beginning." She wiped her eyes again.

That was a real understatement. Lauren and Carrie Ann had always sniped at each other. They didn't have complementary personalities and it didn't help that Lauren was always flirting with Gunnar even when she was with T. J.

"Gunnar was looking for you last night," I said.

"I know. He told me."

I didn't ask where she'd been, figuring it wasn't any of my business, and she didn't volunteer any more information.

By the time Carrie Ann and I returned to the front of the store, more customers had gathered and I saw Stanley in the middle of the group. He gave me an apologetic, helpless shrug, and by the time I realized why, it was too late to duck.

But in a place like Moraine, it was bound to happen sooner rather than later.

My mother, scowling when she turned to me, said, "Arrested? You were arrested? Oh dear God!"

"Why are you even dealing with Johnny? He's a jerk, he's too emotionally involved, and if he isn't officially part of the investigation, why not blow him off?"

"It's a mess, that's why. Hetty was killed on county land, but Lauren's body was found on town property. We're forced to collaborate with the town official, and unfortunately that's Jay."

"Oh isn't *that* wonderful news."

I gave the man a well-deserved, parting hug for springing me from the town jail and headed into the store . . .

. . . only to find one of the twins bagging groceries and my mother behind the cash register. She had been trying to insinuate herself into my business, both my personal *and* my professional life, ever since I'd moved back to Moraine. Just let me turn my back for one minute, one time, and there she was, acting like she owned the place. Give that woman a foot in the door and she seizes control of the whole building. And as everyone knows, there can be only one queen bee.

The Wild Clover was my hive.

We stared at each other. "Hi," I said. My voice sounded weak.

"You weren't minding the store," she said, reading my thoughts, knowing perfectly well she wasn't welcome to intrude like this, but doing it anyway. None of the Fischer women could be called passive bystanders in the game of life. And my mother was a master player.

"Where on earth were you?" she asked. "I can understand taking a few hours, but . . ." Mom checked her watch.

"I'm here now," I said, before she could dive into a lecture about my poor business practices. "Thanks for helping. I'll be right back to take over."

I scurried for the back of the store.

Holly turned from straightening a shelf, saw me, and grinned. "FTF (*Face To Face*)," she said, too low for Mom or any of the customers to hear. "I thought we'd be having all our future conversations through those jail phones. Stanley was pretty upset about Johnny Jay arresting you."

"I'm not arrested anymore. What's Mom doing here?"

"Grams and Mom stopped in after church and decided we needed major help, since you weren't around and business increased even more after they found Lauren's body. I tried to stop them, I really did, but NFW (*No Freaking Way*) were they leaving. It's kind of a miracle they didn't hear about your latest brush with justice at church this morning."

"Where's Grams now?" If Grams was in the vicinity, she could pack up Mom and put me back behind the cash register of my own store.

"She went home to whip up casseroles. One for us later, one for Rita Kerrigan and another for Norm Cross."

In all the drama, I'd forgotten about Hetty's husband, Norm, and how he must be coping with all this. I really hoped the casserole was low-fat, because every time Norm came into the store, he bought lots of bacon and sausages and anything else that made major contributions to clogged arteries. Real butter, whole milk, ice cream, beef liver. And he weighed a ton.

If we had taken bets on which one would depart this world first, my money would have ridden on Norm. But then I hadn't figured tragic endings into the equation.

Speaking of bets. That reminded me of my cousin and the bet we'd had that all of the seats at my candle-making class would be filled.

"Where's Carrie Ann?" I asked, already feeling several inches shorter, a condition that presented itself whenever I had to deal with my mother on her terms. I felt like a visitor in my own store. "Didn't she show up?"

"She's in the storage room, having a big talk with Gunnar."

"Gunnar's in the back with Carrie Ann?"

"No, they're on the phone."

"What are they talking about?"

Holly shrugged. "Probably the same old. Their kids and Carrie Ann's visitation rights."

"Who taught Mom how to use the cash register?" The golden rule popped into my head. Whoever watched over the money controlled the place.

"Really, Story," Holly said, "you don't have to be a bra surgeon to scan groceries these days. It's all computerize And she's a fast learner."

"Can you get her out of here?"

"Maybe." Holly had a smug look on her face like was at least one step ahead of me, maybe more. "But if you never ask me to help with your bees ever again." grinned slyly.

"Great. Cut me off at the knees when I'm already When I'm crawling to you for help."

"Promise."

"Fine. You win." I slammed into the storage before Holly could see the lie in my eyes.

Carrie Ann was draped in my office chair. Sh straight when she saw me. "Gotta go," she sai phone and hung up. Her eyes were red and sv stood, then promptly fell into my open arms. I fresh booze breath. "When they found Laurer said, backing away, wiping her eyes, "it hit m I thought it would."

I shrugged and shook my head in a sa even know what to say to make you feel b drinking isn't the answer."

"How did you know?"

"Buy some breath mints. That will

"Don't tell anybody. Please. I'm n that horrible road."

"Everybody has relapses," I sai was true. "I'll tell you what? You bet, so you can pay me back by ca

Twelve

Here's what I firmly believe about mother/daughter relationships:

- They work best at a distance. Living close to each other is a recipe for disaster (in my humble, but experienced opinion).

- There is less conflict if you don't have clashing personalities, which my mother and I definitely do.

- From my personal observations, oldest daughters have the most complicated relationships with their mothers.

- Younger sisters, on the other hand, are spoiled rotten.

"I wasn't arrested," I said to the gathering group since they were all listening in. I avoided direct eye contact with my mother. "Johnny Jay wanted to consult with me, like a debriefing. That's all."

Stanley gave me a puzzled look. I attempted to display a certain expression, sort of a brow-knitting plea meant to convey a message just for him. It was supposed to say, *go along with me, don't pursue this subject any further please!*

"Okay, then," Stanley said, either catching on or letting confusion reign. "Good to know. I guess I better check my facts next time."

"Another false rumor," someone from the back said, sounding disappointed.

"Rumor?" P. P. Patti walked in just in time for her favorite topic: gossip. "Did I miss something?"

"No," Aurora Tyler, owner of Moraine Gardens and my neighbor across the street, said. "We thought Story had been arrested, but here she is."

Aurora, late fiftyish, had long, naturally gray-streaked hair, wore flowing psychedelic clothing and thick sandals, preferred accessories made from hemp, and had a firm grasp on anything that didn't lead to a realistic viewpoint. Clairvoyants, magic, vortexes, flying objects. Bring 'em on.

According to Aurora, she'd been involved in a fatal car accident in the Arizona desert. Before her lifeblood drained away, a flying saucer came to the rescue, beamed her up to their ship, restored her life, and returned her to earth as good as new.

"Did everybody hear about Lauren Kerrigan?" Patti said, anxious to have the scoop ahead of the rest. That wasn't going to happen today.

"We heard," Stanley said.

Patti shuffled into the middle of the group. "Two women shot dead almost in our backyard! It could have been any of us, if you think about it."

"Nothing is random," Aurora said to Patti and anybody else who cared to listen. "Every present and future event is determined by a chain of occurrences from the past."

"Huh?" Patti said.

"Aurora means," I explained, slightly disturbed that I understood what she was trying to say, "everything that happens to you or me or anybody else is predetermined. We can't control the outcome."

"So you think Hetty and Lauren were going to die no matter what?" Patti scowled and shot me a look that said Aurora was off her rocker (and this coming from Patti!).

"Free will simply doesn't exist," Aurora said firmly, before wandering off to shop. At Aurora's request, I carried a full array of tofu, tempeh, and seitan at The Wild Clover. Anything for my customers, especially one with alien blood flowing through her veins.

Milly Hopticourt, The Wild Clover newsletter editor and recipe tester, finished arranging bouquets of spring flowers from her massive flower gardens. We stocked them at the front of the store where they were a big hit with people walking by. And not to show favorites, Aurora's native plants were for sale in pots right outside the door, too.

"Maybe Lantern Man killed them," Stanley said to a chorus of snickers mingled with just as many ahas. The snickerers couldn't completely buy into the idea of a ghost wandering the old logging trail, but they still wouldn't set foot in The Lost Mile. The aha-ers were totally convinced that evil incarnate walked the woods.

"Just so it's perfectly clear," I said. "I didn't make up Lantern Man."

"I'm not so sure," Mom added.

"I believe he's real," Milly said.

"He exists," Stanley insisted.

Stanley's comments generated some lively discussion. While they debated whether or not a ghost could actually kill (based on the damage Lantern Man had done to camping equipment, the possibility seemed to exist in some of their minds), I worked on a more immediate problem—how to remove Mom from my store.

"Shouldn't you go help Grams make casseroles?" I said

to her. "She's getting up there in age. That's a lot of work for one woman. Three casseroles might be more than she can handle."

"We chopped and measured everything early this morning," Mom said. "She just has to mix the ingredients together and put them in the oven. We were going to freeze one for later, but now we'll take that one over to Rita, the poor woman. A mother shouldn't ever have to bury her child. So sad." That was the extent of Mom's fluffy side. She clapped her hands together and said, "Now, let's get back to work."

I used my cell phone to call Grams.

"Do you need help?" I asked.

"No, precious. Everything is in the oven, cooking away. But you're so sweet to offer."

So that was that, at least for today. Mom was on the clock and she wasn't punching out any time soon.

Customers kept coming in the store all afternoon, congregating up front or outside on the Adirondack chairs I'd arranged once the weather had improved. Some of them went into the old choir loft, which I'd converted into a cozy area for weekly events, like the seniors' Monday afternoon card games. Customers stayed up there all afternoon playing gin rummy and throwing around more murder theories than cards.

And the theories and motives grew wilder as the day progressed. After a while, I couldn't listen anymore.

Lori Spandle came in to open her mouth in an ongoing effort to get thrown out of my store.

"That Hunter Wallace is one sexy man," she said, knowing full well I was seeing him and wanting to ruffle my feathers. She stuck her big boobs out as far as they went. "Too bad I'm married."

"That never stopped you before," I replied.

Lori flounced away.

The only regular customers I didn't see before we locked

up at five o'clock were the families of the victims, who were presumably grieving and making funeral arrangements, and Stu Trembly, who probably had more business than I did over at his bar and grill. Good thing it was Carrie Ann's day to work or who knows how far she would have slipped into a pitcher of tap beer over there.

"I need your help," I said to her after we locked up, before she could get into her car and drive away.

Carrie Ann looked beat. "Now what?"

I had one of Grams's casseroles in my hands. I'd offered to take it over to Norm Cross before joining the rest of my family for dinner. Mom hadn't argued.

"Help me deliver this casserole to Norm," I said to my cousin.

"Sure, why not. I don't have anything better to do."

With that, we hopped into my ten-year-old, rusted-out pickup truck and headed north out of town. "I can't believe this old bucket of bolts is still running," Carrie Ann said.

"Watch what you say about her!" I said, laughing. "I take good care of my baby." Which was true. She never had to wait past her due date for an oil change.

We crossed the bridge over the Oconomowoc River, followed the curve onto Creamery Road, then cut south again. I could have walked to Norm and Hetty Cross's house faster than I could drive there, since there wasn't any quick-and-easy access to their property from the main road.

The prefabricated home they owned hadn't aged well. Set back among large shadowy trees, corrosion had done its work and I could see rusty joints and sagging where there shouldn't be any. The front steps consisted of cement blocks and a few planks of mossy pine.

Norm opened the front door as soon as we got out of the truck. He filled every inch of the doorway.

"We brought you a casserole," I said.

"Come on in." Norm backed up, creating enough space for us to cram in.

I'd never been inside his house before. The last time I'd been on this property, I'd been half the size I am today and Hetty had escorted me back the way I came, yanking my ear while I squealed, leaning into her to relieve the pain. Now I was all grown up and inside the Witch's lair.

Or rather her kitchen, which smelled of recently fried bacon. Neither Hetty nor Norm would have earned any clean house awards. Norm made room on the counter by pushing aside objects with a full sweep of his arm. I set the casserole down.

And promptly fell over something alive, wiggling on the floor. It had wrapped itself around my legs, throwing me off balance, and I was down before I knew it. The thing attacked, diving on my chest, raking its claws on my skin, and attempting to attack my face. I hid behind my hands and felt paralysis setting in.

"Help," I sputtered, fear cutting off my airway.

Carrie Ann reached down and rescued me, hauling me up from the floor. "Nobody's ever died from face kisses," she said. "Boy, you really flipped out."

"What is that thing?" I asked, safely tucked behind my cousin. It had to be the ugliest dog I'd ever seen, a cross between a Chihuahua and something hairier. An alien from space right out of an Aurora story. Hairy antennas. Whiskers in all the wrong places. Long chin hair like a billy goat.

"Not sure what kind of mix she is," Norm said. "She came that way from the shelter."

"Oh, how sweet," Carrie Ann said. "A rescue dog."

"You girls want to sit down?"

"I don't get along great with dogs," I said, backing up. At least my heart rate was heading back to normal.

"You're around Hunter's dog all the time," Carrie Ann pointed out.

"Ben is different."

My cousin had her hands on her hips now, chastising me. "You need to get over this goofy fear of dogs." Then to Norm, "Story was attacked by a dog when she was a kid and can't seem to get past it."

"Aha," Norm said, understanding.

Carrie Ann didn't let it go. "It's a tiny, tiny dog. How could you be afraid?"

"I'm fine," I said, forcing myself forward again. My cousin was right. Humiliating, really, to be afraid of *that* little thing. But size wasn't always everything. What about piranhas? Or scorpions?

Feeling slightly foolish, I sat down and we exchanged expressions of sympathy. I wished I could have come up with something more original than "I'm sorry for your loss" and "She had a lot of life still in her" but words couldn't possibly help Norm with his grief. Going through the motions was all we knew how to do.

Two minutes later we were out of conversation. Yet how could we leave the man there all by himself?

The hairy little dog sniffed around under the table, lapping up crumbs, which were plentiful. I started to relax and even risked extending a finger so the animal could sniff it. This wasn't so bad.

During a stretch of silence, I eyed Carrie Ann, hoping she would think of something more to say, because my mind was totally blank. Norm started the ball rolling again. "I heard you were there when they found my wife," he said to me.

I nodded, not liking the new direction.

"Did she say anything? Any last words for me?"

I was disappointed in myself for not coming up with something for Norm to hang on to for the rest of his life, even if it had to be a lie. But I was caught more off balance by his question than when the dog tripped me. I dumbly shook my head. "She'd passed on by the time we got there," I said. "I'm sorry."

What a ditz I was! If I'd been the one in his shoes, I'd want to know that my dying loved one had said something important. Like "Tell Story I love her." Why hadn't I thought of something like that?

Norm looked disappointed in me, too. "Hetty hated when kids came into The Lost Mile," he said. "She thought only bad would come of it, like what happened with all you teenagers drinking that time. I don't blame her for worrying so much, because now look what happened. One of you, from that same gang, came back and killed her."

Somehow Norm had clumped me in with Lauren Kerrigan, making me feel guilty by association, like I had personally killed Johnny Jay's dad, then came back to do the same to his wife. And what was with the gang reference? Weren't we just ordinary kids?

"It had to have been an accident," I said, hearing Carrie Ann start to sniffle next to me. If she started crying, I might break down and join her. I shot her a don't-get-started glare, just as the dog tinkled on top of my right flip-flop. Gross! I picked up a soiled paper napkin from the table and blotted my foot.

"She does that sometimes," Norm said, seeing it happen and not even lifting his voice to reprimand his dog. "She must like you."

Yeah, right.

"The police will sort everything out," Carrie Ann said. "In the meantime, do you have any family you can call, someone who can come and stay with you?"

"None I'd want around."

At least Carrie Ann knew what to say, while I sat there acting like my mouth was numb from novocaine, and anything coming out would be pure slobber. Next she said, "There's some talk around town that Lantern Man might have been involved in what happened."

Norm's face clouded over faster than a spring day in Wisconsin, and his tone of voice wasn't pleasant when he said, "Stupid talk. Who said that?"

Carrie Ann blinked. "I don't really remember who started it."

"Stupid because Lantern Man wouldn't hurt anybody?" I really wanted to know, amazed at Norm's strong reaction. "Or stupid to believe he exists?"

"It's time for you girls to go." Norm stood up abruptly in case we didn't get the verbal message.

"I'm sorry we upset you," I said.

"I hate gossip," Norm said. "It hurts people."

"Me, too," Carrie Ann said. "I hate it, too."

"If there's anything I can do . . ." I made the mistake of saying, implying that I might be able to redirect any Lantern Man talk if that would make Norm feel better. Not that I could really do that without raising more gossip, but if saying it helped . . .

Norm jumped in before I could finish. "Now that you mention it," he said, "there is. I'm going to have to take care of a lot of details in the next several days, and Dinky isn't used to being alone. Can she stay with you?"

Dinky? Norm bent down, fumbled on the floor, and came up with the little ratty dog. Oh no!

"Uh-uh," I said, realizing my quick reflex storytelling needed major polishing. I'd have to find time to practice. "But I work at the store every day," I managed to say.

"She likes to visit. See how friendly she is? Your customers will love her."

"Some of my customers will object," I said, thinking about his dog's peeing problem.

I looked at the scrawny thing and didn't feel one iota of affection welling from my heart. Was my heart two sizes too small? Or was my reluctance because my foot reeked of dog urine? I pondered a way out. If only I could find the perfect excuse. If only I had more time.

"Of course she can come for a visit," Carrie Ann said, taking Dinky out of Norm's arms and cuddling her. My cousin had claimed responsibility. I liked that much better. "Does she have any special toys we should take along?"

Norm and Carrie Ann made a big deal of collecting Dinky's dishes, kibble, toys, and a pink, grimy "blankie." We were bogged down with enough dog paraphernalia to open a doggy daycare when Norm thanked us for the casserole and shut the door.

"What are you doing?" I said, hiding my hands behind my back when Carrie Ann tried to get me to take Dinky from her. "You're taking the creature. *You* offered, not me."

"Story, how could you even think of saying no to him?"

"I didn't say no. But I was getting ready to." I pitched the doggy equipment into the back of my truck and got in.

"I saw it in your eyes," Carrie Ann said, getting in with Dinky. "And I couldn't believe you were going to refuse to help him. His wife is dead. Shame on you."

"But look at it." Dinky blinked back at me. "And it peed on my foot, so it isn't even housebroken properly. It's your problem, not mine."

"And she is *not* an *it*."

"She, then. She's your problem, not mine."

"I'm not allowed to have pets in my apartment."

We were down the road from Norm's when I discovered that little tidbit. "What!"

"No pets."

"Then you'll have to hide it . . . er . . . her."

"The landlady lives in the apartment next to me. I'm afraid you're stuck. But don't worry a bit, I'll answer any dog questions that come up."

"Oh dear God!" I yelled, sounding exactly like my mother.

Thirteen

I never showed up for dinner with my family that night. We had been too close for comfort as it was. Mom and Holly had been at the store the entire day, and I didn't want to get into it with Mom, which happened almost every time we had meals together. So I called from my truck and told Grams I was too tired and couldn't make it.

After Carrie Ann and I unloaded Dinky's personal belongings, we returned to The Wild Clover. She drove off, I parked the truck behind the store, checked to make sure everything was locked up tight, then Dinky and I walked home.

The dog scampered along ahead of me on a leash I'd dug out of her stuff. She lunged at the end of it, determined to stay out front as lead pack dog. Sometimes she strained so hard, she gurgled and choked. Dumb dog didn't even know how to walk on a leash. This was bound to be a major disaster.

At home I showed Dinky around the backyard, pointing out better places to do her business than on my foot.

At some point I finally realized that, at least physically,

I had the upper hand in our relationship. I abandoned some of my dog-fear-induced anxiety, because Dinky couldn't take me in an attack like the big vicious dog from my childhood had. And we'd find out soon enough which one of us would win the seat of power and control. I was confident and determined. It wouldn't be the canine.

Dinky decided to take a nap inside the house and I was sitting on my front porch when Hunter surprised me by coming by on his Harley. He offered me a sweet ride on the back of his bike. I had purchased a black leather jacket for just such an occasion, since I absolutely loved motorcycles.

So with the powerful motor beneath me, and my arms wrapped around Hunter's lean mean pecs, we headed north out of town toward Holy Hill, a national shrine perched on the highest point in southeastern Wisconsin. Unlike the small church I had converted into my store, this one's steeple towered high above several small communities, its lights glowing and illuminating the sky for miles.

We rode past the building and drove in a loop across the countryside. For those who don't know about Wisconsin's topology and think the state is as flat as Kansas, nothing could be further from the truth, at least in this part of Wisconsin, where two giant ice sheets collided under great pressure during the Ice Age. The earth between them exploded up and out, creating large deposits of rock and sand as well as deep crevices.

Because of that history, Moraine sits among hills, valleys, steep ridges, and deep and plentiful lakes.

With the clear night and sweet smell of approaching summer, I forgot all about death, disaster, and dogs.

An hour later, Hunter parked his bike in front of my house. The night air was warmer and drier than yesterday, so we sat out on my front porch, handholding on an old love seat, which might eventually (hopefully not too far in the future) live up to its name. Although the thing had failed me miserably in the past.

"Did Carrie Ann call you?" I asked, still concerned about my cousin's sobriety.

"No, why?"

"She's drinking again."

I could see he was disappointed, even though he tried to hide it. Hunter didn't like to throw around personal opinions until he had all the facts. That was the cop part of him.

"I could smell alcohol on her this morning," I said. "She promised she'd call you."

"I haven't heard from her yet."

"Call her then."

"I'm not her parent or her jailer. She'll come to me if she needs help."

"You have all kinds of experience. Can't you fix her?"

Hunter shook his head. "Only she can do that. But if you're worried, I'll find some way to run into her and see how she's doing."

"Thanks."

The investigation into the case of the death of the two women in the woods came up next.

"We're making an announcement in the morning," Hunter said, "so I'd appreciate you keeping what I'm about to tell you to yourself. At least until then."

I glanced over at P. P. Patti's house and saw her pass by a window.

"I won't say a word to anyone," I said, wondering briefly if Patti had planted bugs at my house, then decided that kind of thinking, while perfectly realistic, was way too paranoid. "But keep your voice down anyway, just in case."

"In case what?" Hunter asked.

Had I said that out loud? "Never mind. I'm just tired. Tell me."

"We've ruled out the murder-suicide theory. Lauren didn't shoot herself."

I sat quietly and took that in. Two murders! That meant I was involved on a daily basis with a whole bunch of potential suspects, and I really didn't want someone I knew or liked or lived near to be a killer.

For example, I had sat right down in Norm Cross's kitchen, totally unaware that he could be considered *the* prime suspect. He was married to Hetty, and I knew as well as everybody else who watched enough television that spouses were the first ones the police hauled in and grilled. And even if the cops let them go, thinking they didn't do it, by the end of the show it almost always turned out that they actually had.

"Did you question Norm Cross?" I asked. "Did you find out where he was during that time and if he had a motive?"

"We spoke to him, yes."

"And what did he say?"

Hunter grimaced like he really didn't want to say what he was about to say. "You're edging into confidential territory. I can't discuss that with you."

"Oh, right," I agreed. So what did that mean? Did he have something on Norm Cross?

Hunter and I shifted on the love seat and progressed from handholding to Hunter's arm around my shoulder and my head resting against his chest.

What did I really know about Norm? Not much.

He had lived with a mean woman, he didn't know how to train his dog, and he was overly tolerant of substandard conditions judging by the inside of his house. Norm might have done away with Hetty, and I wouldn't have blamed him one bit, but why would he hurt Lauren?

"It also could have been random," Hunter said.

"Not out here."

"You think random acts of violence only happen in big cities?"

"Norm Cross is worth investigating thoroughly," I advised.

"Well, Sherlock, I'll keep that in mind." We heard a noise coming from inside the house. I tried to ignore it.

"What's that whimpering sound?" Hunter asked.

"You don't want to know."

Hunter got up and opened my front door a crack. That was all Dinky needed to slide through and race for me, leaping up and down on my leg, scratching away with her minuscule toenails until I picked her up. Which by the way was the first time I'd actually held the thing. And it wasn't pleasant. Her fur was coarse, and some spots where she didn't have any at all felt like fish scales to me.

But I suffered through the ordeal.

And told Hunter how I ended up with Norm Cross's unruly dog and how my cousin had manipulated me. I didn't see that much funny about it, but Hunter began laughing and wouldn't stop. Every time he looked at Dinky, who sat on my lap like a crowned princess, with all that wild coarse fur in all the wrong places, having decided I was her newest best friend, he started in again.

"Oh, man," he finally said, wiping his eyes. "I needed a good laugh after the day I've had. That's the goofiest looking animal I've ever seen. But it's good to see you tackling your phobia head-on by accepting the challenge."

"This is all Carrie Ann's fault."

"If you're right about her drinking again, at least she hasn't lost her wit and spunk."

"I have a serious question if you're done laughing at me." Some of the talk I'd overhead at the cop shop came back to me.

"I can be serious," Hunter said, not looking serious at all.

"Lauren wasn't killed right away. She crawled away, right?"

Hunter nodded, no longer smiling. "I'm not sure how you found out, but yes."

"So, why didn't the killer shoot her again?"

"Ah, a fine question. Lauren might have pretended to be dead until the killer left or she could have passed out, regained consciousness, then crawled for help. Or the killer might have wanted to watch her suffer."

My imagination took over and I pictured a trail of blood as long as The Lost Mile. "Who would do a thing like that?"

"You'd be surprised. The world is an ugly place."

I looked down at the thing in my lap. To lighten the mood, I said, "Not half as ugly as this dog."

That got Hunter going again. I stifled my own laughter. Now that I really looked at the situation, it *was* sort of funny.

Holly pulled up in her Jag and got out, carrying a brown lunch bag.

"I brought you a care package from Grams," she said, dropping it down on one of the porch's side tables. "Casserole and cherry pie. Hey, Hunter. You're just the man to confirm or deny the latest. Rumor has it, Hetty Cross and Lauren Kerrigan were both murdered."

Hunter held his arms up over his head and glanced up at the sky, a sure sign of frustration. "The minute I think the thought, it's out on the streets."

"What is that thing?" Holly looked at my lap. "And it's alive. Whatever it is, it just moved."

"I'll tell you the story later. Will you take our roommate inside with you and get acquainted?"

"Roommate? Acquainted? That has a permanent ring to it."

"Only temporary."

"Does it have a name?"

"Dinky."

My sister hooted. Hunter joined in. I had to admit, the dog's name was a riot.

Holly picked up Dinky and correctly identified the critter. Or almost. "A puppy!" she said.

"No, I think she's just a very small dog," I said.

"I bet she's still a pup." Cooing at Dinky, Holly went inside.

Hunter and I watched the stars for a while, sitting comfortably together, then he kissed me good-bye before roaring away on his bike.

A shooting star flew through the sky overhead, reminding me of Aurora. I disagreed with her philosophy. Everybody had choices. If we didn't have free will and everything was predetermined, what was the point of even trying to influence outcomes or do our best?

I did, however, believe in chaos.

Fourteen

Monday morning I woke up feeling slightly hungover from sharing a bottle of wine with Holly after Hunter left.

I strolled through my beeyard, checking on my honeybees and thinking hard about Hunter, which happened every time we got together.

At night, in the evenings when the store closed and I could relax, I dropped my reservations. Then I wanted him for eternity, every last bit of him, the good and the bad— which I had some insight into, since I'd known him my entire life.

The light of day was a whole different animal. I became less sure, remembering how incredibly hard a real relationship was and how badly I'd failed in the past. How I had once thought my ex-husband was the right one. These days I needed distance and space before I could make any more life-altering decisions. Besides, look how many women were horrible judges when it came to picking good men. What if I was eternally doomed to be one of them?

Not to mention Hunter hadn't asked me for any kind of commitment, which just went to show how messed up my mind was when it came to men. Why couldn't I just have fun with him instead of worrying about our future?

The pros and cons of Hunter, as went through my head while observing my bees:

PROS:

- Hunter gave me the space to do my own thing, so he wasn't needy. I couldn't do needy after coming from a line of incredibly strong women. Fischer women don't cater to men.

- Unlike a lot of guys, Hunter wasn't looking for a mother. He was totally self-sufficient. He had his own house, kept it up, did his own laundry, cooking, etc.

- He didn't criticize everything I did or give guy know-it-all advice designed to imply my way of doing things was substandard. (Been there, done that.)

- I was attracted to him big-time, and he had great, sexy feet. There was something about a man's feet that really turned me on. Especially this man's. Summer and its promise of bare feet could hardly come fast enough.

CONS:

- Hunter gave me space to do my own thing, but was that because he didn't want me around much? (See the conflict!)

- The man was thirty-four and had never married. Why not? As far as I knew, he'd never even lived with a woman, other than his mother. So was he afraid of commitment?

• And what about his drinking problem? He said it was in
  his past, but Mom said he'd fall off the wagon eventually. I hadn't seen any sign of that, but were we destined
  for big trouble down the road?

Since I had so many unanswered questions, why couldn't I
just live in the moment instead of worrying about the future?
Today, I'd try to take a break from conflicting thoughts and
just enjoy.

My bees looked good. Almost all of them had made it
through the winter while under my rookie care and protection. A big surprise since it was also the first winter I'd had
such a large beeyard and I was still learning the ropes as I
went along.

Not that I hadn't had a few disappointments. In early
spring when I pried open the top of one of the hives and
found the entire colony dead, my heart hurt for days. I felt
so responsible and helpless.

That colony was gone, and nothing I could do would
bring it back, but they'd been replaced with a new queen
and workers, and life went on. I was happy to see yesterday's
recaptured swarm moving around and adjusting to their
upgraded, spacious new home.

Dinky trotted around the yard, exploring her vacation
property. She seemed to understand that when it came to
my bees, she'd better mind her own beeswax. She instinc-
tively gave the beeyard a wide berth, standing and watching me work from its perimeter as though the area had
been dog-proofed with invisible electric fencing.

My backyard was a kaleidoscope of spring colors, with
blooming lilacs, lavender, verbena, and scented geraniums
filling my flowerbeds. Other perennials were forming buds
and the trees were leafing out.

"Hey, Story," I heard a voice call my name and cringed,
keeping my back to her while I continued to check on each
hive. If I ignored her, would she go away? Fat chance.

"Story!"

"Hi, Lori," I said to my least-favorite real estate agent, who unfortunately stood in my ex-husband's driveway next to the house she hoped to sell for him. The woman had always been a barracuda, but she was even worse since the housing market had taken a hit and business had slowed.

"It's bad enough," Lori griped, "that you have all those damn hives in your backyard, and now we just had two deaths in the vicinity."

I glanced her way. "Yeah, it's a crying shame that Hetty and Lauren went and got killed like that and might have ruined your chance for a big commission. They should have discussed the timing with you first."

Lori had a perfectly round face that was quick to redden when she was angry. If the woman had a speck of self-consciousness, her mug should also have changed color in times of extreme embarrassment—like when she'd snuck through my yard to visit my husband and banged into one of the beehives, creating a scene that would have sent any other human being into extended hiding—but humility wasn't one of Lori's attributes.

"Your bees are making the sale of this property almost impossible," she said. "And I'm *never* going to sell it if you don't clean up your lawn and try to act like a normal person. Nobody intentionally grows dandelions."

"Go away, Lori." I went about my chores, making sure each hive still had enough stored honey.

"I'll pay to have your weeds sprayed. Out of my own pocket. How's that?"

"No way. Absolutely no poisons in my yard," I said, turning fully to address her. Lori wore a prissy face, an ill-fitting pantsuit, and Barbielike high heels.

"Why not kill all those weeds?" she pressed. "Everybody else does."

I couldn't help what I said next. The words just slipped out. After all, I am my mother's daughter. "Look at yourself," I said. "If you want to know why I don't use poisons, look in the mirror. You're living proof of what toxins can do to what was once a living organism."

Lori stared at me. "We're not done with this," she croaked. "I'm taking my complaint to the town board." With that, she stomped off.

This wouldn't be the first time Lori and I had gone rounds. Despite having the town chair (aka her husband) in her corner, she had still managed to lose the last time she'd tried to run my bees out of town. If anything, I thought that beekeeping in towns and cities should be encouraged more than it is, not eliminated. Since neighborhoods have more diverse nectar sources, all those lovely annuals and perennials, honeybees stay healthier and produce better honey than those that have to rely on wildflowers and monofloral crops. And I'd say all that if Lori involved the town board again.

I thought a few very bad thoughts about Lori before scooping up Dinky and heading to the store. My Sleeping Beauty sister wasn't an early riser, so opening The Wild Clover fell to Carrie Ann or me every day. I'd hoped to leave Dinky home, but didn't trust the little female as far as I could see her. During the night, she'd chewed up one of my favorite flip-flops, which was the worst thing she could have done if she wanted to stay on my good side.

Monday mornings usually started out slow at the store. This one didn't.

"Hunter's waiting for you," Carrie Ann said, looking perky with her short, straw-colored hair all spiked. I couldn't help thinking her hair reminded me a lot of Dinky's, only with more unnatural color. "He tried to sneak in the back door, but I'm on to him."

"Did you two talk," I asked, "about you-know-what?"

"Uh-huh. We're good."

I breezed by, relieved. Carrie Ann certainly looked upbeat and sober to me.

"Wait a minute," she called. "Not so fast. Where's Dinky? You didn't do something you'll regret later, did you? Please tell me she's okay. You didn't lose her? Please tell me you didn't."

"Relax." I had the dog stuffed under my arm, where she peeked out like a big ball of armpit hair. I was intent on getting to my back office without any of the customers noticing my hairy new addition. Thanks to my cousin's yelling, several customers had turned our way. "She's right here," I whispered, quickly showing living proof to Carrie Ann before racing away. I opened the door of my office/storage area/break room to find Hunter and Ben waiting. Both looked rugged and manly, especially Hunter, considering he was the man and Ben was a dog.

I closed the door behind me.

"I had planned on stopping at your house," Hunter said, with a teasing, amused grin, "but then I saw Lori next door, standing in the driveway with a rabid expression on her face. It looked like you two were having one of your friendly conversations. I didn't want to intrude."

I made a mental note to add another bullet point to Hunter's pro and con list. Con: he needed to be more protective. "What you really mean," I said, "is that you were afraid you might get caught in the crossfire."

"Exactly. I could have called, but I wanted to see your perky, smiling face before I started my day."

"Aren't you sweet!" I couldn't help grinning at that.

I put Dinky on the floor near Hunter's feet, which were encased in Harley Davidson motorcycle boots. I couldn't satisfy my foot fetish. Darn.

Dinky, with four paws on the floor, promptly peed, creating a now-very-familiar yellow puddle. "According to Norm Cross," I said, "that means she likes you."

"I have that effect on women."

While I wiped up the mess, Ben stared at the goofy-looking creature sniffing around his massive paws. Ben was as puzzled as the rest of us when it came to determining what species the little ball of fur was. He lifted the paw she was currently inspecting and gingerly set it down again. Then he backed away.

"Since when do you allow dogs in the store?" Hunter wanted to know, suppressing a chortle.

"Ben just walked right in, and you didn't ask permission."

"He's a service dog. He can go wherever he wants. I'm pretty sure that Dinky doesn't meet the qualifications as outlined under—"

"Stop, please, I have an idea," I said, interrupting. "I completely agree with you. I don't want anything to do with this dog. Arrest it. Take it away, please."

"Don't look to me for assistance. Ben could eat her for lunch. Just keep her in this room and no one will have to know. But you better hope Johnny Jay doesn't find out. He's gunning for you."

That's all I needed on a Monday morning. Johnny was like an enormous vulture waiting for an opportunity to strike. "So why are you two here so early in the morning?" I asked, shaking off the negative, going for the positive. "It must be really important if it brought you into the store."

Hunter usually avoided The Wild Clover, claiming it was, in his words, "a hotbed of rumor and innuendo and a den of dubious drama." Which was probably true. The Wild Clover was a meeting of the minds and not all of them were firing on all cylinders.

"We need to talk," Hunter said. And he wasn't smiling when he said it.

Yikes! Whenever a man said he wanted to talk, I expected nothing but bad news and trouble. In the space of two seconds, all kinds of thoughts rushed through my head. Were we over before we barely got started? Was this the let's-just-be-friends discussion? Couldn't he have picked a better time to drop a bomb on me than first thing in the morning at the store?

"Talk?" I said, dumbly. "Uh-uh . . ."

"About some stuff from the past. A few things I don't remember too clearly."

"Sure." Did he mean our past?

"But not here. Can you meet me at Stu's at noon? I'll buy you lunch."

"Okay." Was I easy or what? "But can you give me a teensy, tiny hint what it's about?" I could have added "so I don't dwell on it all morning and drive myself nuts," but I left that part out.

"We got a warrant and searched Norm Cross's house. We found something."

"So he killed Lauren and Hetty?"

"I didn't say that."

"What did you find?"

"Not here. You'll have to wait."

"Okay."

"And don't bring Dinky."

I suddenly remembered something. "Oh no, I'll have to find someone to cover for me. I totally forgot I have a dental appointment at eleven."

Hunter lifted his eyebrows. "Okay, then, forget it. We'll talk later."

"No!" And lose an opportunity to help out and get inside information at the same time? No way. "I'll meet you as soon as I can. I'll be there. For sure."

After Hunter and Ben disappeared out the back door of the store, I considered workable options for the few hours I'd be gone. Holly (once she showed up) and Carrie Ann should be able to handle business for a while. They had already assured me they could handle the hour I'd be gone to the dentist. Another hour wouldn't hurt if business stayed steady and not too busy.

I poked my head out of the back room. We were already too busy.

"I could use some help up here," Carrie Ann hollered,

reminding me to oil the squeak out of the door I had just peeked out. I saw a long line forming at the register, a sight we went out of our way to prevent if at all possible. Carrie Ann and I worked nonstop for several hours. When Holly arrived, I took a quick moment to give Dinky a potty break, before which I discovered she had gnawed through a box filled with bags of Wisconsin-made beef jerky and had scattered pieces all over the room. I picked up the mess.

Outside on the lawn, Dinky refused to go.

Back inside, a call to the twins to ask if one of them could come in for a few hours produced nothing but a request to leave a voice message and little hope that one of them would return my call in time. So I was stuck. Now what?

Meeting Hunter for lunch and the lure of finding out what he'd found in the Cross's house was too much to resist. So I did the one thing I had promised myself I'd never do. Never, ever, ever. Which proves I should never ever again say never.

But these were extenuating circumstances.

Sometimes a woman has to do what a woman has to do, even when it means going against her principles.

So I called my mother and arranged for her to work for me.

Fifteen

Doctor T. J. Schmidt had all the stereotypical characteristics of a dentist. For one, his teeth couldn't have been
more perfect. They were bigger, straighter, and whiter than
anybody else's, a constant reminder to his patients that if
we'd just taken better care of our own teeth (brushed more,
flossed regularly) we could have had what he had.

Nobody in Moraine had healthier teeth.

For another, he had a happy, smiley face on all the time,
like he really enjoyed what he did for a living and couldn't
wait to inflict pain and torture on his next patient, which
happened to be me at the moment.

For another, he talked nonstop, asking question after
question I couldn't answer, while he filled my mouth with
metal implements and gloved fingers.

"How's the family?"

"Ahkay." I mean what did he expect, a detailed report on
each and every family member from this position? I wasn't
sure he really cared about my answers, but I was bound by

social conditioning to attempt responses. Although whatever happened to "Don't talk with your mouth full"? The thing that really amazed me was how well he understood the slobbering and babbling coming from my vocal cords while he pressed down on my tongue. *"Isthiedklsithkelsk."*

"Really, that's great." He poked and prodded, x-rayed, cleaned, and polished, all the while asking me a few more cordial questions. Then we got to the meaty stuff. The topic turned to murder, although we didn't have much of a two-way conversation going. T. J. brought it up and this time all I had to do was listen to his opinion on the subject.

"Here's what's going around," he said, sticking a mirror into my mouth and poking around. "Some people think Johnny Jay became so angry when he found out Lauren was out of prison, so crazed to learn she was free as a bird, that he lost control and killed her."

"Tatsanwtkealleitleaois."

"Right. And everybody in town has seen him lose control of his temper at some point. He's a hothead. A ticking bomb ready to explode. You have a tiny cavity in your right molar. Should I take care of it today?"

"Noth rith now."

Just then I heard a ding as the outer door opened, and a moment later T. J.'s wife, Ali, came in. She helped out in the dental office a few hours every day, and I had been disappointed when she hadn't been there when I arrived. She'd been out with her sister during all the earlier excitement, and I'd hoped to catch up with her before T. J. called me in.

"Sorry," she said to her husband. "That took longer than I expected." Then to me, "I heard about Lauren." She shook her head. "What a mess."

I would have liked to make a few comments, both to Ali and to T. J. regarding Johnny Jay as potential murder suspect, but T. J. still had my mouth out of service.

"Ali," he said. "Set something up for Story. She has a small cavity."

"Sure," Ali said, leaving the room.

T. J. freed my mouth. "Rinse." He handed me a paper cup.

Finally! "They think the police chief murdered Lauren and Hetty?" I said after swishing and spitting.

"That's the word on the street. She *did* kill his dad. You know the guy as well as I do, he's a bully and he has a mean temper. And a motive."

"I haven't heard a thing about that at the store."

"Believe me," he said, stripping off the protective gloves and tossing them in a trash can. "People talk in this chair."

Yeah, right. How?

Ali walked in carrying a metal tray. I could see more dental equipment on it. One was a big honking syringe.

"Whoa," I said. "That isn't for me, is it?"

T. J. glanced at Ali. "I asked you to make another appointment for her."

"Oh, sorry," Ali said. "I thought you said set up to fill Story's cavity. I misunderstood."

T. J. picked up the syringe. It could've been my imagination, but I swear I saw a gleam of anticipation in his eyes. "How about it, Story? I can have you out of here in fifteen minutes and you won't have to come back again for six months. Really, it's a bitty baby cavity."

I checked my cell for the time. It could work. That is, if I really wanted to be drilled and stabbed, which I didn't. But why not get it over with?

"Do your thing," I told him.

Fifteen minutes later, T. J. (aka mad torture dentist) was still trying to numb my mouth with a third application of the needle. He eyed up my chart. "I don't get it. We've used this on you before without any problem."

"I donth geth it, either."

"You weren't drinking alcohol recently, were you?"

"Vy?"

"Were you?"

"Vine las nith," I said, remembering the bottle of wine

Holly and I had shared. What did wine have to do with the current situation? My face felt like an overinflated balloon filled with helium. My lips and cheeks were missing in action. I couldn't feel a thing. Nothing, that was, except the drill every time he thought I was numb enough to start. Each time he began drilling, a sharp nerve-racking pain shot through my head. "I quith. Leth me up."

I ripped off the plastic bib. A long string of spit dribbled on the front of my shirt.

"I'll have Ali call you at the store about rescheduling," T. J. said. "And next time don't drink alcohol the night before. I'm sure that's where the problem comes in. That happens sometimes."

Just like everybody else, T. J. had to blame what happened on something or someone else. In this case, me for drinking wine. Believe me, it would take an entire bottle of the stuff to get me back in that chair.

I bolted out the door and hustled down Main Street to meet Hunter. I waved at Ben, who sat in the passenger seat of Hunter's SUV, waiting for his partner. His ears twitched slightly in greeting. Ben wasn't big on public displays of affection.

Stu's Bar and Grill was busy with the lunchtime crowd. Hunter waited at a table by the window where he had a clear view of his vehicle and police partner.

I tried to smile, but it didn't happen. Or if it did, I couldn't tell.

"I ordered for you," Hunter said. "Hope you don't mind. You're running late and I know you're crunched for time."

"Tank ow."

"What's wrong with your face?"

"Dentith."

One of Stu's part-time waitresses came over with two baskets filled with burgers and fries and placed them on the table.

"I guess you won't be eating that?" Hunter said.

I shook my head, holding my jaw.

"Okay, I'll talk for a while. You listen."

I nodded.

Here's what Hunter told me between bites of burger while I alternated between sucking on French fries and swishing ice water in my mouth:

- The cops had obtained a warrant to search Norm Cross's house after Norm refused to let them in.

- Since Hetty was a murder victim, the police needed to search for clues to her death. They had a perfect right to force Norm's hand, whether or not he was a suspect.

- This morning, Hunter, Johnny Jay, and various other law-enforcement officials arrived and searched the premises. Nothing was found to indicate Norm might have killed his wife or to help them solve the case.

- But a poster board in a spare bedroom drew Hunter's attention. Newspaper clippings were arranged on it. And each and every one of them featured a phenomenon from The Lost Mile: Lantern Man.

"Over the years, the local papers have run quite a few stories about Lantern Man," Hunter said. "Especially after the camper attack. Then every time someone claimed a sighting, here came another article."

One side of my face twitched in amazement at all the developing news. Moraine wasn't exactly a hub of interest. That is until now.

Hunter continued, "Why would Norm save the articles and mount them on the wall unless they mean something to him?"

"Unlesh heesh Lantern Man!" If I spoke slowly, I almost sounded normal.

"That's what I'm thinking. I suggested that to him this morning, but he denied it."

"Of courth."

"Get this part, though." Hunter leaned over his plate, closer to me. "I also found a collection of lanterns in the same room."

"No kiddin'."

"He said he'd collected vintage lanterns for years."

"Like Coleman lanternsh?"

"And railroad lanterns. I came on stronger, putting pressure on him, but he still denied any knowledge of Lantern Man's identity."

We thought about that for a while. Why couldn't Norm be Lantern Man? His property abutted the state and county land and he'd told me just yesterday how much his wife hated having kids hang out in The Lost Mile. Maybe Norm hated them even more. Enough to terrorize anybody who ventured in there after dark, scaring them silly so they wouldn't come back.

"Well, now we know," I said, forming the words carefully and hearing them come out just right. "Even if we can't prove it."

"Remember the night the group of us went in there?"

"It's not a nith I'll ever forget."

"Right. But Lantern Man didn't make an appearance."

"No."

"Why not?"

"Busy doin' somefin' else?"

"I'm guessing we made plenty of noise."

I shrugged. We'd been so bombed—or at least some of us had been—that we *would* have been really loud. "I dunno."

"I think I'll see if I can dig up police dispatch logs and records for that period of time."

"Why?"

"This is a small community. What do you do when you're going to be gone for a few days?"

"Tell one person, den everyone knows."

"Exactly. Everybody finds out. Including Johnny Jay. And what does he do?"

"Nothin'."

"I'll rephrase that. What does he do as a service to everybody other than you?"

"I dunno."

"He does drive-bys. Makes sure nothing is going on that shouldn't be."

"He does?"

"Sometimes residents even call in and ask him to check on their places. So if Norm was out of town during our walk in the woods, that's just one more nail in Norm's Lantern Man coffin."

"But why go to all dat twouble?"

"Because Hetty Cross and Lauren Kerrigan are dead. And because Lantern Man was an unknown entity back then and still is. And because all our paths are converging in one place."

"In Da Lost Mile."

I couldn't help being intrigued.

"What we talked about just now is private," Hunter said. "Between me and you. If we're wrong and this gets out, it wouldn't be fair to Norm. He just lost his wife. He doesn't need more troubles. And I know you can keep a secret. That's why I came to you."

That felt good. He trusted me. I spoke carefully, feeling little needles jabbing at my lips and cheek. "I'll keep my ears open at the store."

Hunter chuckled. "Anything coming from the store's gab group can't be taken too seriously. I can't believe I'm saying this, but let me know what's going around, okay?"

I gave him a lopsided grin at that, since normally Hunter hated gossip. His about-face could only be in the line of duty. "K," I said.

By the time I got back to The Wild Clover, my mother had rearranged the shelves.

Sixteen

My mother hadn't reorganized *all* of the shelves. Just the ones nearest the front of the store, those carefully and creatively designed by me. Shelf placement is a science in the grocery business and I'm constantly looking for creative ways to build displays, end caps, and case stacks into attractive sensory experiences that sell products.

As they say, retail is detail.

So the first things my customers encountered when they walked in the door of The Wild Clover were the hard-to-resist items like:

- Fresh flowers from Milly's yard and from Moraine Gardens

- Just-baked loaves of bread from a wonderful bakery in Stone Bank

- Woven baskets filled with old-fashioned candies like candy lipsticks, Pixy Stix, lemonheads, pop rocks, and laffy taffy

- And a special case stack of Queen Bee Honey products: pure wildflower honey, both processed and raw; honey sticks; honey candy; beeswax candles; and whatever else I could make from my bees' honey

But now everything up front had been drastically changed, replaced with toilet tissue and laundry detergent. Talk about first impressions.

"It looks so much better now," Mom said, dusting her hands, finished righting her world, forcing her unbending ideas into *my* world. "More functional."

Adrenaline was unnumbing my face fast.

"I wasn't going for functional," I said with a neutral tone, proud of my self-control, although I had a twitchy left eye. "Where's my honey?"

"With the peanut butter where it belongs."

Carrie Ann shot me an amused glance. Holly had run for cover when she saw me coming in, probably hiding out in the back in case I blamed her for Mom's actions. She should realize by now that I understood.

Nobody controls Mom.

Voices came floating down from the choir loft, reminding me that today was Sheepshead Day for the seniors at The Wild Clover, as it was every Monday, and the games were on. Sheepshead is Wisconsin's official card game, ever since so many Germans settled here and brought the game over from the old country. It's a trick-taking game and, when played five-handed, the way we like it best, the dealer's partner is a big secret, even from the dealer.

I heard Grams say, "Pass," meaning she was passing on the blind.

Mom pursed her lips, her eyes shifting upward. "Your grandmother gets very aggressive when she plays cards. You should hear some of the things coming out of her mouth."

"She's fun," I said, defending Grams, as always. "She's

like the queen bee of her generation. Everybody likes to be around her."

"Humph," Mom said, since everybody knew there could only be one queen bee and she was it, not Grams. "If you girls can handle the store without me, I'm walking down to the library."

A hoot sounded from up in the choir loft, and then someone said, "Thanks for taking me for a ride!"

With that, Mom rolled her eyeballs in disgust and left.

I surveyed the damage to my store.

Somebody rapped on an upstairs table, doubling the pot.

"I'll help you put everything back," Holly said from behind me, sounding apologetic. "SS (*So Sorry*), but she gets something in her head and nothing can change her mind. Believe me, I tried."

"She *is* stubborn."

"Not like us at all. LOL (*Laugh Out Loud*)."

And there was some truth to my sister's tongue-in-cheek remark. She and I came from a long line of Amazonlike matriarchs. Even sweet Grams had a strong-as-a-tornado side, revealed on very rare occasions and only when it came to defending her family.

"I can manage here," I said. "If you help Carrie Ann."

The toilet paper was the first to go to the back of the store with the rest of life's necessities. Out came my containers brimming with wildflower honey sticks, jars of Queen Bee Honey, honeycomb, and honey candy with those marvelous soft centers. I stopped long enough to unwrap one and pop it in my mouth.

While I worked on restoring order, customers came and went, the card-playing seniors grew louder, and the shocking murders of Hetty Cross and Lauren Kerrigan remained everyone's main topic of conversation.

I stayed in the background, doing a lot more listening than commenting. As a local business owner, I learned a long time ago to keep my opinions to myself, especially when it came to sensitive topics. No sense jeopardizing business by coming on strong and opinionated. We had enough loud know-it-alls around to pick up my slack. In public, I tried not to talk religion, politics, sex, or now, murder suspects.

The big question was: Which woman had been the original target?

If it was Hetty, then Norm had most of the town's guilty votes, simply by association. If Lauren was the one who the killer had sighted in on, then Johnny Jay had the most motive and all the opportunity. In both of those cases, people figured that the other woman had been an accidental bystander.

But if *both* women were intended victims—a stretch for all of us—nobody had a clue. As far as anyone knew, the two women barely knew each other, if at all. Hetty kept to herself. As her closest neighbor, *I* didn't even know her well. Hetty didn't have children, hadn't belonged to any church groups, and didn't make appearances in town unless she absolutely had to.

And Lauren had been gone for a long time. When she did reappear, she hadn't contacted any of her old friends, so why would she have hooked up with Hetty Cross?

So first we had to sort out that dilemma.

Lauren Kerrigan's brother, Terry, came into the store and gave us some useful insight, facts we hadn't had before. Which was amazing considering how close-knit and closed-mouthed that family usually was.

"Lauren was scared," he said. "Terrified of what would happen at the end. I don't care what my mother thought, Lauren was too afraid of dying to even consider taking her own life. I kept saying that over and over, but Mom wouldn't listen. She's having an awful time accepting that Lauren was murdered."

"Why do you think Lauren went to The Lost Mile? To meet Hetty?" I asked, since Terry seemed like he wanted to get his thoughts off his chest.

A crowd was forming around us, although none of the customers wanted to be caught red-handed (or rather red-eared) listening in on our conversation, so they pretended like they were shopping. Suddenly, everybody in the store wanted some of my honey products.

Terry shrugged. "No idea. She didn't know Hetty."

"And why did she think she needed a weapon?"

Terry's eyes scanned the store. "I really shouldn't be talking about this. It's personal family stuff."

"Maybe if we all put our heads together," I reasoned. "We'll think of something important that might help figure out what happened and catch her killer."

I heard murmurs of agreement. P. P. Patti slipped into the store, wearing a black fanny pack, a matching visor on her head, and something hanging from a lanyard around her neck.

Terry still had the floor. "I already told everything I know to the . . ." He stopped there and we all could guess what he was about to say. He'd given his statement to Johnny Jay, probably under duress considering how well they got along. Johnny had to be a prime suspect in his eyes just like in mine.

"Okay," Terry said, deciding to tell us for his own reasons. "Lauren came home to die. She wouldn't have even known about Rita's gun. I bought it after Lauren went away. She would have had to search the house to find it. Why would she even do that? And if anybody knows the reason why she took it and went into the woods, you better speak up now."

The room went so quiet I could hear somebody in the loft slap down a card. Even the gamers hushed after that. Nobody around Terry had anything helpful to say. The silence stretched and became uncomfortable.

"When's the funeral?" Patti piped up and asked.

"It's going to be private," Terry said. "Just family." And

with that, he walked out without buying whatever he'd come in for.

Pretty soon Stu showed up to remind us about Chopper Murphy's Irish wake tomorrow night. Chopper had been a regular at Stu's, bellying up to the bar until one day his lights went out exactly where he would have wanted them to. After a few shots of whiskey, his heart stopped beating. He pitched off his bar stool and that was the last of him.

His wife, Fiona, buried him two weeks ago and the whole town turned out.

But she didn't give him an Irish wake. Chopper started haunting her, according to Fiona, and he couldn't rest until she did it up properly.

So Stu was helping her take care of details.

Patti came close enough that I could read the words on the card dangling from her lanyard.

"Press pass?" I asked.

Patti beamed. "Isn't it cool? I made it on my computer."

"So, you aren't actually a member of the press and you don't really have special rights?"

"Not yet, but I will."

Okay then.

After the twins came in to help out, I closed myself into the back room and sat at my desk with Dinky on my lap. Once she stopped trying to crawl up and lick my lips, she settled down and I had time to think.

It didn't seem fair that one night of bad judgment had changed Lauren Kerrigan's life forever. Then to have terminal cancer and end up dead on the ground, murdered. But life wasn't fair, a fact that announced itself over and over even if I didn't want to face the truth of it. Some people just never caught any slack in life. They started out with more than their share of bad luck, and they ended the same way.

There was a light tap on the door, and Holly slipped in.

"She wasn't suicidal," I said to my sister. "Terry said she was afraid of dying."

"Aren't we all?"

"So she took the gun for protection against somebody."

"She must have been really scared."

"Maybe."

I told Holly about Norm, about the Lantern Man articles on his wall and about the lantern collection. I'd promised Hunter I'd keep that a secret, but like all secrets, they instantly go to work on a person and don't let up until they've been shared with at least one other person. If I had to spill my guts to someone I trusted, Holly was the one.

"Patti's out in the aisles," my sister said, "interviewing customers about Lantern Man. She's convinced that Lantern Man came across Lauren and Hetty in The Lost Mile and killed them. Did you know she has a mini-video camera in her fanny pack? And she's been going through old newspapers to get up to speed on his appearances."

"Wow! I'm impressed. Four whole sentences and you didn't revert to text-speech even once. I'm proud of you."

"WE (*Whatever*)," Holly said.

Seventeen

Tuesday morning arrived before I was ready for it. A violent spring storm moved in during the night, zinging spears of lightning at the ground right outside my bedroom window, keeping me awake with crashes of thunder. Rain beat steadily on the roof, then banged louder as drops of rain turned to balls of hail. Looking out the window, I finally saw gray wisps of light announcing an overcast morning. White balls of ice covered the grass.

The Oconomowoc River, swollen and flowing rapidly, rose to the top of its banks. My backyard hadn't flooded for a long time, but this rainstorm would take it to the brink or beyond. My honeybees would spend the morning safely inside their well-constructed hives. Good thing the beehives stood on cement blocks elevated well above the ground or I'd be out there frantically moving them to higher ground. At least I got some things right.

Dinky, I found out right away, was terrified of storms and thought this one was strictly for her benefit. She burrowed down under the bedcovers, trembled all night, and didn't peer out until the thunder subsided. She also apparently hated rain and refused to go outside, giving me the task of cleaning up after her again. Her only redeeming quality at this point was that her very tiny bladder couldn't produce enormous quantities of fluid for me to mop up. I really appreciated my wood floors.

Norm Cross didn't answer his phone when I called to demand that he take her back. Just as well he didn't have an answering machine either, since my mood wasn't up to its usual tolerance level and I might've verbalized some of my dark thoughts about his mangy mutt.

After feeding Dinky, I ate a honey bun, drank multiple cups of coffee, watched the rain, and pondered rogue cops and whether Johnny Jay might have murdered Lauren Kerrigan and Hetty Cross:

- Johnny Jay hated Lauren Kerrigan for killing his father.

- A scenario (with a few gaping holes): Somehow he found out Lauren was back and got her to agree to meet him in the woods.

- She's afraid so she takes a weapon along.

- They struggle. But Lauren's weak from the cancer and treatments. Johnny Jay takes the gun away from her and shoots her.

- Hetty, out for an evening walk, minding her own business, sees him shoot Lauren, so he shoots her, too.

End of story.
Now to prove it.
I'd seen enough cop shows on television to understand exactly how hard that was going to be, mostly because Johnny Jay held all the power cards. My word wouldn't count for squat against a law-enforcement official's.

So I had to prove his guilt beyond a shadow of a doubt.

With a new mission in mind, to bring down a longtime nemesis, I showered and dressed for the day in jeans and a warm yellow hoodie, opened my sister's bedroom door, deposited Dinky in her bed without waking her, grabbed an umbrella, and made my way to the store.

By the time I'd walked those two blocks, unlocked the store door, and slipped in, I was drenched in spite of the umbrella, which turned out to be useless in the gusting wind and sheets of sleet.

While I tried to dry my hair with paper towels, Carrie Ann called to say she'd be late, which wasn't a big deal since the storm had all my regular customers hunkered down, waiting it out. The tourist business would be nonexistent today, too.

Stu Trembly stopped by for his morning newspaper and confirmed that local gossip at his bar supported the Johnny Jay killer theory over Norm Cross, but no one had any concrete evidence to nail our police chief. Also Stu was busy getting ready for Chopper Murphy's wake tonight.

Milly Hopticourt came in with a rhubarb meringue torte she'd whipped up in preparation for the next newsletter, and we declared it a winning recipe.

"I need some morel mushrooms," Milly said, wiping meringue from her lips. "I have an idea for a recipe. Somebody spotted them a few days ago and with this rain they ought to be growing big and plump."

"I'll hunt some down," I said, thinking of my favorite secret spot for harvesting morels.

A while later, the rain still hadn't subsided. Puddles grew in the street outside while my store's awning sagged and overflowed.

I tried calling Norm again. No luck.

Lori Spandle showed up with a warning. "I have a potential buyer looking at the house today," she said. "Try to stay out of the way and don't blow it."

"What time are you showing the house?"

"Noon."

"Good luck." Which I meant from the bottom of my heart. If my ex-husband's house finally sold, I'd have that nasty woman off my back. Although it had been quiet and peaceful at home without a neighbor on that side. I wondered what kind of person would live there next. Anyone was better than my ex-husband.

T. J. Schmidt came in, shaking an umbrella and showing his perfect teeth. "You haven't returned Ali's call to reschedule," he said.

When pigs fly, I thought. "Been busy at the store," I said out loud. "I'll take care of it soon. Any new ideas coming from your patients?" I asked, remembering the last conversation I'd had with T. J. while I sat in his dental chair under extreme duress. He'd said patients really like to talk in his chair.

T. J. grinned, flashing his great teeth. "Nothing new." Then he went down aisle two with a shopping basket over his arm.

By the time Carrie Ann arrived at the store, with Holly and Dinky right behind her, the storm had moved off to the east, leaving the soft patter of light rain behind.

Carrie Ann snatched Dinky and cooed over her.

"I have to leave for a little while," I said.

"Why?" Holly wanted to know.

"I have to go hunt morels for a newsletter recipe."

Holly gave me a you-get-all-the-good-jobs look, one of those mouth-gaping, eye-rolling, this-is-so-not-fair expressions. "And, just so you know, I'm not watching your dog."

"Do you want to do it instead?" I asked her. "Go out and hunt morels?"

Like my sister was suddenly Miss Outdoorsy.

"Once it stops raining and the sun comes out," she said. "Yes. *You* can stay and shuffle stock around. Do all the grunt work."

"The twins do the heavy lifting," I shot back. "Counting money doesn't qualify as grunt work. Neither does scheduling."

"Scheduling is hard work, harder than you think."

"There are only five of us working here! How hard can it be?"

Carrie Ann moved between us and said, "Forecast calls for rain right into the weekend. So whoever goes is going to get wet."

Holly looked out the window.

"Then I might as well go now," I said. "Besides, Holly, you don't even know where to start looking and I do."

I scooted out the door before Holly could volley another round.

I trotted through the rain to my house, changed into foul-weather gear, dug out my woven wood basket, and struck out into the woods with the hood of the jacket pulled up over my head.

My sister's attitude had me grinding my teeth. My mother's did, too. What they didn't realize was that I bore all the responsibility if things didn't go right with the business.

Holly never used an alarm clock. She got out of bed whenever she felt like it. She came in late, didn't assume responsibility when one of us was sick, and gave me grief every time I asked for help with Queen Bee Honey. Total lack of cooperation!

And where did my mother get off rearranging my store's shelves? The nerve.

I made an important mental note to find out when the twins' school year ended so I could hire them full-time for the summer when the tourist traffic was the heaviest. They, at least, were normal, hardworking, dependable employees and, unlike my family members, actually took direction from the owner of the store.

It took quite a bit of stomping through the brush by the river before I calmed myself down and started enjoying the scenery. Being out in nature had that effect on me. Rain or shine, the fresh air and all the wildlife and flora gave me energy and new perspective.

And hunting for morel mushrooms was my favorite spring sport.

Facts about morel mushrooms:

- May is morel month in Wisconsin.

- They only grow wild. No one has discovered how to cultivate them.

- Morels like to sprout near dead American elms and in old apple orchards. If the May apples are up, so are the morels.

- They are almost invisible, blending into the forest floor as efficiently as chameleons.

- Once discovered, they are easily identified as edible morels by their spongelike heads.

- They are absolutely delicious.

- A morel-picking spot must be kept secret, even from best friends and sisters; otherwise they will try to get to them first, and there goes the relationship.

I felt like Little Red Riding Hood skipping through the woods with my basket. Only I wasn't skipping because the rain made the terrain slippery and also because of my klutz disorder. Walking without tripping was my highest priority. And this time I'd remembered to wear hiking boots rather than flip-flops, which gave me a huge advantage.

Anyway, I made it to the small clearing, within shouting distance of The Lost Mile, where several elms had died last year, making them primo spots for morels this year. I found a long fallen branch and used it to flick leaves around, peering underneath them, while the rain fell gently and steadily. Thankfully, I was toasty warm and dry in my waterproof jacket.

There! Several. And some of them were as big as my fist. Once I spotted the first camouflaged one, my eyes adjusted to their size and shape and others popped into focus.

I hunted and picked until I was sure I'd covered every square inch of the clearing.

Then I hid the basket under a dense bush and made my way into The Lost Mile, along the overgrown logging trail, weaving around puddles and muddy spots until I stood beneath the tree where my bees had swarmed above a dead woman.

I wondered where Hunter had ultimately found Lauren's body.

Evidence of the murders was gone—the crime tape, the dark stains on the ground, the gun. All gone. The forest had been restored to its natural order. One thing that impacts me every time I go into the wild is how temporary we are and how permanent the natural world is.

Norm Cross's house and the edge of his property that abutted the tangled web of county and town land should be close by, although I couldn't be exactly sure of the boundaries. Trees, bushes, and undergrowth all melded into one continuous woodland scene, unconcerned over man-made lines of ownership.

I spotted a tiny worn path that turned into a well-traveled deer trail. It headed in the general direction of the Crosses' house and probably had been used by them to access the logging road.

So I followed it until it veered off away from the house. But by then I could see the neglected prefab through the trees. I made my way toward it through thick brush, where I managed to run headlong into a wild rose bush. Thorns embedded in cheek flesh really hurt. Much worse than a honeybee sting.

Rule of thumb—watch where you're going!

It took some effort to pry myself loose and I saw tiny dots of blood on my fingers when I patted my cheek. No big deal, although it felt like my face had been gashed open. I lifted my face to the sky to clean the wounds with rainwater, but as soon as I did, the rain completely stopped. Just my luck.

I kept going, motivated mainly by Hunter's description of Norm's Lantern Man poster board. I really wanted to see it. Although I didn't have a master plan regarding how to accomplish that feat.

If Norm Cross answered the door, I'd talk about Dinky, give him an update, ask him if he was ready to take her back. Then I'd make some kind of excuse to get inside and hope an opportunity arose to get a look at his wall hanging and maybe ask him questions about it.

As an afterthought, I should have brought Dinky along. But I was improvising as I went. This part of my outing wasn't preplanned.

He didn't answer his door. I figured I'd for sure get a chance to see the poster board now because most people in our neck of the woods didn't bother locking their doors. Why should Norm be any different?

When I turned the doorknob though, it didn't open. Against all the rules of small-town living, his door was locked. I peered in through a dirty window.

"One is open in back, if you want to get in." A voice came out of the wet background, scaring me into a high-pitched squeal. Jeez!

I clutched my chest and attempted to breath. "Patti! What are you doing here?"

"I scared you," she said smugly. "You didn't even know I was here."

"Where did you come from? You're right, I didn't hear you coming."

"You're going to make a poor investigative partner unless you start paying attention to your surroundings."

Partner? Not likely.

"I went in through the back window," P. P. Patti said.

That's when I stepped back and noticed she was dressed a lot like me. Rain gear. Outdoorsy jeans. Boots. Dripping water. Except Patti also wore a pair of long yellow latex gloves. "Want to see what I found inside the house?"

"You broke in? Isn't that illegal?" I figured Patti's method had to be much more unlawful than my foiled attempt to breeze in the front door.

"I didn't break in. I crawled in."

"Same difference."

"Do you want to see or not?"

"What if Norm comes home?"

Patti shrugged. "If you're going to be a whiner, forget it."

Look who was calling me a whiner. That woman could win a poor-me contest in a third-world country hands down.

She proceeded to prove it. "This reporter stuff is rough. I have to carry tons of heavy equipment around like my binoculars and recording unit and pads of paper. And people slam doors in my face the minute I start asking questions. I even got a cut knee from a nail jutting out from the window. See?"

She hiked up her jeans and showed me. After she rolled down her pant leg, she said, "What happened to your face? You look like you were attacked by something with claws."

"Is it still bleeding?"

Patti moved in close. "It's kind of dried in ridges. What happened?"

"Rose thorns. What were you doing here in the first place?"

"I could ask you the same question."

"I have Norm's dog," I said. "He didn't answer my phone calls. I'm checking on him."

Her eyes narrowed, like she had entered my brain and found a whole different story. "We should be official partners."

"Partners in crime?"

"In solving two murders."

I'd already decided to stick my nose into the case. Ever since Johnny Jay's name came up as a suspect, I knew I'd have to add fuel to the fire at his feet and help burn him up. But not with Patti helping me! "That's why we pay taxes," I said, arguing against any kind of partnership. "So cops can do that for us."

"Cops," she said with disdain. "Johnny Jay is a major suspect, if you believe what's going around town."

"Hunter's on the case, too."

"Johnny will make it hard for him. He'll tie Hunter's hands up so tight, he'll have rope burns into old age."

That sure was true. I gave Patti a bit more respect for having some guts and for challenging the legal system. Others in town might be speculating on Johnny Jay's role in the deaths and talking tough, but when it came to action, most of them would stay home with their blinds drawn rather than take a public stand.

"The police chief is winning the popularity contest."

"That's no reason to ignore the other suspects. That is, unless we can really eliminate them with solid proof." Patti had this weird way of staring without blinking. She was doing it now. "We'll compare notes later. Do you want to see what I found, or don't you?"

"Okay, let's go in," I said. "Just for a quick peek."

"You first," Patti said, walking around to the back where one of the windows was wide open. A window screen leaned up against the side of the house. Patti had raised the window and removed the screen to get inside Norm Cross's house. What nerve the woman had!

I had to wonder if she'd used the same technique on my house. Spyglass Patti with her binoculars and telescope and her snoopy nose for trouble. Bold. Brassy. And, I hated to admit it, but she'd probably make a really good reporter.

I heaved myself up on the window ledge with a little bit of a butt push from Patti and wiggled in, dropping to the floor hands first. The first thing I noticed was all the water I'd collected out in the rain and how much of it came inside with me. The second thing I noticed were my muddy footprints mingling with Patti's. We'd have to clean up before we left.

Rising up, I had to give Patti even more credit. She'd heaved me through a window right into the room with the poster board. She knew her stuff.

"Aren't you coming?" I asked when I noticed she hadn't made any moves to join me.

"My leg hurts. Not the one that got ripped on a nail, the other one. I whacked it on the window sill coming out and it's swelling up and I'm going to have one monster of a bruise and—"

I walked away, shutting her voice out.

But if I'd just not been quite so anxious to get inside, if I'd waved a fond farewell to Patti and chucked the whole plan to go inside my neighbor's house, if I had known ahead of time that Norm was so paranoid he had installed a do-it-yourself burglar alarm and it wasn't the loud and noisy kind that scared intruders away, but rather the silent kind that auto-dialed the police department and played a prerecorded message which included the exact address of the break-in . . .

If only I could have seen all that in Aurora's crystal ball, I never would have let Patti suck me into her game of intrigue and espionage.

Or at least, I would have handled things differently.

Eighteen

There's something exciting about being where you aren't supposed to be. Exhilarating and frightening all at the same time. My heart pounded in my ears. My breathing grew shallow and rapid. Not at all like yoga uji breath.

I was in a spare bedroom Norm and Hetty had obviously used for storage. Junk was thrown everywhere. A metal-legged table held the following interesting items:

- A green hurricane oil lantern, the kind used for camping

- More lanterns made from metal and painted a rainbow of colors, including blue, red, and yellow

- Some clear globes

- One amber lantern

- Another I thought might be a railroad signal lantern

Judging by the coating of dust, they hadn't been used recently. Or cleaned, either.

Next, my eyes swept to the wall where I saw a collage of newspaper clippings, a composition of facts pasted together like a scrapbook from the past. The articles weren't old or yellowed or brittle. They hadn't been affected by age at all because they'd been carefully preserved with lamination. And each article was framed with bits of red construction paper.

Someone had handwritten the name of each newspaper, all from *The Reporter*, and the date of each article in red pen beneath each news report. Dainty, feminine-looking handwriting. Hunter hadn't mentioned that. Or maybe he hadn't noticed. After all, he'd been looking for clues to Hetty's death, not for mysteries out of the past.

Something about the combination of black-ink typed pages on white poster board with bloodred trim gave me a sudden chill.

I quickly scanned the headlines. All the articles were short, sensational accounts of strange goings-on inside The Lost Mile as experienced, reported, and documented by local residents whose names I recognized.

I really wanted to read every one of the articles, but I didn't have time to stand there and do that. What if Norm came home?

I went back to the window to ask Patti to stay alert and warn me if anybody showed up unexpectedly. My partner in this scheme seemed to be missing from action.

"Patti!" I whispered as loudly as I dared, craning my neck as far out the window as I could without falling out face-first. "Where are you?"

No answer. Where had she gone? First she scared me to death when she crept up behind me, then she talked me into going through the window, then she ditched me? If she was hoping for a partnership, she was going about it all wrong.

That's when I noticed two things.

First, my fingers on the windowsill weren't sheathed in print-proof material like Patti's had been, so if anyone was busted for breaking into Norm's house, that person would be me, not Patti. Even though she had been the one responsible for removing the window and starting this whole thing, I wouldn't rat her out if things went south.

Which they seemed to be doing.

Because the second thing I noticed was the sound of tires crunching on gravel, right next to the house. Jeez! Still poking my head out the window, I saw the front bumper of a vehicle come into view. It stopped short of being visible from the interior of the house, so I couldn't tell who was driving, but I really didn't need to. The Moraine Police Department insignia near the bumper told me enough.

Its engine died. Any minute now I would be in very big trouble.

No way was I going to make a perfectly clean getaway. Mud all over the floor, footprints, a window screen left off. If Patti had an ounce of compassion in her meddling body, she'd show herself at the front of the house and distract the cop while I ran for cover.

I heard a car door click shut. Quietly. Like the driver hoped to sneak up on somebody.

I hopped up on the open window and twisted so my feet went first, trying to slither out as gracefully as a garter snake. Clutching the windowsill, I dropped, losing my balance and hitting the ground butt first. Hunter might be right about my two left feet, but fear of apprehension gave me added incentive to get upright and stay that way.

I would really haul.

Which is what I decided I had to do.

Especially after hearing that all-too-familiar authoritative voice shouting out to me to halt. Who said "Halt!" except a certain bully cop? The same one suspected of being a killer? None other than Johnny Jay!

And no way was I going to stop in my tracks and let him work me over verbally or physically with no witnesses, thank you very much, Patti Dwyre, for abandoning me in my moment of need.

I was pretty sure Johnny Jay wouldn't recognize me if I kept my hood up, my back to him, didn't say anything, and moved fast. Right now my big advantage was that he didn't know who he was dealing with.

I took off, half expecting Johnny Jay to start firing rounds. I dodged around trees, making sharp, abrupt turns just in case. But he didn't fire. In fact, he didn't pursue me, which should have warned me that something was not quite right.

But at the time, my brain was a whole lot slower than my body.

I ran as fast as I could down to the south end of The Lost Mile, pounding into the clearing, turning onto the deer trail, remembering at the last minute to scoop up my basket of mushrooms. Then I banged across the bridge not caring if I woke the dead. By the time I made it to my backyard, my safe haven, I was winded, gulping for air, and feeling seriously lightheaded. I set the basket on my patio table and bent over, gasping.

Just when I thought I might be able to move again, Johnny Jay came around the corner of my house, spotted me, and charged like a raging bull. He had his head down, his eyes narrowed, and at the last moment, I realized he wasn't going to stop. I put up my arms in a defensive motion just as he actually tackled me and we went down. He, having a lot more weight on me, came out on top, knelt on my back, digging his knee in while he wrenched my arms behind me and slapped on handcuffs.

I came up with a mouthful of gunk and proceeded to spit out wet dandelions, blades of grass, and bits of mud.

At this point I couldn't help noticing we had several witnesses.

Lori Spandle stood in the driveway next door, along

with two people I didn't recognize as locals. A man and woman, fortyish, dressed up as though a meeting with this particular real-estate agent was a big event. They stared at us as Johnny Jay brought me to my feet.

"This *person* is the next-door neighbor?" the woman said, her voice raising an octave as she enunciated each word. *Neighbor*, though, came out as a croak.

Granted, I wasn't at my very best, but I resented her quick judgment of me. I happened to be a great neighbor: considerate, as long as no one picked on my bees, kind, and tolerant. I had lots of good-neighbor qualities.

And considering the way Johnny Jay had just treated me, shouldn't one of these witnesses be coming to my rescue? Couldn't they tell a bad cop when they saw one? Instead, they gaped at me like I was some kind of criminal element and deserved what I was getting.

"I got the whole thing on video," Patti yelled from the other side of the cedars. Turning my head and looking up, I saw her hanging out of the second story of her house, dangling a recorder from its strap with one hand and shaking her fist at Johnny with the other. "Police brutality! I've got the footage to prove it this time."

"Shut up, Patti Dwyre," the police chief snarled up at her. "As soon as I'm done subduing and restraining this bad-news character, I'll be over to get you, too."

"All I can say is you better have a warrant and plenty of backup." Patti pulled in the video recorder and slapped binoculars to her face to take in the scene up close and personal.

"And that's the other neighbor?" the woman said, staring at Patti. I thought the woman looked slightly paler than before. Lori Spandle, however, had lots of vivid color going on in her cheeks.

"Let's get out of here," the man standing next to Lori said to the woman.

"But you haven't seen the house yet," Lori said to them.

"We've seen enough," the woman said.

"But . . ." Lori said.

The couple turned and hurried off.

"I'm going to kill you," Lori said to me, which I took as a real threat judging from the redness of her face, the wild look in her eyes, and the fact that I was handcuffed and couldn't defend myself. I was pretty sure Johnny wouldn't protect me.

"You ruin everything," she said, stepping closer. "I'm going to get you for this."

"Go home, Lori," Johnny Jay said, maneuvering me past her, putting his body between us like he was saving me all for himself. I saw his parked police vehicle. "And do me a favor, pretend you didn't see anything here today."

"I want protection," I said.

"Lori isn't going to carry out her threat," the police chief said. "Although I wouldn't blame her." I didn't correct him, but what I really needed was protection from him.

"I'm calling the newspaper," Patti called out. "This is a travesty and *The Reporter* should know."

Patti was letting adrenaline cloud her mind because our newspaper, affectionately and appropriately nicknamed *The Distorter*, never carried up-to-date news, since it came out only once a week. By then, I would have been in Johnny Jay's hands way too long for it to do me any good.

"Call Hunter Wallace," I shouted to her as Johnny put me in the backseat. I wondered what to say to my main man to cover up my latest mess. I considered blaming the whole thing on Patti. Or denying any involvement. Or if I really wanted the right kind of relationship with him, I suppose I could come clean.

Just this once—okay maybe for the second or third time—I really, really needed his help.

Johnny pulled away and made a U-turn. For a second or two I was afraid he might do something to me, like take me to a secluded area and work me over. But Patti knew he had me, and she would spread the word. I became more optimistic regarding my future when the police chief turned toward the police station.

"You didn't read me my rights," I said. "I don't even know why I'm handcuffed or inside your squad car. Is this how you treat all the citizens you're supposed to be protecting?"

All Johnny said was, "Shut up, Missy Fischer."

My sister showed up at the police station before Johnny Jay had a chance to unload me from the backseat. I imagined her Jag had been smoking hot with speed to get her down to the cop shop that fast. Holly's instantaneous arrival, how blazing fast she came to my rescue, was a good indication that our close network of family and friends was fully operational.

Of course, that also meant my mother had the same information. One more nail in the mom-daughter coffin.

"What did you arrest her for this time?" my sister said, relieved to see me in one piece.

"Breaking and entering." Johnny pulled me out of the back seat. "And burglary."

"What did you steal?" Holly asked me.

"I didn't steal anything. He's making things up. I want a lawyer."

"I'm on it," Holly said. "Johnny Jay, you've overstepped your bounds this time."

"All you Fischer women are pains in the you-know-what," he said.

With that, Holly took off. It was then I realized I brought out the absolute worst in our police chief. Oil and water didn't begin to describe us. Salt rubbed into a wound was more like it. What could I have done to make him this crazy? I mean, other than running when he told me to halt, which when I thought about it might be considered a pretty serious offense by some people.

I really, really wished I had paid more attention in

psychology class or read more on the subject of dealing with nasty people like Johnny Jay, because I wasn't very good at it. It didn't take many of his type running around to ruin a person's day. Like right now.

Every time someone acted like they didn't like me, instead of giving that person extra kind attention and working hard to change his or her mind, I made it worse by reciprocating with the same bad attitude. So if I was going to bring out the worst in the police chief, he was going to bring out the worst in me, too.

It wasn't like I did it on purpose. It just happened. Was everybody like that? Or just me?

Johnny Jay wanted respect, something that eluded his grasp, and he hadn't been able to get any at all from me. Was that it? Was I supposed to act like the other Moraine residents and pretend he was an important guy? I didn't do pretend well.

The next few hours crawled by. Johnny kept me in the holding cell right where all the other cops walked back and forth. The cell contained a bare cot and a toilet, which I wasn't about to use in front of everybody. I wondered how long I could hold out. No wonder they call it a holding cell.

Then I heard keys clanging on metal and the creaky sound of the door opening.

"You're free to go," Police Officer Sally Maylor said.

"You're sweet," I said, staying right where I was, eyeing up freedom on the other side. "But I don't want to get you into trouble."

"I'm not helping you break out," Sally said, shaking her head and rolling her eyes. "You've been released."

"Did Holly get me an attorney?"

"She didn't need to."

I hustled through the open door as fast as I could, just in case she came to her senses and made a grab for me.

Hunter and Ben were waiting for me in the entryway. Again.

Not only that, real news teams (not just Patti) had congregated outside the station.

I squinted when we walked out of the building, stunned that it was still daylight, and wondering what had happened to bring out the big-gun reporters. These weren't hicks from the sticks with their news vans and fancy expensive cameras.

Did we have a real celebrity inside our police station?

Had something big happened that I didn't know about?

"What's going on?" I whispered to Hunter.

"Just keep walking," he whispered back.

Nineteen

Milwaukee, only thirty-some miles down the highway, had three local television networks—Channels 4, 6, and 12. And they were all represented outside the Moraine police station.

Hunter took a protective stance as soon as we came out of the building, drawing me in close, while I glanced around wondering who or what had drawn all the news cameras to our little burg.

And wasn't it just the luck of the draw that I happened to get released right in the middle of all this action? Nothing like making a discreet exit after a police booking.

Before I could suggest to Hunter that we go back inside until this party and its lenses were gone, reporters started sticking microphones in my face and snapping pictures. That's when I caught on that little old *moi* was involved somehow in the breaking news story. But no way would a small-time grocery store owner's arrest draw this much attention from anything other than the local paper.

All I'd done was run from a big bully. That wasn't news in my book.

Either Lori Spandle had engineered this in retaliation for destroying a sale, or this was P. P. Patti's warped way of helping my cause.

"Throw something over my head," I said to Hunter in a panic, thinking about how easily my mother was humiliated by my actions and how this couldn't be much worse. "Give me your jacket. Quick."

"Just stay close and ignore them," Hunter suggested.

"Ms. Fischer. Can we get a statement?"

"What's behind these charges?"

"We only want a moment of your time!"

"Is it true?"

Oh, right, like I was going to confess to breaking into Norm Cross's house and right in front of a bunch of rolling cameras. I scowled and kept going, burying my face against Hunter, wanting to tear his jacket off his body. Lust had nothing to do with it, either.

Hunter had a good strong grip and wasn't letting go. He smoothly rearranged me so that he and Ben were closest to the more aggressive reporters, with the canine partner playing defensive line.

Ben's imposing presence and the intimidating gaze as he swept over the crowd worked because reporters and cameramen alike took big steps away from the large animal. I gave a silent cheer of gratitude for Ben.

Hunter opened the passenger side of his SUV, Ben and I jumped in, and as we pulled out I saw the mass of people turn back to the building, losing interest in us.

"What was all *that* about?" I said.

"Is anybody following us?"

I craned around. "No. Why would they?"

"Let's go to my place. I'll tell you all about it there."

Hunter's home was masculine, comfortable, and so tidy that, at first, I secretly suspected he had another woman on the side. No guy I'd ever known kept such a clean house. Not that I was complaining.

"What . . . is . . . going . . . on?" I asked, plopping down at Hunter's kitchen table, emphasizing each word.

"In a minute." I had to wait while Hunter started a pot of coffee. Then he came over.

"What happened to you?" he said, like he hadn't really looked at me before right that minute. I'd completely forgotten about the rose thorn scratches on my face until he cupped my chin gently in his hand and turned my head from side to side, examining the damage. I was pretty sure he thought Johnny Jay did it. I decided not to inform him otherwise. I needed every advantage I could get.

"Johnny Jay assaulted me is what happened to me." Then I stopped and considered. Hunter was a cop and in theory on the other side. "I'm sorry, but I shouldn't tell you any more than that. I need an attorney."

"For what? You haven't been charged with anything."

"*WHAT?*" I practically screamed. "I was handcuffed and locked in a cell for hours. I thought you'd figured out how to bail me out."

"You weren't charged. You beat Johnny again."

"This isn't a competition between the two of us. It's more like a free-for-all. He threw me on the ground, cuffed me, and arrested me for burglary."

"He's about to pay dearly for that," Hunter said. What a guy! I thought. He's going after the rogue police chief. I still couldn't believe I was actually free and clear. "So I'm not in trouble?"

Hunter smiled. "Johnny Jay worked it from every angle but Norm Cross stood firm. I can't believe you broke into his house."

"I didn't exactly break in." I didn't feel too bad about saying that, since technically Patti broke in.

"Anyway, Norm refused to press charges against you."

"Really? That's great news!" Then I thought of Norm's

dog, Dinky, and it took me a minute to remember that I'd left her at the store with Carrie Ann and Holly. They would take good care of her until I got back.

"So tell me about your little escapade at Norm's," Hunter said.

It didn't take long, since I left out plenty, like how Patti started it and how I ran away. "That poster has me thinking," I said at the end. "The captions are handwritten and they didn't look masculine to me. What if Hetty made the poster?"

"Unlikely," Hunter said, "that she and Norm would have pulled off Lantern Man together."

"Just food for thought," I said. "Whoever called the news media must have it in for me. It must've been Lori. She stood right there and watched Johnny Jay tackle me and didn't lift a finger to help. In fact, she threatened my life."

Hunter had an amused grin on his face when he shook his head. "Lori Spandle didn't have anything to do with tipping off the news media. You're going to love it. But wait. Something else happened next. After Norm refused to press charges against you, he came forward and finally admitted that he was Lantern Man."

"Really? Wow."

"I'd done some research into those records we talked about," Hunter said, pouring coffee for me, fixing it just the way I liked it with cream and honey from a jar I'd left at his house. Last time he tried to get me to drink it with sugar. Yuck.

Hunter continued after handing me the cup. "I couldn't find anything to substantiate whether or not he had been home during the camper attack or the night we were in The Lost Mile. We didn't have a thing on him, but he confessed anyway." He looked puzzled. "Sort of strange he chose now to step forward."

"What will happen to him?"

"Not much. His only crime was destruction of personal

property way back when he shredded those campers' belongings. Statute of limitation ran out on that offense years ago. And he's admitted he went overboard and has offered to pay the families involved for damaged property."

"But he terrorized The Lost Mile."

Hunter chuckled. "Not a crime."

"Did he say why he did it?" That handwriting still bothered me.

"Only that he wanted to discourage kids from hanging out and drinking there. He thought he was doing a good thing."

"We wouldn't have been in The Lost Mile in the first place if Lantern Man hadn't been scaring kids. We wouldn't have had a dare to accept. Lauren might not have driven drunk. Johnny Jay's dad might still be alive."

"On the other hand, if we weren't all afraid of Lantern Man, maybe we would have partied there all the time. But I still wonder why he decided to reveal his identity now."

"I brought up Lantern Man to him," I said, "which really made him mad. And you searched his house, so he knows you saw the poster and lanterns. It was only a matter of time before somebody caught on anyway."

"There's dirt all over your face," Hunter said. "We better get you cleaned up."

Hunter washed my face and applied an antibiotic cream. His touch felt nice. I was feeling better and better all the time. Except for my arms, which ached from being cuffed behind my back, and my legs weren't used to running like I had, so they screamed out in pain. To top it off, my favorite shirt had grass stains all over the front and everybody knows they don't wash out.

I rubbed a shoulder. "Something's really wrong with Johnny Jay," I said. "He's been acting more aggressive and hostile than ever. It's like he's snapped."

"That's the real reason for the news crews. Patti Dwyre sent a video over the Internet to all the Milwaukee newsrooms, showing Johnny Jay beating up on you."

"Nothing like police brutality to fire up the masses."

"Apparently," Hunter said, shaking his head in amazement. "But you seem to have survived the incident without too much internal or external damage."

"I told you I was a big girl and could take care of myself," I said, showing off.

"I could tell that was absolutely, indisputably true when I viewed the video. You really took care of him, the way you had him on the ground on top of you. Lots of technique in that trick."

Hunter didn't have to look quite so amused. After all, I'd been through a lot in spite of my boasting.

"Are you going to pursue charges against him?" Hunter asked. "You do have the upper hand."

"Charges? Sure, right, and have Johnny Jay stalking me for the rest of my life?" Although it dawned on me I was already living that life.

"This is your big chance."

"I have to think about it," I said. Since I was into mixed emotions these days, I was happy and upset at the same time, relieved the world was about to see the real Johnny Jay, traumatized that my exploits were going to be on display for every nightly news watcher in our coverage area.

Friends, customers, family members.

I tried to remember all the details after Johnny Jay came around the corner of my house and tackled me, but things had happened so fast. Mostly I recalled eating dirt.

It felt really good to be sitting at Hunter's kitchen table sharing coffee and conversation.

"What if Norm is covering up for his wife?" I asked, focused again on the poster.

"Why would he do that? If anything, wouldn't he blame her for the whole thing? She's dead and can't defend herself against any charges he made."

"That would be cold."

"I agree."

"But if Hetty was Lantern Man, well, I suppose that would make her Lantern Woman, wouldn't it? That might explain why she was out in the woods at the same time as Lauren. That might help determine if someone was really after Lauren when Hetty heard voices out there and got in the way."

"Story, Norm confessed."

"I better think about getting back to The Wild Clover," I said, giving up on that particular line of thought.

Ben deserved several liver treats for bravery beyond the call of duty, so I made sure he got them and finished another cup of coffee. "Do you think the store is safe from reporters?"

"No."

"I have to get back."

"That's a really bad idea."

"Let's go," I said, ready for anything.

Twenty

Hunter was right, not that I would ever admit that to him. A Channel 4 news van crawled past The Wild Clover and was backing into a parallel parking space just as I bolted through the front door of my store.

"Jeez," I thought I said to myself, very quietly, but instead I must've blurted it out pretty loud. All eyeballs shifted my way. "In a hurry," I said, not stopping to chitchat.

Staff and customers stood gaping, their mouths flopping open when I ran past the checkout counter where Carrie Ann and my sister were standing (Did I look that bad?), then skidded down aisle six heading for the back storage room. I locked myself inside much to the delight of Dinky, who jumped down from the office chair where she'd been sleeping and clawed her way into my arms.

From safety behind the closed door, I called my sister's cell phone.

"A news truck is outside," I said. "Don't let them in the store."

"This is a public building. How am I supposed to stop them?"

"Good point. Okay. At least tell them I'm not here."

"'K."

"I'll hide out back here until you call me back and say the coast is clear."

"'K."

Even before we hung up, I heard a sharp rap on the door. "Who's at the door?" I said into the phone. "Make them go away."

"It's Ali Schmidt."

"I don't care if it's the First Lady. Tell her to go away."

"She knows you're in there. She saw you run by."

"Oh."

"Besides, she's applying for a job."

"Really? Cool!" Music to my ears.

I unlocked the door, pulled Ali in, and relocked.

"What's happening?" she wanted to know.

"Reporters. Stalking me. No big deal. Holly said you want to work here?"

"Yes, I do." And Ali dove into a sales pitch that would have dazzled the manager of any national grocery line. She had a voice I was jealous of—husky and sexy. My cousin Carrie Ann had a husky voice, too, but hers was more gravelly, rough from years of smoking cigarettes. Ali's voice . . . well . . . I always wished mine sounded like that.

Ali, it turned out, was qualified for *my* position, if I could believe everything she told me, which right now, didn't matter in the least. Two arms and half a brain would have been all the qualifications she needed.

Her dental office organization skills gave her a giant step up to the head of my employment list. Not that anyone else was on the list at the moment. As it turned out, Ali didn't need money as much as she needed to get out of the house and the dental office.

"I love T. J. to death," she said after laying out her

professional history. "But I need some breathing room and going to work someplace else, like here, will give me that. It's not the easiest thing for a family to live *and* work together."

Tell me about it, I could have said. Working with family members took either nerves of steel and incredible bravery or total stupidity and desperation.

"But you're his receptionist," I said, ready to sign her on no matter what she said next. "What will he do? How will he replace you?"

"I'll still do scheduling for him and paperwork in the mornings. I just want to work here two or three afternoons every week. And I can work Friday nights, since T. J. has rotary club meetings."

I couldn't believe my good luck. Between Carrie Ann, Holly, and me, we could handle mornings and early afternoons. That would give me wiggle room later in the afternoons with Ali and the twins. Things were definitely looking up.

And the biggest bonus of all? A reliable employee like Ali would keep my mother out of the loop.

"I can stay at the store and help right now," my new best friend, Ali, said. "I heard about what happened with Johnny Jay. Why don't you slip out the back door and take the afternoon to regroup? Go ahead, we can handle the store." Ali shooed me with her hands.

A few minutes later, I was slinking down back alleys with one mangy mutt under my arm and two happy care-free feet. I cut through Patti's yard and made it into my house undetected. After showering, changing into clean clothes, and munching on a peanut butter, banana, and honey sandwich, I sank onto the sofa for a nice long rest.

My cell rang. Holly.

"You can come out now," she said.

I'd forgotten to let Holly know I'd made my escape from the store. She still thought I was in the backroom.

"I hired Ali Schmidt," I remembered to tell her, a bit late.

"So that's why she's hanging around asking questions." Holly's tone was a bit frosty, like maybe I should have passed that news by her already. Or first, before making the decision. I ignored her tone. No way was that ever going to happen. Once I let her in on management decisions, I'd lose my reign. Or reins.

"Show her around and put her on the schedule starting immediately," I said as authoritatively as possible.

"ATM (*At The Moment*) I *am* training her. Until now I was fielding reporters' questions. But I'll get to the schedule ASAP."

"You're not saying anything to the press, are you? Please don't talk to them."

"I'm not."

"And don't give them my home address."

"Gotcha."

We hung up, and my thoughts turned to Patti's recent overtures of friendship and the way she'd stuck up for me, even though I knew her motives were a bit self-centered.

When I was married, I let the part of my life go that included female friends, sad as that was to admit. I opened the store and worked such long hours, I didn't have any extra energy for friendships. But for the last few years I've craved more female interaction. I wanted to have a best girlfriend, or as Holly would say a "BF."

Then a flash of insight came to me while I lounged around with Dinky, hiding from the world.

Best friends aren't something we pick out ahead of time, like a prime cut of beef. People traipse randomly through our lives, starting out as basic acquaintances. Sometimes they move up to a new category, sometimes they sink down.

Like Lori Spandle, who'd slept with my husband and would never be one of my friends. She lacked the basic requirements of friendship—loyalty, commitment, and a whole lot of acceptance of me just the way I came.

But others? One day, out of nowhere, some of those acquaintances and casual friends become something more.

In my life, for example, I suppose I have to count my sister as my best friend. Even though we rag on each other, we still love each other to death. Then there's Carrie Ann, my cousin, who I've known my whole life, and can count on in a crisis.

Holly, Carrie Ann, and I have shared experiences, memories, secrets, and we know one another's faults and failures like they are our own.

What about Patti Dwyre? As much as I didn't want to accept it, P. P. Patti had managed to pass through the acquaintance stage, although she was branching into something as yet totally undefined and a bit frightening. We had a ways to go before I'd consider her a true friend—if ever.

"So to sum up my current circle of friends accurately," I said to Dinky, "they consist of a chronic text-speaker, an alcoholic, and the town snoop."

Dinky's ears perked up and she barked back at me like she was actually responding.

To be perfectly honest with myself, I must have an equally flawed character to fit in so well with them, although I couldn't think of exactly what was weird about me at the moment.

Psychoanalysis wasn't my strong suit, especially when it came to my own personality and motives, so I stood up from the sofa, shook off the heavy thoughts, and decided my next step.

I peeked out into the street. No reporters lurking. So I took Dinky out into the backyard to check on my bees.

Spring is a busy time of year for beekeepers, but most of the hard work had been done earlier in the season. I still inspected the hives on a regular basis, hunting for mite invasions and making sure the queens' egg productions were right on schedule, a sure sign that they were healthy and the hive was thriving.

To prevent more swarms (that last one making me feel like a sorry sort of rookie who needed to pay more attention to detail), I added additional honey supers to most of the hives. "Adding honey supers" is beekeeping lingo for adding an extra box for honeybees to store more honey. It's like putting an addition on a family's house, only on a much smaller scale.

Aurora stopped by to say hi. "Heard what happened," she said. "There's something about you that has started attracting negative karma."

"Like I'm being punished?" To tell the truth, I didn't know exactly what karma was, but Aurora was about to give me her interpretation.

"No, no, it isn't punishment. You create karma with every single one of your actions. Even through your thoughts."

"So I'm thinking myself into problems?"

"Nothing happens by chance. You're in the process of learning a lesson."

"Have you been talking to my mother?"

Aurora, usually serious about everything, chuckled. "No, I haven't seen her. This experience is between you and Johnny Jay. The outcome depends completely on what you do next."

I watched her walk away, heading for Moraine Gardens across the street. She'd left me feeling way too responsible for things I couldn't control. Or could I?

By the time the evening news came on, I was back in the house, perched in front of the television set next to Holly, with Dinky in the middle, chewing on a miniature rawhide bone. The newswoman started with the feature story, what she termed *a chilling event* that had taken place in the small community of Moraine.

And our police chief was the star of the show.

Unfortunately, so was I.

Holly and I watched, glued to the TV, while Johnny Jay and I were shown in my backyard. The footage was slightly shaky, since Patty had been excited at the time. And she'd been hanging out her upstairs window, so a tripod was out of the question.

In those few seconds between spotting Johnny and getting bowled over, I hadn't had time to think too much about the confrontation between bully-boy Johnny and me, other than that he had no right and I preferred *not* to eat dandelions, grass, and rainy muck.

And really, he hadn't actually hurt me much. I guess it was all that childhood conflict between him and me that had me accepting his abusive behavior as perfectly normal, considering the source.

Witnessing the scene as a playback was not only surreal, but Johnny Jay looked and acted like a man who had lost his mind as well as control of his actions. I should have been scared to death.

"That must have really hurt," Holly said, watching the police chief kneel on my back. "He had you in a hammerlock. If I'd been there, this never would have happened. I would have used a full nelson on him first and finished with a few illegal moves to make him squeal."

I reached over and gave her a playful punch. "But then you would have deprived me of all this aftermath glow. No way. I'm enjoying it."

"You are too weird for words."

But I wasn't paying attention to her because the action on my television screen went live. Johnny Jay came out of the police station in fully decorated uniform with his hat in his hands, his hair slicked down, and a look of humility on his face. The amazing thing about Johnny was how sane he could appear. His outward appearance was one of trim, clean-cut, well-dressed, boyish good looks, proving that first impressions should *never* count.

I could see residents milling around in the background,

lots of them Kerrigans, who bore their own kind of grudge against Johnny Jay. They were carrying signs that clearly called for his termination. Was he about to resign from his long tenure as police chief? And give up all that brute control?

Wow! I felt more powerful than him for a change, responsible for a revolution about to take place right before my eyes. We were overthrowing our government. Or something like that.

That karma thing was going to work. I focused on positive thoughts. Please, let Johnny Jay get what he's deserved his whole life.

"The town board just arrived," Holly pointed out with a grin the size of Lake Michigan, as town supervisors filed through the crowd, looking uniformly somber.

With our town board members behind him and a whole lot of residents who'd never liked the police chief circling around the news cameras hoping to make televised statements of their own, Johnny Jay took the microphone and started spewing rhetoric:

- How his own father had been murdered by a drunk driver right in our streets. Didn't they all remember that?

- The loss of his parent had inspired Johnny Jay to take over as commander, where he'd maintained law and order in our town for over a decade.

- Which he had done even better than his father, if that were even possible, just look at the statistics. May his dad rest in peace.

- And now a dangerous situation had required him to pursue an intruder, a common burglar with a history of psychological problems concerning authority figures.

"Do I have a psychological problem with authority?" I asked my sister.

"Probably," she said. "Shhh."

- He had successfully apprehended this person, but only after the unfortunate necessity of physical force.

"Yeah, right, what a liar!"
"Shhh . . ."

- The video skewed evidence against him by not capturing the prior events that had forced him to take action.

- He would soon be vindicated.

- But until that time, the police chief saw no option other than to take an extended personal leave.

Holly and I jumped into the air, bouncing on the sofa, high-fiving each other, and yahooing at the top of our lungs. Dinky ran for cover, dragging her bone with her.

I popped the cork on a bottle of champagne I'd been saving for a special occasion. Occasions didn't get much special-er than this.

We toasted to justice, long in coming.

"We don't know what we'll do without him," I shouted. "But we'll be thrilled to find out!"

Our jubilation lasted as long as the first glass.

Because I suddenly realized Johnny Jay would blame all of this on me.

I had to get out of town.

Twenty-one

During champagne pour number two, I mentioned Johnny's revenge issue and how he'd now focus entirely on giving me his worst. "I wasn't exactly safe before, imagine now."

"You can't leave Moraine," P. P. Patti's voice piped up out of nowhere, startling me into a shriek.

There she was, in the doorway, dressed in dark clothes with a black ball cap pulled down low over her face.

"Where did you come from?" I said, narrowing my eyes. Don't tell me my neighbor had let herself in my back door without knocking or ringing. How long had she been listening? "Don't you believe in announcing yourself like everybody else?"

"That's a cold way to greet a friend," Patti said.

Which was perfectly true. Patti had saved the day by exposing my enemy for what he was. I should be grateful. I also should ask her to work on Lori Spandle next. Maybe Patti was my karma.

Although I would have preferred something a little more low key that didn't put me right in a brute's direct line of fire. So even though she'd saved this day, she might have numbered the ones I had left.

"Talk to Story," my sister appealed to Patti, pouring a glass of champagne and handing it to her. "Convince her that she has to stay." Holly swung back to me. "Mom didn't raise us to be cowards. Fischers don't run away from their problems."

I snorted since my sister's idea of a big problem was finding zit cream after eating too much chocolate and discovering a breakout.

"We are in the perfect position to catch Lauren's killer together," Patti said.

"And Hetty's," Holly said. "Don't blow it by running and hiding."

"How do you come up with this stuff?" I said, amazed that these two were suddenly in agreement. "Do you seriously want me to hang around until Johnny Jay murders me in my sleep? Sure, I'll be fish bait. Works for me," I said in a voice I hoped was dripping with sarcasm.

"Well, you aren't far off," Patti said, missing the drip. She sat down between Holly and me on the sofa. "The police chief has to be raging mad at you and he'll plot to get even. He'll want to make you suffer miserably. So either way, whether he's the killer or not, you're in big trouble. But"—Patti stuck a pointing finger in the air for dramatic effect—"also in a great position for crime fighting."

"I'm not the one who wants to be an investigator. You are. I don't want to fight crime."

"And," Holly said, ignoring me, talking over my head to Patti, "if he's not the killer and just wants revenge, it's not like she'll lose her life. But if he's really the killer and he tries to actually kill her, we'll know he's the one. TP (*Think Positive*). We'll find out the truth based on his next move."

"Oh great," I said. "I feel so much better now."

Patti nodded. "After a killer kills that first time, it gets easier. But he also gets more careless. Trust me, if Johnny Jay tries to kill you, we'll have our proof."

"Just a sec. The murderer could still be Norm," Holly pointed out. "We haven't totally ruled him out, have we?"

Patti gasped, "Oh, what if he is? Oh my, he could kill Story to make it look like Johnny Jay was getting his revenge. And don't you think he's wondering what you were doing in his house, Story? If he's the killer, he might think you found evidence. That would explain why he didn't press charges. He's biding his time."

"I'm out of here just as soon as I pack," I announced.

"What about the store?" Holly said. "Are you really going to abandon The Wild Clover, leave me to manage it all by myself? I'll have to ask Mom to help, and you know I can't control her."

"Mom?" I hadn't thought about that.

"Besides," Patti said, "if you stay, we'll protect you. What are friends for? You have Holly *and* me. Best friends."

"BFs," Holly agreed, looking a little doubtful when her eyes turned to Patti.

"I'm calling Hunter," I said, not sure whether I was overreacting. "*He'll* know what to do."

"Sure," Patti sneered. "Ask a man what to do. He'll know best."

Holly snickered in agreement, which was totally out of character for her. I took the champagne bottle out of her hand. It was empty.

"I don't answer to Hunter," I said, hating that Patti had put me on the defensive. "But I respect his opinion just like I respect yours."

"Then why do you need a second opinion?"

"Um, I don't."

"Besides, you owe me. I saved your life. You wouldn't have made it out of your backyard alive if I hadn't interfered."

That was so not true! I'm sure, given more time, I would have used my brain to best Johnny Jay. Eventually. But

Patti was on a roll. "The least you could do in return," she added, "is stay and fight for truth and justice. And you didn't even thank me."

I mentally gritted my teeth. "You're right. I've been so stressed and preoccupied I forgot. Thank you, Patti, for taking that video and using it to finally bring down Johnny Jay."

Holly had something to say to Patti. "But you never would have accomplished that without Story's help. She's the one who got beat up. Good going, sis."

"Thanks. I think."

Patti stood up. "So what do you say? Stick around and help us. We'll take turns protecting you and it won't be long before the killer surfaces. We'll be heroes."

Holly pounded in the last nail. "We want Johnny Jay busted. This time he isn't going to win."

I eyed up my sister, then Patti. That's all I needed. Two female bodyguards, following me around the clock, cramping my style. And how much time with Patti could I stand before I went totally insane?

And if I ran and hid? I really didn't have anywhere to run away to. And even if I did, Johnny Jay had connections and high-tech methods. If he wanted me, he'd find me.

Better to face him head-on.

Look him in the eye.

Conquer him.

And it helped to know I had backup.

"I'll give it a few days," I said. Aside from wanting a killer cornered, leaving the store in Holly and Mom's hands would be a disaster. Holly would forget to open. Mom would bring the toilet paper back out front. They'd run my business into the ground.

Then where would I be?

Living with Mom, that's where.

As soon as Patti, satisfied that I'd stay and wait for the slaughter to begin, had left my house, I headed for my bedroom.

Dinky followed on my heels. My new shadow.

My bedroom was my favorite room in the house. Except that it faced Patti's house. Therefore, it was the least secure room in my home, but I'd compensated with quality blinds.

Holly had helped me decorate using feng shui, which according to her, should harmonize with my personality, whatever that meant. After I had picked out new bedding, she recommended cream walls because they were supposed to calm me. Lots of pillows, table lamps on dimmers, yellow and blue accents, beeswax candles. The room became my personal, private sanctuary.

Except now I had to share it with a little neurotic dog that was still peeing all over my floors. And earlier, she had pulled a pair of my panties out of a pile of dirty clothes and chewed holes in them. The third pair of undies she'd ruined.

Tomorrow, I'd insist Norm take Dinky back. That was, if he hadn't been detained or jailed for his Lantern Man antics. But with the police chief on leave, his chances of attaining freedom were much greater than before.

I called Hunter on my cell. "Johnny Jay is going to murder me," I said first thing when he picked up. "I need police protection. How did I get in this situation?"

"This is only one of a long line of difficult situations you've gotten yourself into. As far back as I can remember."

"This one wasn't my fault." Was that a whine in my voice? Was what Patti had contagious? I'd been around her too much lately. "Well it really wasn't my fault this time."

There was a significant pause on the other end, one intended to silently dispute my no-fault claim. So I had a short time to reflect on my role in today's events. I suppose I could have refrained from entering Norm's house for starters, but how was I to know he had it wired in to the police station?

"Any breaks in the murder case?" I asked, not ready to analyze my share of the blame.

"It's moving forward."

"That means you don't have anything. Can you please speed it up?"

"Believe me, I'm putting all my effort into it," Hunter said. "Johnny Jay isn't going to bother you. Don't worry."

"Yeah, right."

"I'll warn him off."

"Oh, that will help. Could you get a restraining order for me?"

"Doesn't work that way. They aren't easy to get, although in your case, you might get one. You'd have to prove he's a threat. You'd have to go into court and face him, tell the judge you're afraid of him."

"Never." Let that creep know he scared me? No way.

"You could stay with me."

"Tempting." Believe me, I *was* tempted, but I had work to do. It was time to check on all the beehives that I'd leased out to various farmers in the community. Hopefully, they were all healthy and pollinating crops. Hunter couldn't watch over me 24/7.

"Or Ben could stay with you," he suggested as an alternative.

"That's an option. Or my sister and Patti Dwyre say they'll protect me."

"See. You don't need me. Not with those two." Hunter laughed, bringing a smile to my face. They *were* unlikely bodyguards.

In the end, I realized that only one person could take care of me and that was me. I'd stay around as many people as possible and watch my back just in case. That's all I could do.

"Who's in charge now that Johnny's gone?"

"Sally Maylor," Hunter said.

I liked that. Sally was a regular customer, a good cop, and she didn't get involved in personal vendettas like Johnny. And she was a female like me. I always rooted for the woman.

By the time we hung up, Hunter almost had me convinced that my life wasn't in danger.

Twenty-two

The next morning dawned cloudy but drier than the day before, with the sun trying to make up its mind whether or not to shine. The weather could go either way—more springtime rain or sunny blue skies. But that was Wisconsin weather. Ever changing.

First thing, I let Dinky out in the backyard, too late as usual, but who's keeping track? I wiped up the mess, and she sniffed around the yard while I started coffee. Then I creamed together softened butter, honey, and a shake of cinnamon, and smeared the gooey treat on a piece of sourdough toast. The perfect breakfast. I made a mental note to incorporate a few honey butter recipes in the next newsletter.

After letting my increasingly unwelcome guest back in the house and feeding her, I formulated a plan of action, a simple one really. When push came to shove (and also because it was daylight and the world seemed right when dawn broke), I refused to live in fear of retribution from

Johnny Jay. We'd been at each other's throats our whole lives, why should this time be any different?

So number one: Stop worrying and let karma rule by sending out positive vibes.

Number two: I'd accomplish a few things on my to-do list, which demanded my attention. Mostly bee related. I needed to check on the outlying areas where my bees were busy working for hire.

Number three: Just to be on the safe side, I'd watch my back. Better safe than sorry, right?

Before I left the house, I called Norm Cross again. This time he answered.

"Thanks for not pressing charges against me," I said.

"The police chief gave me a hard time about that, but I didn't budge because I thought you must have a good reason for what you did. So what *were* you doing inside my house?"

"Uh, making sure you weren't hurt," I punted. "I'd been trying to contact you all day and I started thinking maybe you fell down and hit your head or something. I got worried."

That sounded pretty good. Norm bought it.

"I guess you heard I'm Lantern Man," he said. "The whole town knows by now. It's not something I'm proud of."

"Good thing Johnny Jay was part of a bigger story. Yours is already yesterday's news."

The police chief's video trumped Norm's announcement by a long shot.

"Can I bring Dinky back yet?"

"I have to take care of final funeral arrangements today. Can we meet later in the afternoon?"

With all the excitement I'd forgotten that Norm had to bury his wife. How awful! What could I say? "Of course," I said. "No problem."

After hanging up, I headed for the store with the basket of morel mushrooms in one hand and Dinky in tow on her leash. Everything had quieted down since last night's news report. No vans in front of the store. No reporters lurking. They were all off chasing the next breaking news story now that they had destroyed careers (Johnny's) and lives (possibly mine).

No bodyguards, either, I couldn't help noticing. After all the talk last night about protecting me from harm, Holly hadn't managed to crawl out of bed. And who knew where Patti was. Apparently, actions really did speak louder than words, and those two were practicing motionlessness.

Good thing I really hadn't counted on them for help.

I opened up the store and went to work getting it ready for business.

Carrie Ann was already there, but that didn't become apparent until she staggered out of the backroom. Her short spiky hair was still spiked, but not in a good way. One side of her hair was mashed down, the other side had hairs pointing in every direction except the right ones. Mascara streaked her face and her eyes were red-veined slits.

"Oh no," I said. "What happened to you? Are you drunk? Hungover? How could you do that after all your hard work?" And ours, I thought. She wasn't the only one suffering from her addiction.

"I'm not drunk or hungover," she said, leaning against the wall. "But I didn't get any sleep last night."

"Were you in back all night?" I asked, noting her rumpled clothes, the same ones she'd been wearing yesterday.

Carrie Ann nodded.

"Why?"

"Gunnar was hauled in for questioning last night."

"For what?"

"I'm not sure, but it has something to do with Lauren Kerrigan and Hetty Cross. Hunter ordered him to appear at the sheriff's office."

"Ordered? That doesn't sound like Hunter."

"Gunnar called to tell me he was going and said he was

worried because he didn't have anybody to vouch for his whereabouts when Lauren and Hetty were murdered."

"That doesn't make any sense at all. Hunter can't think Gunnar did it. Johnny Jay . . . oh, never mind." I almost said Johnny Jay killed them. But it might be a smart move to lay off him for a while, at least publicly.

"I bet the cops are going to round us up one at a time," Carrie Ann said, with wild eyes. "Everyone who was in The Lost Mile the night Wayne Jay died. You. Me. T. J. Gunnar, who they already have. Hunter doesn't count since he's the rounder-upper. We're all under suspicion."

Carrie Ann, in my opinion, was in some kind of delusional state. That's what happened to alcoholics. Lost brain cells. Delusions.

"That's nonsense," I said. "He doesn't think one of us killed Lauren. The Wayne Jay tragedy happened a long time ago. And if that night does have any bearing on what happened here now, it still has nothing to do with us. Besides, why do you care if he wants to ask you questions? You didn't do anything wrong, did you?"

"No, but . . ." Carrie Ann let the rest of the sentence hang.

Now that I thought back, Carrie Ann *had* been missing in action in the late afternoon and evening when Lauren and Hetty died. She had refused to stay and help at the store, saying she had a meeting. And the next morning, she'd had alcohol on her breath. Where had she been? Not at an AA meeting, that was for sure.

"I'm lying low until this is over," Carrie Ann said.

"You don't have anything to hide. Besides, you're scheduled to work this morning."

"Ali has to take my shift. I can't."

I sighed. Staff rotations were starting to resemble musical chairs without the accompanying peppy melody. "Ali works at the dental office mornings," I told her, adding as much authority to my voice as I could. "You're stuck. It's time to open, but run home first and change your clothes and put on fresh makeup. And hurry."

As I opened the store's doors for the day, I really hoped my cousin would come back. Carrie Ann had been doing really well with her recovery as long as nothing out of the ordinary happened to shake her calm. It seemed like she couldn't handle a single bit of adversity or conflict without slipping back into her old ways.

But I didn't have any more time to think about Carrie Ann and her problems because customers began overrunning the store. Since everybody knew that The Wild Clover was where all good gossip was accumulated and dispersed, and since last night we'd had information overload, the locals were filing in to exchange tidbits. Also, I was sort of an instant celebrity, basking in my fifteen minutes of fame and glory.

Which lasted only about five minutes because Mom arrived with Grams.

"I went out of my way to leave you alone last night," my mother said, which wasn't even close to true. I had just refused to answer my cell phone, but she should realize I could still see how many times she'd tried.

When I hadn't answered, she started calling Holly, who told her I was asleep and refused to wake me.

Mom went on, "We need to have a little talk." That's mother code for "You're in big trouble, Missy."

"Mom, see the line of customers here. Not now, okay."

"Well if it isn't Helen Fischer," someone said to Mom, drawing her attention away from me. "I heard you were taking over the store!"

"Not exactly." My mother's eyes shot over to my narrowing ones. "I'm helping Story keep things on track. That's all."

"You must be very proud of your daughter. She's a real trooper."

"Tough as nails," someone else said. Was that a compliment? Or a criticism? Hard to tell.

"Too bad she had to go through what she did, but thankfully justice was served," another customer said.

"We should name a street after her."

"She was *breaking the law*!" I heard someone say just when I thought the entire world had sided with me. I turned to see Lori Spandle standing behind me, glaring. That had been her flapping lips. Figures.

Mom humphed and elbowed her way in to take over at the cash register.

Grams, wearing a fresh daisy in her bun, took snapshots of me with various combinations of customers and promised everybody copies. My grandmother would be an avid photographer until the day she died, which I hoped was a long way off.

Milly came in to get the morel mushrooms I'd picked so she could work her recipe magic, since the next newsletter due date was coming up soon and our customers expected it right on time.

"Can you make something with morels and honey mixed together?" I wanted to know, thinking everything went well with honey from my beehives.

Milly made a face. "Doubt it. Some things simply don't go together, even if they look alike."

I hadn't thought of their similarities until Milly mentioned it. Morels *did* have a certain honeycomb-like appearance.

Holly showed up before her regularly scheduled time, gaining her extra credit from Mom, who didn't know today was the first time ever that my sister had been on time, let alone early. That girl sure could work our mother.

The scratches on my face from the wild rose bush were still inflamed and red, a fact pointed out by Grams.

"They look infected, sweetie pie," she said. "Did you put honey on them?"

"I totally forgot to do that." Honey was more effective than hydrogen peroxide when it came to dealing with germs. What I should have done was spread honey on a gauze pad and tape it to my cheek overnight.

"It'll heal right up and you won't have a scar." Grams went to my honey display, selected a small jar of honey, popped it open, and waited for me to apply it to my facial wounds.

"Right now? You want me to put it on here? Now?" I said. "I'm working. I'll look silly."

Mom humphed, like I couldn't possibly look more foolish than I already did. Or at least that was my personal take on her sound effects.

"Go on," Grams said. "Do it."

So I did, smearing honey along the thin tears in my skin. My grandmother can't be denied. She's too precious.

The store stayed busy through the morning. Carrie Ann never did come back and, at this point, I had to assume she had fallen off the wagon and our family would have to plan another intervention.

During one lull, I took Dinky outside for a pee break. While I carried her outside, she licked pretty much all the honey off my face. Since that animal's tongue had been in some pretty disgusting places, I rewashed my face when we came back inside and dabbed on more honey to offset any critter infections.

Congratulations and sympathies for what I had endured continued to pour in, with the occasional negative reaction. Why is it that one or two snarly comments can destroy the mood induced by multiple positive ones? I refused to let them, since the negatives came from the same people I expected dirt from, like Lori Spandle.

Or Mom, when she muttered under her breath, "Anything for attention."

An anonymous bouquet of flowers arrived. Some residents had taken Johnny Jay's speech about how he was forced to use physical aggressiveness as absolute gospel and wanted to know what I had done beforehand to cause him to rough me up like that.

"Johnny Jay doesn't need a reason to get nasty," I announced. "And he had to release me without a single charge. Isn't that enough proof of my innocence?"

Once my televised event had been talked to death, comments swung to Moraine's double murders and who might have committed the crime.

At least half the residents now thought Johnny Jay had killed Lauren and Hetty, many coming around to that decision after witnessing his temper toward me on live television. A few customers thought Norm Cross had some answering to do. Others weren't expressing opinions, deciding to wait and see how things played out.

However, most of us expected an arrest sometime soon.

The sooner, the better, if you ask me. Pity-Party Patti might want to solve the case single-handedly to ingratiate herself with the local newspaper, but I was perfectly willing to let the proper authorities handle it.

And with Sally Maylor in charge and Hunter's expert assistance, I really hoped for a rapid solution.

For a while I forgot about my precarious position. And my mother was too busy to turn her full attention in my direction. By the time Ali and the twins arrived mid-afternoon to take over, I was exhausted. Ready for a hot bath, a cup of honey-laced tea, and a quiet evening at home.

Only that wasn't about to happen.

Because Dinky had disappeared.

Twenty-three

"I really don't want to part with your sweet little Dinky yet," I said into the phone, lying up a storm. "I really want to have her a little longer, if that's okay with you. We're bonding." Which wouldn't have been true even if I had known where she was.

"That would take a load off my mind," Norm said, on the other end. "And I know you're taking really good care of her. She couldn't be in better hands."

"The best," I agreed before hanging up.

"You what?!" Holly said when I told her.

"The little rat fink can't be far," I said, hearing panic rising in my voice. "Oh my God, how did this happen?"

"Shhh. PLS (*Please*). Keep your voice down. If customers find out you lost Dinky, someone is bound to tell Norm."

"I didn't *lose* her. She escaped."

"I'll check around inside the store. Maybe she's under

the cheese counter looking for crumbs or a handout. You check outside."

"'K. No wait, she has to be in the store. She couldn't have snuck out the storage room door *and* through the back door, too."

"Don't assume anything."

How had this happened? And when? I had been taking her outside every three hours to accommodate her minuscule bladder and the last time had been—I glanced at the time—a little over an hour ago. So she must have gotten loose sometime in the last hour. Someone must have gone into the back room for supplies and hadn't been diligent about closing the door all the way. The mangy little mutt!

Holly went one way, I went the other. We met in the middle of the store. No Dinky.

"Dinky, want a treat?" I said in a whisper, hoping customers wouldn't catch on. Rustling open a bag of doggy treats didn't produce a real dog, either.

I ran outside and immediately lost the bet with myself that I'd find her rummaging near the Dumpster. She wasn't there, so I circled the building and scanned the neighboring cemetery for any tiny balls of movement. All the while thinking I was burned toast if I didn't find her.

Thinking she might have been smart enough to find her way to my house (which was a stretch, but I was desperate), I trotted the two blocks. Circled the house. Circled my ex-husband's ex-house. Circled mine again. The pipsqueak was still missing in action.

Was it possible to piss off any more people than I already had? Lori Spandle had verbally threatened to kill me when I ruined her house showing. Johnny Jay wanted my head on a platter for multiple reasons, the latest being a video totally embarrassing him and causing his forced leave of absence from his job. And if I had permanently lost Norm's dog, which was all he had left now that his wife was gone, I'd *have* to run away and never come back.

This couldn't be more terrible.

I slipped into my house and called Hunter's cell, careful to keep my voice calm, although a band of tension wrapped itself around my forehead and was getting tighter by the minute.

"How's the investigation going?" I said, trying to sound as normal as possible.

"It's going." Hunter had on his professional law voice, so I knew he was busy.

"I heard about Gunnar. What's up?"

"Story, I really can't discuss this subject with you."

Okay, then. Wow. I was out of the loop. "I was just thinking about Ben," I said, implementing my plan. "Is he home by himself?"

"Yeah."

"And you're working?"

"Yeah."

"I thought I'd go over and pick him up. We could spend some time together."

"Really?" He was all warm and fuzzy now. "That would be great. This case is taking all my time. I feel bad about leaving Ben alone so much."

"I'll go right over, if that's okay."

"More than okay. You remember where to find the key to the kennel?"

"Yup."

With that, I rushed back to the store to get my truck, drove north of town, taking the Rustic Road up the hill, passed Holy Hill, turned into Hunter's driveway, and released Ben from his kennel out back.

Ben jumped into my passenger seat without any coaxing at all, and we were off.

My plan better work or I was in *so* much trouble.

The drive back to my house seemed to take forever.

"Smell this," I said to Ben, showing him the latest pee stain on my bedroom floor. I'd dabbed it up but hadn't had time to give the wood floor a scrubbing, a good thing considering the circumstances. Hopefully, tracking dog Ben would get a scent from it. "And smell this," I held out a bath towel I'd used to dry Dinky after she'd been rained on.

Ben sniffed and sniffed, then gave me a knowing, confident gaze that meant he was ready to get down to business. Or at least, that's how I interpreted it.

"Ready?"

As soon as I opened the door, Ben went to work in my yard. He'd automatically assumed that was his starting point and I'd failed to mention where I'd done the actual dog losing. For all I knew, he understood everything I said.

"Not here, Ben," I said to him. He kept going in circles.

"What's going on over there?" P. P. Patti yelled from her backyard.

"Nothing," I said.

"Since you're home from work, I better take over for Holly and start protecting you like I promised. But come over here and help me first. I have slivers in my fingers from some rotting wood I carried and it's going to get all infected and wouldn't you know it, they're in my right hand, which is my strongest. I'm useless with my left. Why does everything always happen to me?"

"I have Ben to protect me today. He's a police attack dog. Ben can take down the biggest, baddest villain. I won't have to worry about Johnny Jay for the rest of the day. And I'm in a real hurry. Or I'd help."

"You can make time."

"I really, really can't. I'm in the middle of something."

"Well, then what should I do about these slivers?"

"Go to the store. Holly will get them out."

"Okay then. Well, you let me know when you need me."

"Right."

"Ben, let's go." I had his leash in one hand, which I snapped on him, and the towel in the other. We hurried to the store. Or rather I did. Ben, on his harness and leash, kept up without breathing any harder. I snuck into the back of the store where I'd last seen Dinky and we started the sniffing process over again.

Ben led me directly to the Dumpster, which must have been Dinky's first stop just as I had predicted, then across the street, through a few backyards and along the river. Once we were out of the residential area, I set him free. Sometimes he sniffed like he was looking for Dinky's scent floating in the air. Other times his nose was to the ground. Once he stopped and *really* took his time smelling around, alert and excited, and I would have bet a buck Dinky had left her pee mark in the vicinity. Amazing, since she usually reserved that for inside my home or store.

Then we turned toward The Lost Mile with Ben zigzagging along. It didn't take long for my brain to catch up with Ben's. He was leading me to Norm's house.

Of course Dinky had headed home. How dense could one woman be? Although I really didn't think the dog had it in her. Even the two blocks to my house should have been a tremendous strain on her pea brain.

Ben beat me there and immediately started barking.

Sure enough, Dinky was stretched out on Norm's moss-covered, rotting porch, cool and calm as can be, patiently waiting for her owner to return.

Good thing he wasn't home or I'd have some explaining to do.

"Bad dog," I said to Dinky, who didn't care in the least.

"Good Ben." The K-9 cop's tail wagged.

I glanced at the house and thought about my options, a no-brainer really when entrenched as deeply as I was in the current drama. Norm's door sprang open when I turned the knob, not like last time when the house had been locked up. That might mean Norm wouldn't be gone long. I'd have to hurry.

And I really hoped the unlocked door meant the alarm wasn't activated. At least if it was, Johnny Jay wouldn't be the one responding and I had a perfectly good reason to be there. Or I'd come up with one, if necessary.

In Dinky and I went. "Stay, Ben," I said, knowing he'd remain close by for as long as I asked him to. Dinky was another story. Totally untrained and wild. I wasn't giving her the opportunity to escape my clutches again by leaving her outside. She probably wouldn't run off, but I wasn't taking any more chances.

I lost her the minute we got inside, when she scampered around a corner and disappeared. So I gave up and made my way to the spare room to get another look at the lantern collection and poster board.

This time, I read each of the articles. Except for the one about the campers, all were based completely on superstition rather than any actual facts. Wild noises not attributable to local animals, unexplained lights and movement at night, a "creepy sensation" as one person put it in an interview.

Had Hetty helped Norm create the bizarre wall hanging? Had she known about his adventures as Lantern Man? Probably. The mean Witch would have loved the very idea of tormenting kids in the dark as much as she enjoyed hauling them through the woods by their ears. She might even have encouraged Norm the first time.

I really could see her forcing him into it.

I finished reading the last article. If Norm arrived, I decided to give him the same excuse as last time, the concerned neighbor spiel. I took a few minutes to study some pictures hanging on the wall. There was a younger version of Norm, wearing a Boy Scout troop leader uniform, framed in several different photographs, each with the same Boy Scout troop.

Hetty hated kids and Norm had been a Boy Scout leader! Talk about opposites! So why would he attack campers in the woods? What a contradiction. Although, appearances weren't everything. Just take a look at Johnny Jay.

I thought of comments made by my customers and how

some of them thought Norm was a killer. I wasn't completely in that camp, but it was a good thing that I had Ben with me anyway. Just in case they were right and I was wrong.

I decided to stick around. By the time Norm pulled into his driveway, I was sitting on the porch steps, throwing a ball for Ben and Dinky to chase.

I couldn't exactly come out and ask Norm about the things that bothered me, like why would a Boy Scout leader terrorize kids, because then he'd know I'd been snooping where I didn't belong.

So I handed over Dinky.

"Where are her things?" Norm asked, cuddling Dinky in his massive arms. "You know, her blankie and other stuff? Did you leave them inside?"

"Um, gosh, I forgot. I'll bring them over a little later. Just as soon as I get back from a few errands."

"It sure is good to have my little pup home," Norm said, looking like a great big teddy bear.

"How old is she, anyway?"

"Nine months." Holly had been right. She was still a puppy.

Looking at Dinky, who had settled contentedly in Norm's arms, I felt something strangely familiar tugging at my heart. The same feeling I got after spending time with Hunter and watching him take off on his bike.

"I'll come and visit often," I said to Dinky, realizing I actually meant what I said. Her ears changed position and she squirmed like she heard, understood, and approved.

Ben and I drove slowly away, with me watching Norm and Dinky grow smaller and smaller in my rearview mirror.

Twenty-four

I found Stu Trembly's brother, Eric, on a tractor, spraying apples in the orchard at Country Delight Farm on Creamery Road. He'd worked there as long as I could remember, starting out bailing hay as a teenager and progressing to manager of the farm. Based on an article hanging on Norm Cross's wall, Eric had been one of The Lost Mile campers the night Lantern Man had stalked them and destroyed their camping equipment.

After describing the details of the night, Eric said, "I'll never forget it as long as I live." Eric wasn't exactly an easy scare, so coming from him it really must have been a terrifying experience.

"Describe the sound it made," I asked, still trying to pin the local legend on Hetty Cross.

"I don't know."

"Did it sound like a banshee?"

Eric and I didn't have an Irish bone in our bodies except on Saint Patrick's Day, when the whole town pretended they had Irish blood. But since so many Irish immigrants had settled in the southeastern part of Wisconsin (right along with my German ancestors), we all knew what a banshee was—an Irish spirit, which sometimes appeared in human form and wailed across the countryside to foreshadow death.

"It sounded kind of like this." Eric let out a loud lingering howl, not piercing at all.

"Could a woman make that sound?" I wanted to know.

Eric hopped off the tractor and leaned against it. "I'm not sure. Maybe." We watched Ben nose around an apple tree and lift his leg. This was the third tree he'd marked since we arrived and, knowing the dog, it wouldn't be his last.

"Thanks, Eric."

"Sure. What are you up to?"

"Just fact-finding, feeding my curiosity."

"Well, I better get back to work. Nice seeing you again."

Halfway to my truck, I remembered something. "Hey, Eric, you were on a Boy Scout camping trip that night, right?"

"Yeah. The whole troop can vouch for what I told you just now."

"Was your troop the only one camping?"

"No, a bunch of them were, but ours was the only one in The Lost Mile."

"Was Norm's troop out?"

"Probably."

Two and two were beginning to add up to four.

I thanked Eric for his time and called out to Ben, who came running. The tractor started back up. My brain churned, the squeaky gears started turning.

I became more and more convinced I was right, in spite of Hunter's brush-off.

Norm Cross had as much potential for filling the legendary Lantern Man shoes as I had for morphing into Wonder Woman. In other words, no chance whatsoever.

He was covering for somebody and that somebody had to be his wife, Hetty, who had been a much nastier human being than Norm ever would be. The role suited the old biddy perfectly.

The Witch had been Lantern Man.

Or rather, Lantern Woman.

Hetty had been out patrolling her woods that night, making sure intruders weren't lurking around once the sun set in the west. Maybe she heard voices, Lauren's and her assailant's, and went to investigate.

Hetty spotted trespassers, all right. She had probably been thrown off by that, because no one had dared trespass on her turf for a very long time. Judging by layers of dust accumulating on those lanterns, they hadn't been used in the recent past. She must have stumbled into a confrontation, maybe even witnessed Lauren's death and could identify her killer, therefore leaving the murderer no choice but to kill her, too.

And I thought *I* had bad luck!

That would mean Lauren was definitely the prime target, and only one name stood out in boldface on my list of persons of interest in that case.

Johnny Jay.

He wasn't going to be a free man long if I had any say in it, which I didn't, but aspirations and short-term goals are always good incentives. What if he'd already been arrested by Sally Maylor and Hunter and charged with two counts of murder? I could imagine the scenario—Johnny in that very public holding cell instead of me, stripped of his dignity and position, having to use that open toilet right in front of everybody.

Johnny Jay had gone too far and would get his comeuppance, a word my mother used frequently.

If Johnny really was a killer, Hunter had better arrest him before Johnny had a chance to hunt me down.

For the first time ever, I considered buying a weapon for self-protection.

Although, thinking about it, a weapon hadn't helped Lauren. Her gun had been taken away and used against her.

As I pulled into The Wild Clover's parking lot, Holly came out of the store. She flung a filled garbage bag into the Dumpster. I rolled down the driver's-side window, and she moseyed over.

"What are you up to?" she said. "And why are you chumming with Ben? That isn't like you."

"I love Ben. He and I are plotting an arrest, but I'll tell you more about it later. We found Dinky. She had gone home, so I left her there with Norm."

Holly banged her open hand against her chest in a show of relief. "Whew. I was really worried about her."

"Not as freaked as I was."

"BTW, Stanley Peck needs your help, something about beekeeping advice. He said he'll be home if you get time to stop by and take a look at one of his hives."

"Want to ride over with me?"

Holly rolled her eyes, as if that was the silliest question of the day. "NFW (*No Freaking Way*). I hate bees."

"Oh, come on. You have from now until tomorrow morning totally free. Ali and the twins don't need your help and your man's still out of town. Have you two made up yet?"

"Sorta. We're talking. He'll be home AND (*Any Day Now*). Thanks for letting me stay with you. It's helping to have family around."

"Hop in."

Holly still stood by the window, not moving. "I can't go along with you. The store might get busy. One of us should stay close by in case."

"Since when did you become Ms. Responsible Store Partner?"

"Since two seconds ago when my only other choice involves bees."

"You're my bodyguard."

"AIR (*As I Remember*) you promised not to make me help with your bees if I got rid of Mom the other day. Which I did."

"These aren't my bees."

"Same difference."

"Well, you promised to protect me after I made my promise, so your promise to stick close to me overrides mine. Besides, we're family. I need you."

Those were the magic words, because Holly made a face and that familiar lip pout while she went around the front of the truck, opened the passenger door, and got in. "I'm only doing this," she said, "because you played the family card. Cheap shot."

On the way over to Stanley's, I told her about Norm's alleged Lantern Man lie, which I planned to prove soon, and how the real culprit wasn't a man, it was a woman. Lantern Woman (aka Hetty Cross). And how I couldn't understand why Hunter was wasting time interrogating Gunnar when he could be taking care of the real killer and keeping our streets safe.

When we pulled into Stanley's driveway, my cell phone rang. The number on the display wasn't familiar. I shouldn't have answered, but I did.

"We need to talk, Missy Fischer," Johnny Jay said without identifying himself. I'd know that voice anywhere.

"Johnny, you need to stay away from me. Or I'm getting a restraining order." Yes, I needed a restraining order pronto. Even if it involved face-to-face confrontation in a court of law.

Holly, on the other side of Ben, sat up straight when she heard me say Johnny's name. She stared at me.

"I'm hanging up," I said, but that wasn't true. I needed

to find out just how angry he really was and to what lengths he'd go to get his revenge.

"I think you want to hear what I have to say," he said next.

"Uh, no, not really, but if you insist, say it."

"Not this way. In person."

Oh, right, like that was going to happen in this lifetime. The next thing I said just popped out. "Is that how you got Lauren to meet you in the woods? Pretending you had something important to tell her?"

That was really the wrong thing to blurt, because I should have kept him off guard until I had more information. I hated when I blurted.

The pause was pronounced, as in uncomfortable and awkward.

Then he said, "So you've been sitting down at that store of yours, pointing your finger at me, telling all your customers I killed Lauren Kerrigan."

And Hetty, I could have pointed out, but what was left of my common sense took over. "Townspeople are smart. They don't need me telling them what's as obvious as the noses on their faces."

"You're making a big mistake, a very big mistake."

"I'll take that as a threat then," I said and hung up.

"I need a really long vacation," I said to my sister. "Peru or Brazil. Columbia. Someplace safe."

Holly snorted. "Those places aren't safe. They have terrorists and drug dealers."

"They'd be minor problems compared to this."

"Relax. You'll be fine. Don't overreact."

Easy for her to say. She didn't have a care in the world other than deciding what color Jag to buy next time and whether or not to be mad at Max the Money Machine for working hard and keeping her in the style that she'd become accustomed to.

With a sigh, I stepped out of the truck and greeted

Stanley, who had waved to us from an outbuilding next to his house. "Come on, bodyguard," I said to Holly.

"I'll wait here."

"No you won't. You're the one with the wrestling degree. Stay close. Johnny Jay could be around any corner."

"Yeah, right." But she followed me.

Ben moved over behind the steering wheel and watched out the open window, his tongue hanging out about two feet.

"I have two problems," Stanley said, standing next to one of his hives.

I could tell what one of those problems was by the fact that the hive had been disassembled in a crude and rough way. Holly, I noticed, was as far away from the flying honeybees as possible, which sort of countered my plan to get her more involved with bees. She wanted a partnership and she was going to get it full blast.

"Come take a look, Holly," I said. "You should learn this, too."

"No," she answered.

I bent down and spotted raccoon tracks. Stanley was a total rookie, even worse than I'd been as a first year bee-keeper. "Raccoons. They lifted the top right off the hive to get at the honey, then just kept taking it apart, one level at a time."

"You'd think all those bee stings would have chased them away."

"Raccoons have thick fur, dense enough to make it hard for bees to penetrate. Not much stops them. And they are as smart as some humans I know." Smarter than a whole lot of people I knew, actually, but I kept that to myself.

"What should I do?" Stanley said, worried. "They'll be back tonight and do the same thing to the rest of my hives."

"Bricks on top," I answered.

"Ahhh." Light bulbs went on in the dimness of Stanley's mind. "I thought you put bricks on top of your hives so the tops wouldn't blow off, which didn't make much sense since the tops are pretty heavy. I should have figured that out."

Holly had edged an inch or two closer due to my constant gestures to join the conversation.

"That one was an easy fix," I said. "What's your next problem?"

"Mites," Stanley said. "I found mites on my bees. Come look."

"I'm out of here," my sister said.

"Ben has more loyalty," I called after her retreating back.

Sure enough, Stanley's bees had what all beekeepers had to deal with sooner or later. Varroa mites. Parasites almost invisible to the human eye. They attached to bees' bodies like bloodsuckers or wood ticks, but instead of sucking blood, they sucked hemolymph. Varroa mites could weaken a colony so much that if the bad news bugs weren't discovered and treated quickly, they could wipe out an entire hive.

Stanley didn't like my diagnosis, although he suspected it. "If it's not one thing, it's another," he said.

Which was true.

Here's a list of only a few predators that prey on honeybees:

- Skunks—I had that challenge last year. They actually knock on the hives to draw out the bees and then they eat them.

- Bears—There aren't any in this part of the state, so we don't have to deal with that one, thank goodness.

- Raccoons—These bold, beastly critters are highly intelligent and creatively persistent.

- Rodents—Mice and rats like to make winter homes in hives.

- Birds—Martins, swallows, and woodpeckers eat the bees right out of the air.

- Beetles—The small hive beetle, in particular, takes over an entire hive, eating the honey stores and chasing out the honeybees.

- Varroa mites—Imagine carrying a fifty-pound blood-sucker on your back and you'd have some idea what a honeybee goes through.

I told Stanley what to do for starters—sprinkle the honeybees with powdered sugar. The sugar made it harder for the mites to stay attached and it gave the bees a reason to do some extra grooming, which also caused them to fall off. "Let me know if that doesn't work," I said, walking with Stanley out to the truck where my sister sat inside, talking on her cell phone while studying her fingernails to make sure they were picture perfect.

"I heard Carrie Ann might be drinking again," Stanley said.

If Stanley knew, then everybody knew. "She'll be fine," I said, hoping that was true. "Lauren Kerrigan's murder really stressed her out."

"We're all a little edgy with a killer running loose."

"This can't be over quick enough for me."

"That reminds me of something," Stanley said. "Way back when Lauren ran over Wayne and plowed into that tree, I was the one who towed her car off to scrap it."

Thinking back, I remembered that, at the time, Stanley still ran his farm instead of renting it out to other farmers like he did now, and he had his hands into everything where money was to be had, including the towing business.

I nodded. "I remember."

"Usually when a car is totaled like that, the family comes by and strips out personal belongings, but none of the Kerrigans ever showed up even though I let them know I had her stuff. I guess they had other things on their minds. So I went through the car and boxed up whatever was loose, which wasn't much. Rita said she didn't want the junk back and it's been here every since."

I looked at the outbuilding. "You've held on to things from Lauren's car for sixteen years?"

"Yup. And now that she's gone for good, I asked Rita again and she said to throw whatever I had away. Guess I'll do that."

"Don't," Holly piped up. "Rita might change her mind someday."

Stanley shook his head. "It's nothing but junk. I'm cleaning out that building, making room for other stuff, and it's going."

"Throw the box in the back of Story's truck. She'll hang on to it for a while."

Gee, thanks, sis. I wondered why she couldn't store it herself.

But in the scheme of things, it wasn't a big deal.

Stanley limped away to get it, came back with a cobwebbed cardboard box that had seen better days, and added it to the junk in the back of my truck.

One of these days, I'd have to clean out the back end and get organized.

Twenty-five

It had been one of those days when I started out with good intentions and ended up with very little accomplished. I had a list a mile long and hadn't made a dent in my chores. I'd wanted to start checking my outlying bee-hives, but that would have to wait until tomorrow. And I didn't want to even think about all the paperwork piling up at The Wild Clover.

At the rate I was going, I had just enough time to take Ben home and return Dinky's belongings before getting ready for Chopper Murphy's wake at Stu's. First stop was Norm's house while Ben waited on the porch, pressing his nose against the screen, inhaling the odor of freshly fried meat.

"Here you go," I said, handing over the scraggly mutt's food, pink blanket, and accessories, looking around Norm's kitchen floor for the tiny terror. "Where's Dinky?"

Almost before the words were out of my mouth, Dinky

barreled at me like I was her long lost mother, squealing and panting. I scooped her up.

"She really likes you," Norm said, watching her wash my face while I tried to dodge her pink tongue.

"As long as she doesn't pee on my feet, we get along just fine."

Norm put her things on the floor and she wiggled to get down and take possession. I obliged. She ran off with her rawhide chew toy.

"We're having a wake for Chopper tonight at Stu's," I said to Norm. "Are you coming?"

"No, I'm not in the mood to party. Those Irish . . ." Norm shook his head like I should automatically know how to finish the rest of the sentence.

I hadn't intended to bring up the subject of Hetty's reign of terror or Norm's dishonest cover-up, wanting to give him some grieving time before making accusations, but the words came flying out before I could stop them. "I know you aren't Lantern Man," I blurted.

Norm's eyes narrowed and his face reddened almost immediately. "I admitted it in public and those reporters even put it on television. What more do you want from me? I don't know what you're talking about."

"You have good intentions, but Hetty was the one who destroyed those scouts' camping equipment. Not you."

"That's a lie!"

"You were on a camping trip at the same time as those campers who had their supplies destroyed by the so-called Lantern *Man*." I put special emphasis on the last word. "You weren't even in the area."

I'd guessed at that last part, but my remark struck true as an arrow. Part of me wondered why I was giving the man more grief to pile on what he already had. "I know you did it to preserve your wife's good name. I won't tell anybody else."

I was so intent on watching Norm's reaction I didn't notice his dog approaching until I felt warm liquid on my flip-flopped foot. She hadn't peed on me once while she stayed with me. On everything else, yes, but not directly on me. I had to remember to wear more protective footwear on her home turf.

"You must really like kids," I said, "to become a leader."

"I've always liked them," Norm said. "Hetty did, too."

I almost snorted at that. Norm read my expression.

"Hetty was a very private person," he said. "And kids didn't respect that as much as they should have. She just wanted them to stay away."

"I'm absolutely convinced you didn't pull any of those mean pranks."

"Get out of my house," Norm said, exploding the same way he had when Carrie Ann and I visited with the casserole and told him people were talking about Lantern Man maybe being involved in the murders.

He didn't even try to control his temper. Or it just blew out before he knew it was happening. He had some of the same signs I've witnessed from Johnny Jay when he'd lose control over his emotions. Overly red face. Clenched jaw. Bulging neck veins and enlarged Adam's apple. Raised voice. On a scale of one to ten with ten being raging, Norm would rate an eight or nine.

The guy was headed for a massive coronary at this rate.

Good thing Ben was right outside the door. If I needed him, I better get closer, so I could make a run for it. I didn't think Ben could get right through the screen to protect me.

"I didn't mean to upset you," I said, after totally upsetting him and considering how to do damage control. "I just want to understand."

"Get out." Norm took a few steps forward, towering over me, and I shuffled backward, tripping only once before he slammed the door and left me on his porch with Ben and a foot wet with urine.

I'd really handled that well.

Before I got into my truck, I rubbed my germ-infested bare foot in the grass in Norm's lawn while Ben marked some shrubs to let Dinky know who was boss.

Hunter called my cell phone and, as soon as he found out I was on my way to his house, arranged to meet me there for an *interlude* (his words). I wasn't fooled by his romantic word choice. The man was ultra-focused on crime solving, as he should be.

Once Johnny Jay was in custody, we would have time for something much longer, like a rhapsody. Or so I hoped.

Absence, I was finding out, really did make my heart grow fonder. And my mind clearer. I hadn't had conflicting thoughts about us as a couple for almost a whole day.

"Have you arrested Johnny Jay yet?" I said, the second thing I did after getting out of my truck. The first thing I did was check out Hunter and proclaim him as hot as ever.

He had his arms wrapped around me in a miss-you bear hug when I asked about Johnny. He relaxed his grip and stepped back, gazing into my eyes. Then holding my hand, he led me to a patio table where he'd put out a pitcher of lemonade and two glasses. We sat down close to each other.

"You decided to press charges?" he asked.

"No, but most likely he killed Lauren and Hetty."

"I suppose you have proof to back up any accusation you have against Johnny Jay." Hunter poured lemonade and handed a glass to me.

"Process of elimination," I said, like I really knew this stuff. "He hated Lauren because she killed his father. So when she came back, he lost control and killed her. Revenge is a powerful motive. You've said that yourself. I know you have to actually prove he did it, but could you please hurry up?"

"Has he come near you again?"

"No, not exactly, but he threatened me. Verbally. He

called my cell and wanted to meet me, pretending he had to tell me something."

"Maybe he wanted to beg for your forgiveness."

I snorted at the thought of that unlikely possibility. "He could have apologized over the phone. And are you suggesting I should have agreed to meet him face-to-face after what he did to me last time?"

"He didn't murder anybody, Story, so get that out of your head. But no, meeting him would be foolish. He's a vengeful guy who needs anger-management training."

I could have told him Johnny Jay wasn't the only one with excessive anger problems. Norm Cross was a hothead, too. But I didn't want to muddy the water. "If you plan to let Johnny run loose like a rabid dog, I've decided to go for the restraining order."

So far, our interlude wasn't going so well, thanks in part to me. Okay, thanks *all* to me. But Hunter hadn't arrested the killer, even though I was the next target and slated for death. I was scared.

Hunter rubbed his face, looking tired. "A restraining order takes time."

"Pull some strings."

"I can't do that. Like I told you, you have to fill out paperwork, go before a judge. Johnny will have an opportunity to defend himself against whatever charges you make."

That wouldn't be good. In fact, that would only make him madder. I was running out of options. Leaving town was back on the table.

I couldn't help that my eyes were filling with tears. Not the boo-hoo, poor-me variety, but the totally frustrated kind. To give Hunter credit, he noticed and tried to cheer me up. "You and Johnny have been going head-to-head as long as I've known you, and up until the other day, he hadn't displayed any signs of physical aggression. Right? He's just loud and obnoxious. Right?"

I didn't want to admit that Hunter was right. "He's always been a jerk and is rotten to everybody. Me more than most."

He continued by saying, "Johnny lost it and he's paying dearly. The guy's smart enough to stay away from you. He wants his job back and the key to returning to his office is making things right. He told me you deserved a public apology from him."

"Oh, sure, like that's going to happen."

"But he didn't kill anybody."

"How can you be so sure?"

"Story, you're making this hard for me. Everything about this case is confidential at this point. You can come up with all the circumstantial evidence in the world, but unless you bring me something concrete, I'm not jumping to conclusions."

"Humph," I said, sounding like my mother.

"Story, I have to believe that cops are the good guys. If I started doubting my own team, I might as well give up and quit."

"Okay. I understand." And I really did. Hunter's world was more black and white than mine was. I sighed heavily. "Carrie Ann's in trouble again. I think she's drinking."

"I'm keeping an eye out for her. Is she at the store?"

"Not right now."

I thought about Carrie Ann wanting to hide and about Hunter questioning Gunnar, and I wanted to ask all kinds of questions. But now wasn't the time. Hunter looked tense.

"I should be on your list, too," I said, putting a little sug- gestiveness into my voice, so the implication was clear that I wasn't going to bug him anymore.

"You're at the very top," he replied, catching my drift. Men could do that—change direction mid-stream as long as the subject interests them.

"Then why aren't you grilling me?"

Hunter grinned at me playfully, only it wasn't all play

on my part. I really wanted to know why he needed information from Gunnar and Carrie Ann, yet not from me.

"You heard that I was asking Gunnar questions," he said, on to me from the start. "I don't have any reason to question you, because I knew exactly where you were every step of the way."

I reached over and took his hand, rubbing his palms, massaging the stress from each of his fingers, until he relaxed. Fifteen minutes later we pulled out of his driveway, Hunter going one way to seek truth and justice, me going another to get ready for an Irish wake.

The only thing I knew for sure was that Hunter was looking for clues in the past. And what did he mean about knowing where I was every step of the way? What was my almost boyfriend up to?

Twenty-six

All I know about Irish wakes:

- They are special vigils held the night before a funeral. Although, since Chopper Murphy had already been buried weeks ago, this was definitely going to have a few differences.

- It is also a big party with plenty of alcohol, at which we recognize and celebrate the deceased's life.

- Crying is allowed, but so is laughing and singing. Wailing is common.

- As a sign of respect, all mirrors must be covered with cloth, and clocks are stopped.

- An Irish wake cocktail consists of orange juice, gold rum, 151 rum, blue curaçao, and maraschino cherries.

• I'm familiar with two important Irish blessings:

> *May those who love us, love us.*
>
> *And those who don't love us,*
>
> *may God turn their hearts.*
>
> *And if He doesn't turn their hearts,*
>
> *may He turn their ankles*
>
> *so we'll know them by their limping.*

and

> *Here's to a long life and a merry one*
>
> *A quick death and an easy one*
>
> *A pretty girl and an honest one*
>
> *A cold beer and another one!*

The first blessing reminded me of Stanley Peck and his limp. Tonight he'd be walking straighter than ever, so we wouldn't think badly of him. The second one made me more aware than ever that Lauren Kerrigan's death hadn't been quick and easy like Chopper's. She'd stayed alive long enough to try to crawl for help. I couldn't even begin to imagine what she went through in the last moments of her life.

Holly, Patti, and I walked into Stu's Bar and Grill twenty minutes after the wake officially began, and we were already way behind everybody else in the celebration department. Stu and his staff were struggling to keep up with requests for Irish wake cocktails and the drinks were going as fast as they could make them. We waited our turns then grabbed our drinks, dropping bills on the counter to pay for them and stuffing dollar bills into a coffee can set up for donations to Chopper's immediate family.

I expressed my condolences to Chopper's wife, Fiona,

and to several other members of the Murphy family, saying pretty much the same thing I'd said at his funeral. With one addition. "I hope this wake is what Chopper needs to move on," I said.

"Me, too," Fiona agreed.

Grams and her card-playing buddies had set up at a table in the corner and were dealing hands of gin rummy. One seat was vacant, but that didn't stop them from dealing in the invisible player. Another wake tradition—the extra place was for Chopper Murphy, in case he decided to join the game from the spirit world.

"This tastes too alcoholly," P. P. Patti said after taking a taste of her Irish wake and making a sourpuss face. "Like really strong booze."

"Well, yeah," my sister said. "One-fifty-one rum. You can actually flame it with that kind of alcohol content."

"I don't want it," Patti replied.

"Give it to me," I said. Patti handed it over and I quickly became a two-fisted drinker. Just in time to be greeted by Mom.

"Drinking a little heavy, Story?" she said, disapproval stamped on her gathered eyebrows.

"Umm. This one's for you." I attempted to hand it to her.

But Mom didn't bite, at least not that way. "You know I don't drink."

"It has maraschino cherries in it?" A drink would do wonders for my mother's disposition. It might put some color in her pale cheeks and a real smile on her face.

"Hi, Mrs. Fischer," Patti said. "I'm not drinking one of those strong things."

"Some of us have more sense than others," Mom said.

"Alcohol robs you of brain cells," the brownnoser said. But camaraderie has never worked on my mother. She ignored Patti.

"I'm sitting at a table behind Grams," Mom said to me. "Why don't you join us?"

So what could I say? No? "I'll be over in a minute."

"You have a really nice mom," Patti said, watching her make her way to the table behind Grams.

"Peachy sweet," I agreed.

"It must be hard for her, living with your grandmother."

Unbelievable! Talk about having no people perception skills!

"Oh, look," Holly piped up and said. "A Celtic band is setting up."

Sure enough, I saw fiddles, guitars, and an accordion.

My two bodyguards vanished into the crowd, leaving me to fend for myself. Didn't they know my mother was harmful to my health? In spite of that, I made my way over to her table.

Where, I noticed right away, she was sharing the table with Jackson Davis, who was the county medical examiner. Suddenly, I really wanted to sit at that table.

Jackson was a good-looking guy in his mid- to late forties, with thick dark eyebrows, the kind that formed one continuous line across his forehead, and a five o'clock shadow, no matter what time of day. He'd lived in the area long enough to know our ways, but he'd been born and raised in Chicago, making him a permanent outsider right along with Patti Dwyre. The difference between the two of them was he didn't seem to mind at all and didn't go out of his way to offend people by trying to overcompensate.

Could it be that medical examiners have outcast personalities to begin with? Jackson had what Carrie Ann accurately described as "the suckiest job in the world." He dealt in graphic gore, so he needed a strong stomach and a thick hide. And when it came to murder, he had to understand criminals, combine pieces to create a whole, and draw valid conclusions. The medical examiner was the first person a murderer had to fool.

"How's business?" I asked.

"My patients don't complain," Jackson said.

I groaned. Add another characteristic personality trait—a morbid sense of humor.

"I bet they're just dying to do business with you," I said, handing him the extra Irish wake cocktail, which I hoped would make a good bribe. If my overflowing generosity didn't do the trick, the alcohol sure would loosen him up. I proceeded with caution. "Ever been to an Irish wake before?"

"No, this is my first." He took a cautious sip, found it tasty, and took a real drink.

The musicians started up. I recognized "As I Was Walkin' Round Kilgary Mountain."

Glancing at Jackson, I noticed his drink was almost gone. "Good, isn't it?" I yelled over the music. But just then the song ended and I was still shouting. "You have to get drunk at wakes. It's a rule."

Mom was leaning over the back of Grams's chair, trying to tell her what to play, but she took time to swivel her head and make sure her daughter was behaving. By her frown, I assumed she had overheard me. Not exactly hard to do considering my poor timing.

"Don't believe a word of it, Jackson," she said, confirming my assumption. That woman had some keen hearing to go along with her snake tongue. "That stuff is pure poison."

I leaned closer to him when Mom went back to her backseat card playing. "That drink in your hand is called an Irish wake. They hardly have any alcohol in them at all. Don't worry."

"Okay." Another solid drink. "It's really good."

"Any updates on our double murder?" I asked.

"I can't talk about that subject, Story. You know I can't compromise an active criminal investigation by releasing confidential information to the general public."

I didn't know that, but I did now. "I understand," I said. "Hunter said you would try to squeeze details out of me," Jackson continued, laughing. Then I noticed several empty beer bottles in front of him and that his eyes were slightly brighter than sober eyes should be.

"Let me buy you another drink," I said, scooting away before he could refuse. "Save my seat."

I ordered two more—one for me and one for Jackson. "Make one of them a double; no, change that to a triple," I said to Stu. "Lots of one-fifty-one rum."

"You aren't messing with your mother, are you?" Stu asked.

"I wouldn't think of it. I'm a good daughter."

The noise level in the bar had increased about a zillion octaves since I first arrived. Between the talking, wailing, and music playing, I expected the roof to come down at any moment.

Volunteers were setting out platters and bowls of food on a long table against the far wall. Since Stu didn't have the capacity, staff, or equipment to cater food to a crowd this big, he'd agreed to allow a potluck inside the bar as long as the drink tabs kept adding up. That wasn't going to be a problem.

But if they didn't get the food uncovered and ready to serve soon, so wake-goers had something inside them to sop up some of the alcohol, half the customers would be in drunken stupors before long.

I loved the Irish culture.

Jackson did, too. I could tell. He had a big smile plastered on his face, and his head was bobbing to the tunes piping through the sound system. Since it was too loud to hold the conversation I had hoped to have with him, I gave up and watched the action.

Holly and Patti swung across the floor, dancing together, attempting a really poor example of an Irish jig. Hands on hips. Legs flying. They looked more like electric-shock patients undergoing treatment than real dancers.

Looking around, I saw a few Kerrigans, but none of

Lauren's immediate family. I wondered how they were coping with their loss.

The band finished the set. They went off to take a break, giving some of us the opportunity to toast Chopper.

"Hope he gets to heaven before the devil finds out he's dead," someone called out, paraphrasing a typical Irish toast. Cheers went up and everybody took a drink of whatever was in his or her hand.

One of the Murphys started singing and everybody joined in:

In Heaven there is no beer, that's why we drink it here.

Most of those celebrating were customers of mine as well. Some had small businesses in town. My dentist came into view, and I hunkered down a little. If he saw me, T. J. would run over and start blabbing about my cavity, and badger me into setting up an appointment. Knowing him, he probably had his appointment calendar in his pocket.

Three residents were noticeably missing (other than most of the Kerrigans and Norm Cross, who had already told me he wasn't coming): Hunter wasn't in the bar, but that was because he had work to do on the case. I really hadn't expected him. And Carrie Ann hadn't made an appearance, which, on one hand, surprised me because if she was drinking again, wouldn't she be bellied up to the bar? On the other hand, last time I saw her she was spooked and talking about going into hiding.

The only other resident missing was Johnny Jay. If he was as calculating as I suspected, he'd stay away. Nobody thought too highly of him at the moment.

The band started back up with "Danny Boy." I went to the ladies' room and met up with Patti inside. "I saw you sitting over with the medical examiner," she said. "What did you learn?"

"Not a thing. He won't say a word."

"Ply him with alcohol."

"I'm working on it."

Patti looked into the mirror and met my eyes. "Let's kidnap him and make him talk."

"Please tell me you're kidding?"

Patti didn't blink.

"Let's reserve that in case we get really desperate," I suggested, meaning it was never going to happen.

Suddenly, right in the middle of "Molly Malone," the music stopped. I found out why when we walked back into the bar. Because one of the missing residents had arrived after all.

Johnny Jay had the mic. And the floor. Every head in the place rotated toward the ladies' room, so I had to be involved in whatever was taking place. Patti stepped away from me, blending into the background. Before she disappeared, leaving me alone—not for the first time, either—I saw her whip out her handy video recorder.

Jeez, I hated being the center of controversy. I really did. Sure, I liked attention just like everybody else, but not this kind.

Johnny Jay's head swung and he followed everybody else's gaze until his cold eyes locked onto mine. And I read the message they conveyed loud and clear. I knew exactly what was coming next, and he wanted me to know none of it was for my benefit.

"I'd like everyone's attention for a moment." His voice boomed with the added amplification provided by the mic, which the man didn't really need.

You could have heard a maraschino cherry drop, the place went so quiet. I froze.

"I came to pay my respects to the memory of Chopper Murphy," he said, "and I want you all to know that I mean it from the bottom of my heart. Chopper and I got to know each other pretty good."

He didn't mention that they had plenty of time to get acquainted because Johnny kept arresting Chopper for public drunkenness, but we all knew that.

Nobody said a word. Patti was standing on a chair with her arm extended, the video rolling.

"What the hell!" That's what Johnny Jay said next, with his eyes fixed on Patti. "Are you video taping me?"

The raging bull was snorting and stomping at the surface. It sure didn't take much. The only positive thing about this was that I realized I wasn't the only one in town who could rile him. Patti had a gift for it, too.

"Put that thing away! *Now!*"

Patti lowered her arm and jumped down from the chair.

Johnny Jay struggled to control himself. And actually won.

"Chopper was a forgiving man," Johnny went on. "So he would have appreciated what I'm going to do next. You all know Missy . . . I mean Story Fischer and I had an altercation recently and I want to apologize to her in public. And this is the best place to find everybody together. Can you come up here please, Story?"

Jeez, he was looking straight at me. All I wanted was to disappear from view, get down and crawl out the door, because no way did I want to accept an apology from Johnny Jay. He didn't mean one word of it.

Somebody gave me a little shove, so I walked up to the center of attention on numb legs.

"Story Fischer, I am sorry for any harm or hurt I caused you. Will you accept my sincerest apology right out in front of the whole town?" He grinned at the crowd. "Or do you want me to get down on my knees and beg your forgiveness?"

Someone yelled, "Yes, do it!"

And everybody laughed and thought it was one big joke when he actually got down on the floor and pleaded with his hands clasped together and that stupid grin still on his face. When I looked around the room, I could tell he had them eating out of the palm of his hand.

And he waited, still smiling, but his eyes when they pierced mine weren't laughing along.

I licked my lips.

"I'll think about it, Johnny Jay." I saw him flinch when I called him that, but right now he wasn't police chief, and I didn't have to bother with titles and respect. "But I'd like you to start over again from the beginning and let Patti Dwyre preserve your heartfelt apology for eternity."

He really hated that, almost lost his place in the script, but for the moment I was directing and he went along, doing as I said.

"You can get up now," I said, after he repeated the performance for Patti, who took her job very seriously. "And I'll give you an answer after I've thought on it long and hard. In the meantime, the next round of drinks is on The Wild Clover and Story Fischer."

And that was the end of that scene, because buying the whole place a drink beat out just about anything else in the world.

I showed Johnny Jay my back and returned to my table.

Mom slowly shook her head at me, implying that either I hadn't handled the situation well or I shouldn't be buying drinks for everybody. Or both.

Jackson had pushed back his chair and was standing. His body language told me he was leaving and by the way he was swaying without any music, he'd had too much to drink. Partly, or mostly, thanks to me.

I couldn't let him drive.

"I'll walk out with you," I shouted to him since the band had resumed. I watched Johnny Jay make his way to the door and leave, so I stalled until I was sure he wasn't in the parking lot any longer. Then Jackson and I walked out together.

I decided to try one more time to pump him for information.

"Are you sure you can't tell me just a little about what you found in the autopsies?" I asked.

Jackson stopped next to his car.

"I'm sure," he said, digging through one pocket, then another, searching for his car keys. "But I can tell you I still disagree with the jury's findings in the case against Lauren Kerrigan."

"You and all her family."

"Especially how she ran over Wayne Jay."

"What about it?"

"Why did she run over him twice?"

"Everybody wonders that," I said. "Even Lauren didn't know."

"See, that question has bothered me all these years and it's never been answered. The way it happened didn't make sense. I wasn't a medical examiner at the time, way too young, but I was studying up and watching her case."

Jackson leaned against his car, and he tried to focus on me with glazed-over eyes. He actually closed one, thinking that might improve his vision. He hadn't slurred any of his words. What came out of his mouth was well formed and thoughtful, but the rest of him . . .

"Why don't I give you a lift home?" I said, thinking he would tell me more on the drive over to his house.

"I'll be fine. Think I'll go back in, though, and see if there's any coffee on that table."

"If not, ask Stu to make some."

"Good idea." Jackson pushed off from the car.

"Wait a minute. Don't go yet. You were telling me about the trial and your theory."

"Oh, right. Here it is. Based on angles," Jackson used his hands to supplement his speech, making imaginary angles, "Lauren ran over his legs the first time, so the man was still alive. Right?"

I nodded, remembering what came next, which had a lot to do with earning her an extra-heavy sentence.

"Then she put the car in reverse, backed up, shifted to drive, hit the gas, and ran over him again. That time she killed him."

"Yeah," I said a little impatiently. "Nothing new there."

"Okay, Miss Smarty Pants. My question was, she had so damned much alcohol in her bloodstream, how did she even drive at all?"

I shrugged. "Drunks drive plastered all the time. It's unfortunate, but they do." Like this very minute when Jackson was nearly going to get behind the wheel and drive when he shouldn't. The hardest thing about someone soaked in booze is that they don't realize how drunk they are. So they resist everybody's efforts to help them.

"It had rained earlier that day," Jackson continued, still swaying, but still speaking perfectly fine. "So the ground was soft. The shoulder of the road from The Lost Mile into town was soft, too. There wasn't a single sign, not a hint of a recent tire mark. She hadn't swerved off the pavement from the time she left the rest of you until she came to the curbed street in town. Not once. She drove perfectly straight until the very end. Then she swerved right into Wayne Jay. It didn't add up then and it doesn't add up now."

"So what are you saying?"

"You tell me? You're a smart woman."

Jackson stood, swaying, waiting for my answer.

Explaining why she ran over him twice was easy.

"The prosecuting attorney argued that after she hit Wayne Jay, Lauren knew she had seriously injured the police chief," I said. "She panicked and ran over him again because she was afraid of what would happen to her if he lived to tell the truth. A dead man couldn't accuse her."

"Think outside the box, Story. Forget what everybody else thought or said, and work with the information I just gave you."

My shoulders slumped. "I don't know. Maybe the booze

didn't hit her until then. Come on, Jackson, just tell me what you think."

He swayed once, then stood tall. "I thought then," he said, "and I still think . . . that when her car ran down Wayne Jay, Lauren Kerrigan wasn't the one behind the wheel."

Twenty-seven

With that stunning declaration, which I hadn't even seen coming, Jackson took off back inside. I followed him long enough to snatch his keys when he set them down next to the coffee pot and to ask Grams to see him safely home. She agreed, and I handed over his keys to her.

Grams and Mom were probably the only ones in the bar who would pass a Breathalyzer test. Someone with more foresight than me should have set up designated drivers and a shuttle service. Just as well I hadn't driven Jackson home myself—I could feel the effects of the Irish wakes kicking in. I planned to walk home.

Later, I'd blame my lack of caution on the cocktails, not on my own impulsiveness, although it was completely in character for me to act first, think later. But, really, what could happen in two short blocks?

And so I set out walking.

And analyzing possibilities.

What the medical examiner had shared with me was

mind-boggling. He thought Lauren had been too drunk to operate a car that night? If Jackson was right about a different driver (and in my opinion, that was up for serious debate), who was it?

And what about Hunter's recent actions? Interrogating Gunnar and Carrie Ann, two of our original group of friends. None of us could have been involved. We'd all been together, right? Weren't we together the entire time? I thought so. Well, most of the time.

Pure nonsense, I decided. Rubbish, as Mom would say. Jackson might have sounded sober, but he was drunk as a skunk when he came up with that baloney. Or I should say blarney, since we were into Irish tonight. I wasn't buying the idea that it was a different driver. Lauren Kerrigan went to prison for it.

I had to get my hands on my cousin and make her talk. She'd been acting strange. She knew something.

If I could find her.

Where was Carrie Ann?

I crossed Main Street, not paying too much attention to my surroundings, because I knew the town inside and out. Moraine's streetlights were bright, and traffic was light, as in next to nonexistent. Businesses along Main Street, including mine, were dark, closed up for the night. Crowd noise drifted over from Stu's Bar and Grill as people went in and out of the bar. The sidewalk under my flip-flops felt like it was undulating to the heavy bass vibes from the music.

A full moon grinned from the sky, creating tall shadows from short objects.

And right then I paused, remembering unpleasant things through my pleasant alcoholic haze. Johnny Jay was out here somewhere, stalking me, plotting revenge against me for ruining his life. Not to mention the humiliating apology he'd had to endure. Twice.

I hadn't fallen for his little act and he knew it. He'd even wanted me to understand that. He wasn't nearly finished with me.

And here I was, alone, in the dark, not paying attention.

Isn't that exactly how women got in trouble all the time? By not being cautious?

I hadn't even told Holly or Patti when I left.

Nobody knew where I was, where I had gone.

I picked up speed. No longer lollygagging along, I turned onto my dead-end street, passed by Patti's dark house. No one was around. Every house was dark and silent, everybody had gone to the wake.

Wouldn't this be the perfect place and time for an attack? That was, if Story Fischer was actually foolish enough to walk home alone in the dark. Suddenly that short walk seemed like the longest ever.

Just as I talked myself into believing everything was fine, a car started up ahead of me at the end of the street. No lights, but I heard the engine.

It sped out of the darkness, like a bat out of the depths of hell, aiming straight at me.

My reflexes weren't going to be as sharp as they would have been if I hadn't been drinking. That was for sure. I glanced around for options. Nothing brilliant popped out.

So I did the only thing I had time for.

I got behind the nearest streetlight, not too close to it, but not too far away, either, and I closed my eyes, waiting for impact. With a bit of luck, the metal pole would stop the car's forward momentum and save my life.

I backed up a few feet, thinking if I lived through this I would never, ever put myself in this kind of position, ever again.

Tires squealed. My eyes shot open in time to see the car veer off right before hitting the pole. I thought the driver might lose control after that, because the car swerved back and forth several times before it straightened out and sped off into the night.

"What a total moron," I said, really talking about the driver but I could just as well have called myself that for being utterly stupid. In this case, I was addressing the driver because I'd actually found time in my terror to read the license plate number with my fine but trembling mind.

I even got cocky about it, while repeating the number several times so I wouldn't forget it. What kind of pathetic attempt on my life was that? A real serious murderer should have planned for possible failure. If that had been me behind the wheel, I would have removed the plates beforehand. Just in case I messed up.

I ran up onto my front porch and collapsed in an Adirondack chair, panting, my heart pounding as the full realization struck. I had come uncomfortably close to dying.

I pulled my cell phone from my pocket and slouched down out of sight. Then I started second-guessing my first impressions, trying to turn it into something more benign.

Maybe teenagers had been parking at the end of the block, making out. It wouldn't be the first time or the last. Then along comes me, and they get scared, thinking maybe I'd recognized them or might approach their car. So they rushed to leave, tearing out of there, a little out-of-control like new drivers sometimes are. The driver oversteered before correcting and gunning away.

Okay, that had lots of potential.

The cell phone in my hand rang.

"Where are you?" Holly shouted into the phone, the background noise not exactly in the background, more like front and center. I could hardly hear her.

"Around," I hedged. "Why?"

"I can't hear you. Wait, let me move someplace not quite so loud."

I waited, hearing the din die away. Then I said, "What do you want?"

"Max came home to surprise me." Holly sounded happy.

Max the Money Machine, Holly's workaholic husband.

Holly's attitude always adjusted when Max came home, as brief as his visits usually were. Then he'd get back on the road and she'd start moaning and complaining again. "That's sweet of him," I said, concentrating on lowering my blood pressure to somewhere under three hundred over one hundred. The car incident had really affected me. "Does that mean you two are back together?"

"Yup. So I won't be staying with you tonight. It's make-up sex time."

"I didn't really need to know that," I said.

"See you tomorrow at the store. I might be a little late." Holly hung up.

So then, to get this all in perspective: I could understand Holly wanting to spend time with her husband, but it meant that I didn't have a roommate, and I also didn't have a bodyguard. Not one. Never again would I take comfort from Patti's and Holly's promises. Ever.

I seemed to be full of nevers and evers and planned on sticking to them from now on, as in forever. Patti was just as bad as my sister. Probably snooping too much to remember about me.

Next, I called Hunter. "There's a strange car parked on my block," I pretended. "Can you run the plates for me?"

"What color is it?"

"Dark."

"Like black dark?"

"Sure. I guess."

"What kind of vehicle is it?"

"A car."

"You already said that. What kind?"

"Uh, a car-car." So I hadn't been as observant as a man might have been. Hunter would have been able to tell me what kind of rims the car had. "You don't need all that extra stuff. Just run the plate number."

"Let me get this straight," Hunter said. "You got close

enough to the vehicle to read the license plate number. But you don't know the make or model and you aren't even sure of the color."

"How should I know what kind of car it is? They all look the same. It's a standard sedan. Do you want the license number or not?" Then I quickly proceeded to give him the number, not about to give him time to answer with a *not*.

"I'll get back to you," he said.

I stayed slumped down in the chair, cloaked in darkness, listening to sounds from Stu's, which still floated in the air.

The car thing had done a real number on my nerves. I concentrated on relaxing, breathing deep and slow.

When my phone vibrated, I almost shrieked. "Yes?" I said, after checking the caller ID and making sure it was Hunter on the other end.

"The car belongs to Johnny Jay," he said. "Is anyone inside the car at the moment? Don't go near it or expose yourself, but if you see anybody, I need to know."

"It's gone now." I didn't like Hunter's tone of voice. He sounded upset. As he should be, since my fears about the former police chief were coming true.

"Whew." Hunter let out a big sigh into the phone. "Because Johnny Jay reported it stolen a few minutes ago. He had parked it down the street from Stu's. When he left the bar, the car was missing. Good thing it's gone from your block. I wouldn't want a car burglar hanging around anywhere near you."

"Yeah," I said, with a sick feeling in the pit of my stomach. "Good thing."

"Anyway," he said, "I passed on the information you gave me to Sally Maylor. She promised to patrol your block."

"Where's Johnny right this minute?" I asked.

"At the station. Filling out paperwork."

We hung up.

A car turned from Main Street and headed my way, so I slunk down even lower in the chair. It came slow, crawling along and still managed to hit the curb on the corner during the turn.

I'd know that car and driver anywhere.

Grams.

She bumped her Cadillac Fleetwood (See, I can identify at least one kind of car, Hunter Wallace!) to the curb in front of my house. I walked out to greet her. I haven't been so glad to see anybody for a very long time.

The passenger window slid down and Mom said, "We have Jackson in the backseat. He's practically passed out, thanks to you and those drinks you forced on him."

Grams leaned across Mom and looked out at me. "We don't know where he lives, sweetie."

"I'll show you," I offered, relieved to have family surrounding me. Any family!

I got in the back next to Jackson. The smell almost blew me out of the car.

"Jeez," I said to him, noticing he still had one eye open. "What happened to the coffee?"

"What coffee?"

"He refused to drink any," Mom said.

"Turn right at Main," I told Grams, before leaning back in my seat and thinking.

Had Johnny just set up this whole thing? Orchestrated an attempt on my life after calling in his car stolen, planning to run me down? Or was he telling the truth?

I thought of all the years we'd been butting heads. Did he really hate me enough to kill me?

"Johnny Jay isn't through, either," I muttered to myself.

"He apologized to you," Mom said, overhearing. "What more do you want from the poor man?"

"Handcuffs and a nice orange prison outfit?" I said, looking out the back window and noticing one dark vehicle after another.

And that's when I decided to spend the night at my grandmother's house with Grams and Mom.

Twenty-eight

While Grams made blueberry pancakes on a griddle, Mom grilled me over hot coals.

- Jackson Davis was such a nice man, or had been until I forced my bad habit of drinking too much on him.

- When was I going to straighten up and fly right?

- Why was I denying I had some problems? That's the biggest step, you know, admitting you have a problem.

- Maybe if I didn't surround myself with other alcoholics, I could get my act together.

- Carrie Ann, for example. That girl might be family, but she was bad news.

- Hunter for another. He might be sober for the time being, but that was bound to end. He'd revert back.

- We used to be such a respectable family. What happened?

• Now the whole town knows our affairs.

• It's a crying shame, is what it is.

"Helen," Grams finally said to Mom, "you have to concentrate on being happy. You find negative in just about everything. What happened to that smiley-faced little girl I raised?"

I dug into a stack of maple syrup-doused pancakes, the syrup straight from Gram's red maples, which she tapped every February. Mom? Smiley faced? When was that?

"This isn't a happy world," Mom responded.

"It's whatever you want it to be," Grams said, keeping her tone friendly and sweet as always.

"Oh, for cripes' sake," Mom said, and at first I thought she was crabbing about Grams's comment, but she was looking at something out the window when she said it. "Speak of the devil and he's on the porch with *that* dog."

I followed her gaze and saw Hunter and Ben at the door. Since Hunter was on Mom's s-list, I headed outside with a cup of coffee in one hand, wiping sticky syrup from my lips with the other.

"Did you ever consider calling me back and letting me know where you were staying?" Hunter said by way of a greeting, looking about as happy as Mom was at the moment. He launched in before I could reply. "I stopped at your house late last night to check on you and guess what? You weren't there. And you weren't at the store. And you didn't answer your cell phone. And after Jay's stolen car showed up in front of your house, what do you think went through my head?"

"You were worried about me?" I liked that a lot. The only other person I made worry was Mom, and she didn't worry *about* me. She worried *because* of me. Big difference.

"After that, I couldn't sleep," Hunter said.

He did look a little rough around the edges. Red eyes, shadow of unshavenness starting on his chin (which I thought looked sexy), ruffled hair like the wind had gotten a hold of it. Only it wasn't windy.

Ben didn't look like he'd stayed up late stressing over me. I gave him a pat on the head.

"My cell battery died," I explained. "I totally forgot about it. And the last thing I expected was a visit from you that late. If you were so worried, you could have checked here."

"Your truck was still parked at the store. How did you get here?"

"Grams picked me up."

"I almost *did* come over but figured I'd upset your family if you weren't with them, or your mother would shoot me for showing up so late. And why is she giving me the evil eye through the window? She never did like me."

"She doesn't like anybody."

I pulled Hunter out of Mom's view and we walked out to his SUV. I knelt to exchange proper greetings with my four-legged friend—an ear rub for Ben, a face wash for me. Then I thought of Dinky and admitted to myself that I missed her. Sort of.

I stood up. "Hunter, you have to let me know what you're thinking about this case. I feel like I'm right in the middle of a thick forest without a compass or sunlight to guide me."

He was still crabby. "Should I keep you informed just like you keep me informed?"

"Right. Yes." Well, I could be better at that, I suppose. No question. Like what happened last night with the car. Why wasn't I telling him all the scary details? Sometimes, when I waited too long to share something, the timing got all messed up, and suddenly it felt too late. This was one of those times.

"Please, tell me," I begged, hearing a whine in my voice. "Last night at the wake, Jackson Davis said he thought someone other than Lauren Kerrigan was driving the car the night Wayne Jay was killed."

Hunter looked surprised, then thoughtful. "Why would

he say something like that? Even if he believed it, he wouldn't spread stuff like that around town. Jackson's a total professional."

"He'd been drinking."

Hunter stared at me like he was working over the details of my discussion with Jackson. Sometimes I forget his line of work includes analyzing situations and figuring out motives. Hunter was good, because he said, "Let me guess. You attached yourself to the medical examiner, made sure he was well watered, then pumped him for all kinds of information."

"That is so far from the truth," I lied.

"And how much alcohol did the guy consume before he shared that particular tidbit?"

"A little."

"Are you sure it was only a little? His car is still parked at the bar."

"Grams took him home."

"Case closed."

I didn't let up. "You're questioning Gunnar and Carrie Ann. Do you think one of them killed Lauren and Hetty? You can't believe that!" I wanted to press on to convince him of Johnny Jay's guilt, but we'd been down that path before without accomplishing anything.

Hunter opened the door of his SUV. "What are your plans for the day?" he wanted to know, changing the subject without answering any of my questions. Men! And this one was one of the most frustrating on the planet. At least for right now.

I gave up. "I'm working at the store until Ali and the twins come in. Then checking on my bees, the ones out in farm fields."

"Can Ben hang out with you today?"

I smiled. "That would be perfect."

"You're a stubborn woman, Story Fischer." Hunter shook his head at me like I was a hopeless case.

"What do you mean by that?"

He got in his SUV and closed the door. I leaned in the open window, watching him put the key in the ignition. But he didn't start it up. He turned back to me and said, "If I asked you to stay out here with your mother and grandmother, would you?"

"You're kidding, right?"

"Then go someplace with your sister."

"I can't. Her husband is back home." Why was Hunter pushing so hard?

"After what happened last night . . ."

What was he getting at? I'd only told him the car had been parked near my house. Why should he be so worried? I was still waiting for the perfect opening to tell him the rest. "I have things to do, a store to run."

"So, your answer is no. See? Stubborn." He paused, then said, "I know about last night, and a lot more happened than you said. When were you going to tell me the truth?"

Too late. "At first I thought it was kids," I said, realizing my defense was lame. "Parking and making out, and no big deal."

"So exactly when were you going to tell me?"

"Soon. How did you find out, anyway?" I'm not sure why Hunter hadn't solved Moraine's recent murders, since he seemed to know everything that went on in town. At least everything that pertained to me. "Nobody saw it happen. No one came running over to help me."

"Larry Koon was down on the corner of Main. He couldn't remember if he locked up his custard shop, so he was on the way to check the doors. He saw the car aim directly at you and veer off at the last second."

"Only because I got behind a pole. Did Larry get a look at the driver?"

"No, the car had tinted windows. We found it this morning, abandoned on a side road."

"You were so sure Johnny Jay wouldn't bother me," I reminded him. "Now look. I was almost killed by him."

Hunter shook his head. "He wouldn't do a thing like that."

"You should re-watch Patti's video if you've forgotten how crazy he is."

"Not crazy enough to take that kind of risk," Hunter insisted. "At first I thought he might have been behind the wheel. But he wouldn't have had time to call in the report, hang around waiting for you, then attempt to run you down *and* dispose of the car."

"Somebody took that risk."

"And I'm going to find out who it was. My top priority is your safety."

I planted a kiss on his cheek. "Another crime to solve," I said lightly, even though I didn't feel light. "I believe in you."

That didn't even earn me a smile or a return kiss. "Stay close in touch," he said, "answer your phone when I call. And make sure it stays charged."

After Hunter left, I asked Grams to drive Ben and me home. In the light of day and with Ben at my side, I shed all my earlier anxiety. I showered, changed, and headed for the store with Ben on a leash next to me.

Joel Riggins, junior reporter for Moraine's weekly newspaper, waited by the door, ear buds in, sunglasses on, and holey jeans hanging loose. *The Distorter* distributed papers not only to Moraine but also to the surrounding communities and liked to hire young, overzealous college kids to work the main streets. Joel fit the bill in the over-eager department.

I immediately switched directions, doing a one-eighty, with Ben and his fast reflexes right there with me. But Joel spotted me.

"Ms. Fischer!"

I turned back reluctantly.

Ben's ears stood at attention and I suspected he not only could understand us, but could sense potential conflict.

Joel sized up Ben and took a step back.

"Let me go past," I said.

"Please. Just a few questions for the next edition."

"No comment." Ben and I slid by him and fumbled with the locked door.

"What are you so afraid of?"

I paused with my hand still on the key. That question caught me off guard. Me? Afraid to speak with the media because of . . . what? Consequences? The kid was good, playing to my ego like that.

"You think I'm afraid of Johnny Jay?"

He shrugged. Glanced at Ben. "Maybe."

Joel followed me in.

By some miracle, long-lost Carrie Ann showed up right behind him, looking fresh and pert, like nothing had ever happened to freak her out. Just wait, woman. I'd get an opportunity soon enough and when I did, she was going to tell me everything she knew, right down to her bra size.

But for now, Carrie Ann helped me open up the store. I ignored Joel, hoping he'd go away. He didn't. Finally I gave him the attention he wanted.

"Why are you still here?" I said. "I'm not talking to you."

"All you have to do is confirm or deny."

"What's that supposed to mean?"

"Patti Dwyre and I are working on an article about the police chief. She gave me a lot of material, but we need corroboration. A quote from you would be awesome."

Then I remembered what Patti had said about Joel helping her get a job at the paper. I groaned. Leave it to Patti.

"You're going off to college?" I asked.

Joel grinned. "I can't wait."

I took him into the back room. By the look on his face, he thought I was going to cooperate fully. "Tell me what you've got so far," I said.

So here's what he had, according to Patti's point of view:

- Johnny Jay had a history of bullying going back to adolescence (nothing new there).

- He had an ongoing battle with me. Our relationship was as explosive as dynamite, as toxic as pesticides on honeybees (still nothing new).

- Johnny Jay was out for retribution and had been lying in the weeds waiting for his chance to attack me out of video range (probably true, but not for public knowledge).

- And last night he made an attempt on my life, tried to run me down on a dark street. (How did she know about that?)

"I'm not participating in this interview," I said.

"It won't look good in the paper, you refusing to comment."

"He'll sue the paper if you print that." Not to mention that Johnny Jay would come after me even harder. "And you can leave now."

Joel looked disappointed, like he was a soda can and I'd just crushed him between my hands. "I'm going to interview the police chief next," he said. "If you won't give me a quote, I'll have to paraphrase."

"You and Patti better run that article past your editor," I warned him.

"He's on vacation."

Great. Just great.

Once Joel left and I had a chance to tell Carrie Ann about the article, she said, "When Johnny Jay reads that, he's going to kill somebody."

"He was going to anyway. Now he has another target, too. Patti. Plus, I look at it this way, if everybody knows he's after me, maybe he'll think twice before making a move."

"No, he won't," Carrie Ann reassured me.

"We need to talk. You and me. Privately."

"Am I fired?"

"No," I said, grudgingly. "As soon as we slow down again, let me know."

With that, The Wild Clover sprang into its daily live action.

Milly Hopticourt came in with her morel mushroom creation.

"Try this," she said.

My taste buds exploded. "Oh my gosh, what is this deliciousness?"

Milly looked pleased. "Morel sauce. Butter, wine, heavy cream, this and that."

"It's an absolute winner. Use it. How's the rest of the newsletter coming?"

"Almost done." And she bustled off with a shopping basket over her arm, leaving the rich sauce for me to sample again. Yum. It was hours before I had a chance to get Carrie Ann alone.

Twenty-nine

Holly arrived (late as promised), glowing and not overly chatty, which was fine with me. Let her bask in the sunshine of her renewed relationship with Max. Not once did she mention anything about guard duty, but maybe she figured Ben had taken her shift.

My protector sat near the front of the store acting as greeter. The kids loved him even more than the candy bins, swarming around him like he was a queen bee. Or king, if honeybees had male rulers, which they didn't.

"Dogs aren't allowed inside grocery stores," Lori Spandle announced when she walked in for her daily potshots. "This is totally illegal. I'm calling the health inspector."

"Americans with Disabilities Act," I said. "I can't turn away a service dog."

"Who's disabled and with what?" she wanted to know.

"You can't ask that."

"I want to see his papers."

"Nope." The Act was clear about special dogs. If I

couldn't ask customers for proof that they needed a service dog and if I wasn't legally allowed to request registration papers, neither could troublemaking Lori.

"I'm taking this to the town board." With that she took several photos of Ben with his new buddies and marched out without buying anything.

I was sure Ben had the proper paperwork. Or at least pretty sure.

If Lori didn't spend so much time going head-to-head with me, coming into the store and destroying the atmosphere, maybe she'd sell the house next door. Although I kind of liked the added privacy with it empty.

When Ali came in, I finally had an opportunity to have that conversation with my cousin.

"Now what did I do?" Carrie Ann asked, making me realize the distance between us had become almost as wide as one of our great lakes. My cousin and I had been good friends for so long, but our relationship had changed. That really bothered me. Especially since Carrie Ann hadn't been a stellar addition to the staff, and I was forever taking calming breaths to cope with her constant problems.

At least the twins were easygoing and didn't have issues.

We went out in front of the store and sat down on a wooden bench, soaking up some springtime sun rays and sizing each other up. Business had slowed by mid-afternoon. Ali and Holly were inside. Ben sat at our feet, alert but calm, in his standard mode of operation.

"Carrie Ann, I'm so worried about you," I said to her. "My concern has absolutely nothing to do with your job performance. We need to have a personal talk, an honest one, because no matter what happened, what you might have done or not done, we're family and I love you."

"I need a cigarette," my cousin said. I knew for a fact (the smell factor) that Carrie Ann hadn't smoked for at least six months, maybe longer.

"You don't need a cigarette, you need to talk to me."

"Okay, what do you want to know?"

"For starters, where you were the afternoon and night when Lauren and Hetty were murdered?"

My words came out suspiciously close to an accusation. I hadn't intended to sound so harsh. Damage control time. "I mean, I missed you. Everybody in town was bonding and banding together and you weren't around. Then Gunnar came into Stu's and he said he couldn't find you, either."

Carrie Ann started looking around for an escape route.

"Don't even think it," I said. "I'll chase you down." Okay, that wasn't much of a threat. I glanced at my flip-flops and added the clincher: "And if I can't catch you, Ben will."

She glanced at Ben. "You wouldn't."

"Try me."

I'd have to ask Hunter for a comprehensive list of commands Ben understood. Other than the basics like sit and stay and the attack command, which I'd discovered on my own, I was clueless. If Carrie Ann decided to test me, I really didn't want to ask Ben to attack her. Just fetch her in a nonaggressive, but firm way.

Carrie Ann raked the fingers of her right hand through her short spiky hair and considered her options. She didn't find any.

"I've been sneaking a few drinks," she said, like that was some kind of big surprise. "And I had an alcoholic blackout. And don't look at me like you don't believe me. It happens sometimes. Ask Hunter about blackouts. Alcoholics get them."

That was the first time I'd ever heard Carrie Ann call herself an alcoholic. It might have been a first for her, too. Outside of AA, I mean.

"I believe you," I said. "So you have no idea at all where you were or what you did?"

"Nada. All I know is I woke up in my own bed the next morning, still in my clothes, and . . . oh God, please don't tell anybody . . . "

"You can trust me," I said.

"I was all dirty, like I'd been stumbling around in the woods . . . and what if I'm the one who"—she started choking up—"killed them?"

I gaped. Closed my mouth. Opened it again. "That's the dumbest thing you've ever said."

"But it could be true."

"No, it can't. Besides, Johnny Jay is the main suspect." At least in my book, he was.

"Things are looking really, really bad," Carrie Ann said.

"You aren't a killer."

"Are you sure?" Carrie Ann sniffed.

"Absolutely," I said with complete conviction. "If you were a killer, you would have murdered Gunnar after he had your visitation rights taken away when you were drinking so heavy."

"That's true," she said. "I think."

"Okay, forget that for a minute," I said. "Hunter questioned Gunnar. He told me he was looking for you, too. What was that all about?"

"He questioned me." Carrie Ann chewed the inside of her cheek. "Wanted to know where I was that afternoon and evening. He wasn't like the Hunter we all know. It was almost like he was accusing me of something."

"Were you and Gunnar together at all during that time?"

"Not according to Gunnar. I told Hunter about my blackout but I didn't say a word about the condition I was in when I woke up."

"He would have hauled you in."

"You aren't going to tell him, are you?"

I shook my head. "No, we'll work this out together."

"And he wanted to know what I could remember from when Lauren ran over Johnny's dad."

I thought about what Aurora had said—how the present was predetermined by the past. And now Hunter was looking hard for the truth way back in time. Was it possible the connections were more complicated than I thought, that there was some basis to the medical examiner's theory?

"What did you remember about that night in The Lost Mile?" I asked her.

"Nada," Carrie Ann said.

"Let me guess. Another blackout."

"Noooo. But we *were* drinking and it was a long time ago. If I can't remember what happened less than a week ago, how am I going to remember way back when?"

She had a point.

"Okay," I said. "Then concentrate on last Saturday. Try to remember."

"I've spent hours trying to remember where I was and who I was with." Carrie Ann frowned. "That's the worst blackout I've ever had."

"Someone must have seen you. Keep trying to remember and let me know if you do."

"I will," Carrie Ann said. "How's it going with Hunter?"

I smiled, taking a moment to savor the image I had of him in my mind. Being appreciated was good for the ego. "Going good," I answered.

"Don't you sometimes wonder why a man like Hunter, in his mid-thirties and as hot as he is, hasn't been married by now?"

I shrugged. "The right woman hasn't come along? Or he's the type of guy who can't commit." That last part really bothered me. What if Hunter got to a certain point on the relationship path, then backed out?

"Boy, you're dense," Carrie Ann said. "The right woman was there all along, but she wasn't paying any attention to him."

By the expression on Carrie Ann's face, I assumed she meant me. Hunter and I had split up the spring of our senior year in high school, not that that was so unusual. Lots of couples went their separate ways around then. It had been a transition I needed. I did the breaking up, I left for college, and I married another man. A really bad one, but that's a whole other story."

Carrie Ann wasn't finished. "Hunter went out with every available woman in town and beyond while you were away. He never got serious with any of them. And it was because of you!"

"No way!" I said, suddenly jealous of those other women but secretly pleased by Carrie Ann's observations. "No man would wait that long just for me."

"He told me himself."

"Thanks for letting me know," I said.

All Carrie Ann and I needed to do to cement our recovered friendship was hug, which we did—a long, hard squeeze to let each other know we'd be there, no matter what. She'd watch my back. I'd watch hers.

Carrie Ann wouldn't hurt a fly, let alone a human being.

After that, Ben and I headed out to check on bees.

Thirty

I love all creatures, big and small, so deciding to raise bees was a hard decision for me, mainly because I can't stand to witness living things die. And honeybees die all the time. Every fall when they prepare for winter, the girls kick the boys out of the hives. Every last one of them. The drones stay close to the hive, hoping for a reprieve that never comes. They starve or freeze to death.

Which might leave you wondering where the next batch of males comes from. That's one of the fascinating things about bees. The queen can actually determine the sex of each egg. If she fertilizes it (and most of them are fertilized because she needs workers and nurses), the egg becomes a female. If she doesn't, they're male.

I also have to watch my bees expire from old age way before they reach what we would consider old. The life span of a honeybee isn't anything to aspire to. If they are born in the fall, they can live through the winter, otherwise they only live about a month, usually working themselves to death. Not much time to smell the roses.

Then there are the times a beekeeper opens up a hive and discovers every one of the bees, girls *and* boys, flopped over dead. That hasn't happened to me as much as it has to other beekeepers, but just one dead colony had me undone for weeks.

A beekeeper has to have a thick skin. Which sometimes I don't.

And my sensitivity extends to other species as well. Dinky, for example. I'd had some really bad thoughts about that dog, but if anything happened to her, I'd hurt like crazy.

So I'm always a little apprehensive out in the field, where I haven't been able to check on my bees on a daily basis and monitor their progress. Although I felt lucky to have as much business as I did. Renting honeybee hives out to commercial apple orchards was a good chunk of my business, keeping it financially viable. Not only did I make some cash, I got to keep the honey, and my bees were helping out where they were really needed. The farmer, the bees, and me, we all came out winners.

I pulled into the first stop, a large apple orchard west of Moraine, and tucked the truck back far from the road so it couldn't be seen, going the safe rather than sorry route. Just because I had a protector with massive hooked teeth didn't mean I wanted a confrontation with Johnny Jay. Or, as my missing bodyguards had ventured, the killer who wanted it to look like my old nemesis had done me in.

A frightening possibility if Johnny Jay turned out to be innocent.

Looking around the field I didn't see a soul, benevolent or otherwise.

I let Ben out of the truck to do his business and explore and lowered the tailgate to get my supplies.

I had fifteen acres to cover. With one or two hives per acre, I needed to check roughly twenty-five hives. These girls weren't used to me like the ones in my backyard and, since I was a bit of a bumbler and stumbler, I played it safe. This time I wore the full beekeeper's uniform.

At each hive, I lifted the top and inspected inside, making sure the colony had enough food and the queen was laying eggs. All of my hives were treated with tender loving care, but some were stronger and healthier than others. But that was part of this business. At least none of them I checked on had died off.

After making the rounds, I sat on the truck's tailgate and pulled off my veil and hat. That's when I spotted the box Stanley Peck had given me, the one that was sixteen years old and held items from Lauren's totaled car. I pulled it out, sat swinging my legs on the tailgate, and rummaged through it.

Here's what I found:

- An empty vodka bottle without a top (Figures. That girl had loved her vodka.)

- The usual glove box items, like car manuals, registration info, pepper spray (Okay, that wasn't everybody's standard car necessity, but not uncommon either. Note: it didn't work anymore.)

- Female things that we all kept in our cars—hairbrush, lipstick (pink), eye shadow (blue)—whatever we needed to make up our faces in the rearview mirror while we were driving

- Clothing: a pair of jeans, a sweatshirt, a swimsuit. All girl must haves. What female teenager drives around without a small wardrobe for quick changes?

I started putting everything back in the box, deciding to throw it away. The booze bottle was empty, the paper products were yellowed and brittle, and mice had gotten into the clothing, making a nasty mess on the bottom layer of the box—droppings and chewed up material. Yuk.

Just then something caught my eye through the disgusting mouse stuff. Trying to avoid the droppings, which proved impossible, I pulled out a chain with a small, delicate locket—gold-plated, heart-shaped, and engraved with roses. Inside the locket was a tiny picture of a much younger T. J. Schmidt.

Lauren's locket. A souvenir of the brief period of time she'd managed to snag T. J., before all the bad stuff happened to her.

Holding that tiny lovers' locket in my hand brought back memories of my own, of Hunter Wallace and me, how excited I'd been that the sexiest guy in high school was attracted to me, how just holding his hand sent electric shocks through my body. Still did, in fact.

I ran my fingers over the locket and remembered my own box of high school treasures. I should pull them out someday soon, go back in time, down memory lane. Didn't I have a locket something like this one? Didn't we all?

Before heading home, I took care of two tasks.

First, I stopped at a large Dumpster near the apple orchard and tossed in the box and its contents, tucking the locket in my pocket. I wasn't sure why. T. J. certainly wouldn't want a keepsake from a brief encounter that had ended in murder. But maybe Lauren's mom might appreciate it. For all I knew, the locket could be a family heirloom. It looked older than just sixteen years. Although years inside the box had probably aged it. Still, I couldn't bring myself to throw it away.

The second thing I did was pull into a hardware store where I found a restroom and washed the mouse gunk off my hands. Then I took a lesson from Lauren's glove compartment stash and bought a pocket-sized canister of pepper spray. Except this one worked. I made sure of that in the store's parking lot, sending a narrow spray into the air. Testing, testing.

Armed with attack-ready Ben and my pocket-sized version of tear gas, I was ready for anything.

"Where have you been?" P. P. Patti wanted to know, calling out from her backyard the minute I hopped out of my truck. Like she'd been trying to track me and had failed even with all her electronic devices. At least she hadn't tinkered with my truck and installed some kind of locator.

"Checking bees," I said. "And buying protection." When Patti popped through the cedar hedge, I held up my new pepper spray.

"That isn't going to even slow down an attacker," Patti said.

"Are you and Joel really going to print all that stuff he told me about?"

"Of course. This could be my big break."

"Aren't you worried about Johnny Jay's reaction?"

"We're saying we got the information from an anonymous source."

I sighed in frustration. "Won't he figure that source is me?"

"Probably. Here, you need this." Patti handed me a large spray can.

"Wasp spray?" I read from the label on the can. "For what?"

Honeybees are constantly blamed for the actions of wasps, which are a far more aggressive insect, but it isn't in my nature to spray them dead.

"Spray that at Johnny Jay," Patti said. "And he'll stop dead in his tracks. And it's good for twenty feet so get him early before he has a chance to get too near. If you aren't on the ball, if you freeze up and don't get him right away and he *does* close in, you'll have to use the knee-to-groin tactic and you better hope you connect."

"Where do you come up with this stuff?" I asked, giving the air a small spray from the can to make sure it worked. Patti would make a great self-defense instructor, if she could be pried away from her snooping habits. She had unique techniques.

"I've been in some tight spots and always feel safest with my trusty can of wasp spray."

"It doesn't exactly fit in my back pocket."

"I don't care how you carry it, just do."

"All right."

"Where are you going?" Patti asked when she saw me putting a leash on Ben.

"To check on things at the store."

"I'll come along. Give me that wasp spray. I'll protect you."

"I have Ben."

"You need all the help you can get."

We had barely made it past Patti's house when a car pulled up and Johnny Jay came charging out of the driver's seat like an angry bull.

I didn't even have time to turn and run.

Thirty-one

Johnny Jay was in my face before either Patti or I had a chance to raise our weapons and aim at him. My mouth didn't even have time to open, so Ben didn't get the attack command from me, not that I would have remembered that special, powerful word under the circumstances anyway.

There Johnny Jay was. All that bullying, bulky brawn way too close for comfort.

And to say he was P.O.'d wouldn't even come close to describing his current emotional state.

"Haven't you done enough damage?" he had time to yell, so close to my face I could count his gold fillings. Instead of counting, I came to my senses and blasted him with the pepper spray. Only I didn't get it in his eyes, because his arm came up and blocked my trigger finger. But he sure backed up fast. That move left him open to a flank attack from Patti, who fired a round of wasp spray at the back of his head. Some of it settled on me.

Ben, sensing he should run interference, growled. That scared all of us.

"Stop!" Johnny shouted, and for some strange reason we did. "That's enough. Don't move. I'll charge you both with assault. And call off your dog."

"You can't charge us with anything, Johnny Jay," I shouted back, since he was shouting. "You aren't in charge anymore! No charging. No arresting. How does it feel to be common?"

"I'll file a complaint."

"You're the one after me! I'll get you for stalking."

"I have a pocket video camera," Patti lied. I knew it was a lie because she didn't have any pockets in the capris she wore. But Johnny didn't notice. "Touch a hair on her head," my neighbor warned him, "and you'll make the front page one last time."

Johnny's mouth opened, closed, opened again, but nothing came out until his eyes shifted to me. Then he said, "Fischer, you've completely ruined me."

I used to be Missy to Johnny Jay until the big public apology; then I became "Story." Now I was just Fischer? Well, he'd always be Johnny Jay to me whether he wore a uniform or not.

And the nerve of the man, blaming me for his own actions, not taking responsibility. I hated when people didn't take responsibility. Grams called it a pervasive social problem and she was right. "You ruined yourself, Johnny," I said. "I didn't make you use unnecessary force on me. If you're stupid enough to beat up on a woman, and in front of witnesses with electronics, then you deserve what you get."

"Should I nail him again?" Patti yelled, spray can at the ready.

"No, wait," Johnny said, still loud, and I could tell his eyes were at least irritated, because they were red as if he'd been crying and he couldn't keep them open without a lot of blinking. I felt a little eye irritation myself from

Patti's overspray. "What the hell did you spray me with?" he asked Patti.

"Wasp spray. And there's more where that came from, so back off, buddy."

Another big surprise, Johnny backed off. "Damn," he said.

Ben growled again, watching me for guidance. "Sit, Ben," I said, now that there was space between the bad guy and the rest of us. Ben sat and turned his head to stare at Johnny.

"We need to talk," Johnny said to me.

I saw Carrie Ann and Ali Schmidt round the corner at a dead run. Carrie Ann was in the lead; she overshot and ran right into me, which I saw coming only at the last second, not nearly enough time to dodge her. She knocked me backward into Patti's bushes.

After almost taking a direct hit of wasp spray from Patti, and Carrie Ann's overeager rescue, I wasn't sure I needed any more help from my friends.

"One of the customers said you were in trouble," Ali said, panting.

"And I forgot my cell phone at the store and just happened to be inside picking it up," Carrie Ann said, pulling me upright. "So we came to help."

"What is this?" Johnny Jay said. "Some kind of vigilante block watch group?" He glared at me, then shook his head. "This has gone too far."

"You got that right, bud," Patti said, still talking tough.

"What are you doing harassing Story again?" Carrie Ann asked him. "Don't you know enough to keep your distance?"

"Did you hear about the article about to run in *The Reporter*?" he said. "Did you hear what she said about me?"

"Nothing that wasn't true," I said, wondering when Patti was going to step in and admit her big role in that article. I glanced at her. She wouldn't meet my eyes. "My car was stolen," Johnny said.

"Convenient," Carrie Ann said.

There we all stood in a big circle, four determined women and one pathetic bully. How does it feel? I wanted to ask him, but Johnny wouldn't have understood. He didn't have the capacity to feel anything other than frustration and rage.

"Get back in your car and take off," Patti said to him. "And don't come near her again." She held up the wasp spray, her fingers on the trigger. "Or next time, I won't miss."

"Wasp spray?" Carrie Ann said, with an incredulous expression on her face. "You're using it for self-protection?"

Johnny glanced at me, and for a brief second I thought I saw pleading in his eyes, but then they turned back to their standard mean glare.

"Don't think this is over," he said to me.

"Did you hear that?" Carrie Ann said. "He threatened her right in front of us."

My friends edged toward Johnny. He didn't seem so confident without his badge and gun and with four of us and a canine attack dog staring him down.

In next to no time, he was peeling away and we were watching him go.

After a round of high-fives, my knees got weak and I had to sit down on the curb. "What if I'd been alone?" I asked. "What would he have done?"

"You don't have to even think about that," Ali said, sitting down next to me. "Because you weren't by yourself. Good going, Patti."

Patti beamed. "Having you and Carrie Ann show up didn't hurt, either."

"Next time," I advised her, "spray an attacker from the front. Blasting him in the back of the head didn't accomplish anything."

"I was unnerved," Patti said.

"Who's watching the store?" I asked Ali.

"Brent and Trent," she said. "Business is winding down. They told me they would close up. So I'm off now."

"I want a drink," I said, standing up and wondering if Mom was right about me having a problem.

"Let's go to Stu's," said Carrie Ann.

"Not a good idea," I said.

"Trust me," Carrie Ann said. "I can handle going there. Do you really think it's possible for me to stay away from drinkers forever? Look around you. Everybody and his uncle drinks alcohol."

"Not *everybody*," I said. "Hunter doesn't."

"So there are two of us out of zillions. Besides, Hunter goes to bars. He just drinks soda. I can do that."

What could we say? At least there'd be plenty of us to watch over Carrie Ann. We headed down the street. Ben trotted along next to me.

Carrie Ann had one last comment before we swung through the door into the bar. "I'd be perfectly content to inhale second-hand smoke. Too bad nobody can smoke inside anymore. Trust me, though. I won't drink a drop."

My cousin was using *trust me* way too much. I had my guard up.

Inside, a bunch of Kerrigans sat at a table—Terry, Robert, Rita, Gus, and several more.

"I'll catch up to you," I said to my group. "I want to talk to Gus for a minute."

My cohorts found a booth next to a window facing the street, while I joined the Kerrigans.

Out of respect for Carrie Ann, and partly to prove to myself I didn't have any kind of problem other than Johnny Jay, I ordered seltzer water with a twist when Stu asked me what I wanted.

Mom should see me now. Why did she always arrive at inconvenient times when I seemed to be at my very worst?

"Johnny Jay tried to ambush me a few minutes ago," I told everybody at the table. "Lucky for me I was with my friends and Ben. Or who knows what he might have done."

Murmurs rose around me, expressions of outrage, several

head pats for Ben. I'd found my fan base. Why hadn't I thought to appeal to Lauren's extended family earlier?

"We want him behind bars," Gus said, rubbing day-old growth. "It's not enough that he's stepped down."

"He hasn't stepped down," Terry corrected Gus. "He's on leave, like a vacation. But if we have our way he won't be back."

"He killed Lauren," Rita added, her voice thick with conviction.

"We can't prove it," Robert said. "Not yet anyway."

That got me thinking about how much effort and luck it took to actually prove a person guilty of a crime. Even when the whole town knew the truth, without the right evidence or a confession from the killer, a cold-blooded murderer could go scot free to hurt other people. Scary to think about.

Terry was going over his own bullet points, making me smile. I thought I had a monopoly on those. "Number one," he said, "Jay never forgave Lauren for killing his father. Number two, where was he when Lauren was killed? Nobody knows the answer to that because of his job. He was alone on the road all the time. Where's a solid alibi?"

"Number three," I said, stepping in to help with the various points. "He had the means. Johnny's trained in firearms. Those two women didn't stand a chance."

"But how are we going to prove he did it?" Gus asked. "That's the thing."

Nobody had an answer for him.

Thirty-two

Since I wanted to help Carrie Ann remember the period of time when she'd blacked out, I waited until Stu had a few minutes free, then I asked him if he remembered her being around last Saturday.

"She was here late afternoon," he said, glancing over at my friends sitting by the window.

"Was she drinking heavily?" I asked.

Stu groaned dramatically. "You know I don't like to talk about my customers," he said. "It's bad for business."

"She's part of my family. You have to tell me. Come on Stu."

"She might have had one or two."

"Carrie Ann says she can't remember a thing. It had to have been more than one or two."

Stu shook his head. "She wasn't here long enough to have had more than one, maybe two."

So Carrie Ann had changed locations; started at Stu's, ended someplace else. But where had she gone from here?

I caught my cousin's eye, motioned to her with a little head move, and she came over to the bar.

"Stu remembers seeing you in here last Saturday afternoon," I said to her.

"Okay," she said slowly, and I saw her eyes swing up in her head like she was trying to see inside her brain and that would help her remember.

"Keep at it," I told her, and we went back to our table. Carrie Ann started moping over the 7UP in front of her. She should be thrilled that I'd discovered her starting point. She'd been in here Saturday afternoon. Why couldn't she remember any details? That was the weird part. Unless she did remember and wasn't telling the truth.

Ali scooted over, making room for me to sit down. "Sounds like you have the Kerrigans on your side," she said in that husky voice of hers.

I nodded. "Just have to prove Johnny Jay did it. How hard can that be?"

"Pretty hard," Patti said. "A police chief can concoct alibis and all sort of things."

Ali looked doubtful. "I don't know about that. He'd need people to lie for him."

Carrie Ann said, "Well, someone might. You guys would lie for me if I asked you to, right?"

"Not if you murdered someone," Patti said, definitively. "Unless, of course, they deserved it. Like if they were killers themselves or they hurt kids or small animals."

A little later I saw Rita Kerrigan head for the ladies' room. I followed her in and explained about the box of items out at Stanley's and how most of it was junk, with one exception. I tried to give her the locket I'd found.

She wouldn't even look at it. "I don't want anything to do with anything from then," she said, actually closing her eyes rather than risk actually seeing what it was. "And I told Stanley the same thing. Throw it away, every bit of it."

Okay, then. Stanley had been right about Rita not wanting

to confront any memories that might pop out of that box. I felt insensitive for reminding her of other bad times and putting her on the spot.

When I returned to the table I dropped the locket down in the center.

Stu came over. "You ladies want another round?"

"Four more sodas," Patti said. "And more sweet potato fries."

"Whose is this?" Carrie Ann asked after Stu went to fill our order and she'd picked up the locket.

"I found it in a box of things Stanley pulled out of Lauren's car," I said. "The night she ran over Wayne Jay."

And then I told them about Stanley wanting to throw it away and how Holly had volunteered me as custodian while she'd been lounging inside my truck hiding from Stanley's bees. And how I'd had to scrounge through mouse poo to find the locket.

"Rita won't take it," I finished. "What should I do with it?"

"It doesn't look valuable," Patti said, as though she had any idea what jewelry cost. Patti's body was totally unadorned with extras. No jewelry at all. "A trinket. Pitch it."

Ali took the locket from Carrie Ann and studied it. She opened it up and saw T. J.'s tiny picture. I thought she looked wistful and a little sad. "He's always been cute, hasn't he?" She showed it around and everybody agreed, including me. I'd never thought of her husband as good looking, other than his teeth, but as long as Ali thought so that's all that counted.

Then she dropped the locket on the table and pushed it away. We kept ordering food. Nothing beats good old bar food when your energy reserves are low. I ordered a big burger decked out with all the trimmings, including bacon and cheese.

But I resisted the urge to eat the entire giant hip-widener, so I shared it with my cousin, who said she wasn't hungry but took half anyway and picked at it. I hadn't seen her that down in the dumps since Gunnar put her on a short leash with her own kids.

As it turned out, she had something to worry about.

Because about an hour later Gunnar rushed in, scoured the place until he spotted us, bolted over, and told Carrie Ann the cops wanted her for questioning and she should give herself up.

"Who says?" I asked while Carrie Ann tried to hide under the table.

"Sally Maylor came by my place looking for her."

"I'm as good as dead," Carrie Ann said from below. "I'll live out the rest of my life like a goldfish in a bowl, like a monkey in a cage."

"Gunnar said they only want you for questioning," I offered, but it was a lame attempt to comfort her. "I'll go down there with you."

"No, I'll go," Gunnar said.

"You stay with your kids," I said. "They need you."

For once in my life I'd made the right decision by not drinking alcohol, because I had to drive her to the police station, where I found out Johnny Jay was running the whole show from the sidelines when all along he'd led the entire community to believe he was on voluntary leave from duty. He even had on his uniform.

"Fischer," he said to me, standing too close for comfort. He took a big whiff my way, nosing around in hopes of catching the smell of alcohol on me. "You seem to follow trouble wherever it's hanging out. And get that dog out of my station."

"What are you doing here?" I demanded.

"Questioning suspects, apprehending criminals. Want your own suite? I think a cell is available."

"We want to talk to Sally instead of you," I said. Carrie Ann hadn't said boo. She stayed behind me, looking like a cornered animal. A guilty one.

"You don't have any say, Fischer. Come on Carrie Ann, let's go."

And he left me standing in front all by myself. My cousin turned back once with pleading eyes before they disappeared from view.

My plan had been to stick by Carrie Ann's side through the whole unpleasant episode. My new plan was to camp out with Ben right where I was.

That all changed when Sally Maylor came through the door into the building and stopped to chat.

"He's been running the show the whole time," she admitted when I asked. "Guys like that don't go down easy."

"Isn't that illegal?"

Sally gave me a crooked grin. "No," she said, like she wished it were. "Eventually the newspaper will figure it out and report that he's back. By then the police chief will have a spiel ready."

"Why does he have his clutches in Carrie Ann?"

"He has a potential witness who says he saw her in The Lost Mile right before Lauren Kerrigan and Hetty Cross were murdered."

That was not what I expected or wanted to hear. "But . . . but . . . who said that?"

"Can't say. Go home. We'll call you when she's released, if you want."

I called Hunter.

"It's been a week since Hetty and Lauren were killed," I said. "What's happening with Johnny Jay?"

"Johnny Jay didn't do it."

"All the Kerrigans believe he did."

Hunter let the silence grow and so did I.

"Johnny is questioning Carrie Ann right now," I finally said.

"I know. I'm sorry."

"Come down here and get her out. Or at least run interference for her."

"You're there? At the department?"

"Waiting for you."

"Carrie Ann's too close to me personally. I'm a lifelong friend and her AA sponsor. I consider it a conflict of interest to involve myself professionally at this point. The only right thing to do is distance myself from her while Johnny Jay does the questioning."

"Where are you?"

"On my way to see Norm Cross."

Call it intuition or premonition or whatever, but at that moment I knew exactly who the blabby witness was. Norm Cross had seen Carrie Ann in The Lost Mile.

Or so he said.

Thirty-three

Ben rode shotgun. We drove through Moraine and out the other side of town. I took Creamery Road, but didn't turn down Norm's road. I didn't want Hunter to know what I was up to.

Whatever words those two exchanged, I'd get from Norm after Hunter left, since my almost boyfriend wasn't exactly sharing content with me. In fact, he'd driven me into the shadows, literally, because that's where I found myself.

It was pitch dark when I parked in Country Delight's apple orchard, where I could watch the road without anyone watching me. Pretty soon I expected Hunter's SUV to pull out onto Creamery Road. Then I'd go in. Even though I was doing this strictly to help my cousin out of a really bad jam, I felt like a cross between Nancy Drew and V. I. Warshawsky. Not a bad feeling. Of course, *they* solved their cases. I wanted to follow in their footsteps.

So I waited.

Only Hunter didn't come back out onto the road. Had

I missed him already? It had taken me less than ten minutes to hightail it out of the police station and hide in the orchard, and Hunter hadn't been at Norm's yet when I talked to him on the phone.

If I really had missed him, then Norm hadn't been home when Hunter showed up and he'd left right away. What if I sat here all night thinking Hunter was with Norm when he wasn't?

What to do?

I could drive past Norm's and see if Hunter was there.

That's what I decided to do.

As I crept slowly toward Norm's, I kept my truck lights off to be on the safe side. I didn't want Hunter to spot me if he was outside. Which isn't what I should have been most concerned with.

Because the sound of sirens was coming my way. Sirens never were a good thing.

I pulled over and called Hunter.

"What's with the sirens?" I asked, really hoping they weren't cop sirens.

"Ambulance," Hunter said, which wasn't any better. "Norm Cross had a heart attack. At least, that's what I think happened."

"Is he okay?"

"He's alive, but barely."

"Do you want my help?" I said.

"No, it's late. I'll stop by your place as soon as I can."

So with that, I swung around and headed home, passing an ambulance and cop car on the way.

Norm Cross finally had one slab of bacon too many. I wondered if he'd make it and, if not, who would bury him, since he and Hetty hadn't had any kids. Surely they had family someplace?

I was about to turn onto my street, when I remembered something important.

What about Dinky? Was she okay? What would happen to her with Norm in the hospital or worse, dead?

I swung around in the road, doing a complete one-eighty, and headed back. Ben gave me a questioning look from the passenger's seat. "We have to make sure Dinky is all right," I told him, wondering why I was explaining myself to a dog.

The ambulance's strobes were still running but they'd killed the siren. No one was around the vehicle. I walked onto the porch and peered in. Lots of voices and motion inside. I waited.

Finally they brought an unconscious Norm out on a stretcher and loaded him into the back of the ambulance. Hunter came out last. He had Dinky in his arms.

I got the most grateful look as he handed over the baggage. "Found her hiding under the bed. Thanks for coming."

I nodded but really wanted to jump for joy that Hunter was appreciating me. Even if it was only because he wanted to pawn off Dinky on me.

"What happened?" I asked.

"I came to talk to him and found him on the floor."

"With his size and the junk he ate, he's lucky to still be alive."

Hunter gave my arm a squeeze. "Thanks again. You'll keep his dog for a few days?"

"Sure." We watched the ambulance pull away, lights flashing, sirens wailing.

"Why did you need to talk to Norm?" I asked, digging for info on the Carrie Ann witness. "Is he still under suspicion?"

I could tell Hunter was conflicted over how much information was too much. Finally, he said, "Norm saw someone in the woods behind his house the night Lauren and Hetty were killed."

"And he thought it was Carrie Ann," I said.

Hunter nodded. "He wasn't completely positive of the ID, but he was pretty sure the person was a woman with short, yellow hair."

"Lots of women have short, yellow hair," I said.

"Really? Who else around here?"

He had a point. Carrie Ann *did* have a certain unique flair.

"Why didn't Norm come forward before now?"

"He did. We just didn't act on his statement until now."

How could my cousin have gotten herself into such a mess? And more importantly, how was I going to get her out? "I'll go inside and get Dinky's food and toys," I said.

I knew exactly what to pack: food, chew toys, pink blankie, which was dirty again. How could it get that dirty that quickly? Norm's bedroom, where I found the doggy blanket, was a pigsty like the rest of the house. Junk was piled everywhere.

Dinky ran under the bed and wouldn't come out.

"Here, doggy, sweetie," I said, pitching my voice higher while remembering why this animal drove me crazy. On my knees, I could see her peering at me, but she was out of reach. So I had to move the bed away from the wall and attack from that side. After a little back and forth, I had her.

When I moved the bed back, I jostled a nightstand and heard things falling to the floor. Not that anyone would notice if I left them scattered where they fell, but I started picking up what I could and putting things back where they'd been. Most of what dropped turned out to be prescription meds. One was a bottle of medicine used for hypertension. Another's instructions said to take when needed for anxiety.

"It's late," Hunter said when I handed him the bottles of medication. "Why don't I follow you home and make sure you get inside safely, then I'll drop these at the hospital and check on Norm."

Which we did. And when he left I had custody of a

wire-coated miniature terror named Dinky and a more welcome houseguest, Ben.

Hunter also left me with a nagging suspicion about events from the past, something buried deep in my mind that was trying to surface.

Thirty-four

I woke the next morning to a wet, slurpy tongue rolling across my face. For about six seconds I thought I was
dreaming that Hunter was kissing me. Until I opened my
eyes to a hairy face and cold, wet snout.

Oh jeez, it was Dinky.

Ben, on the floor, had his head down and one eye on us.
He looked comfy.

I hadn't slept this well since the bodies had been discovered in The Lost Mile. I was sure last night's dreamland
was because of Ben's alert and guarding presence. How
could I have been afraid of dogs for so long? I'd really
missed out on the simple pleasure of an adoring compan-
ion who loved me no matter what I said or did. Uncondi-
tional. Through thick and thin.

I popped out of bed and started my daily routine, but not
before letting Ben and Dinky out the back door. I started
coffee, let them back in, showered, pulled on a yellow top
and jeans, and fed the dogs. After refereeing so that Dinky

didn't steal Ben's share, something I never expected Ben to allow, I made myself toast and spread it with honey butter.

Ali Schmidt called, and I told her what little I knew about Carrie Ann and then went on to relate what had happened to Norm, leaving out the whole bit about Norm thinking he'd seen Carrie Ann the night the women were murdered. Hunter had trusted me with inside information and I wasn't going to blow that trust.

"Carrie Ann didn't kill anybody," I said to Ali instead.

"She has a lot going against her," Ali said.

That really was true, but I wouldn't give up. And I told Ali that. "We have to sit down and talk," I said, "about the night Wayne Jay died."

"Why? Let the past alone, Story. Besides, I wasn't there that night. You know that."

But T. J. was, I wanted to say.

Then Ali said T. J. had a cancellation later today and she'd inked—not penciled—me in to take care of my cavity. Not only that, she didn't leave me the store as an excuse to dodge that novocaine-injected experience. She'd run over, she went on to say, and cover for me once I was snug in the dental chair.

Thank you very much, Ali, I thought, hanging up.

I hadn't heard from Sally or anybody else from the police department advising me of Carrie Ann's release, so I had to assume she was still at the station.

Hunter knocked on my door. He was dressed for field-work in jeans, Harley Davidson boots, and a light windbreaker issued by the sheriff's department.

He gave me one of the sweetest kisses ever, one I wanted to curl up with until life returned to normal. Normal meaning the case closed, Johnny off my back, and a killer put behind bars.

"I'm picking up Ben," he said. "We have a training session this morning."

My heart sank into my stomach. "But, but . . . I need him."

"Sorry, I can't leave Ben with you today. Why don't you plan on staying in public places? And no more agitating people who have anger management issues. Okay?"

"Okay," I said, meeker than usual.

"I'll escort you to the store," he said, putting Ben in the passenger seat of his SUV to wait. Dinky was perfectly happy to ride in my arms.

"What's the story with Carrie Ann?" I asked.

"She's being held. That's all I know. Can we talk about something else?"

"I'm not supposed to be concerned about my cousin?"

"I checked on her this morning. She's okay." Hunter grabbed my free hand and encased it in his own strong one. "Norm is still critical."

"I hope he makes it."

"Me, too."

"It'll be his word against hers, you know."

"This whole thing will be over soon," Hunter assured me.

We walked in silence the rest of the way. When I put Dinky down, safely on her leash for one last effort to do her business outside instead of in, Hunter gently put me up along the building and pressed into me.

"I miss you," he said. "Let's get away tonight, have a nice dinner at my place. I'll cook."

"That sounds wonderful."

He put his fingers to my lips. "And no shop talk. Just you and me. Us."

"I like that."

"It's starting to rain."

"You better hurry back."

By the time Hunter turned and walked away I had forgotten how annoyed I was with him. My mood had improved considerably. All he had to do was throw me a bone and I was all his. I watched him go, thinking he was strong and competent and he'd find the real killer soon. But at this point, whether he liked it or not, I was on the case, too. Carrie Ann needed me.

Rain broke from the sky as I scooted under the store's awning and started my day. I had my own plans to help Carrie Ann. Ideas had come to me before I had gotten out of bed.

First, I didn't know anything about investigating a crime or even following Carrie Ann's trail on the crucial night she couldn't remember. I hadn't been trained, so I was learning as I went along. Second, I realized the only way to make headway was to be thorough, asking the right questions and following up on the replies, which I hadn't been very good at.

Not to mention I was stuck at the store, a serious handicap.

Rain came down in buckets as the store's lights went on. I'd be working alone until Holly showed up, which wouldn't be anytime soon. I missed Carrie Ann already.

"Get over here as fast as you can," I announced to Holly over the phone. "They took Carrie Ann in for questioning and it looks like they kept her. I'm alone at the store."

"I'll be right there," my sister said. Amazing. A little attitude worked.

Or maybe not. Business was light for the next hour and a half, but Holly was still a no-show. Stu came in for his daily paper and we traded what we knew about Carrie Ann, which was next to nothing. I wondered when the man slept, since he closed his bar late and opened for lunch by eleven and was always the first one there in the mornings.

Owning your own business was a lot more work than people thought, unless they happened to end up in the same situation. They had to experience it to appreciate the time, money, and dedication it takes to become successful.

Aurora came in, dressed in tie-dye and hemp. She greeted me and wandered off to the natural organic section of the store. When she came back, our conversation involved the latest development concerning Carrie Ann. Aurora said again, "It's fate."

"Do you have a crystal ball?" I asked. "Because if you do, I'd like to look into it."

Aurora smiled mysteriously, reminding me of the Mona Lisa. "Don't I wish! Or maybe that would be a big mistake. Because then I'd know the outcome and still not be able to stop it. That is, if I didn't like what the future held."

I thought she might be right.

"Everything that happens is a reaction," she said, happy to have someone paying attention.

"The past determines the present and future," I said. "I remember you saying that when Lauren was killed."

"That's right. If you want to understand current events, study what happened before. But I warn you, nothing you do will change the outcome."

With that ill boding comment, Aurora walked out into the rain with her small bag of groceries, slowly, like she didn't mind getting wet. Or maybe she just didn't notice.

The past kept coming up.

All right, I decided, let's go there.

I'd assumed, just like everybody else, that Lauren had killed Wayne Jay. If the medical examiner was right and someone else had been driving instead, who could it have been? Anybody, that's who.

But to let an innocent young woman spend all those years in prison for a crime she didn't commit? That was wrong on so many levels. Evil.

I kept up small talk with the handful of customers who came through. Then Holly arrived. Finally. And I brought her up to speed about Carrie Ann's problems and Norm's heart attack.

"Now what?" Holly asked.

"I'm going to dissect every minute of that night sixteen years ago. How hard can it be?" What I really wondered was if Holly would draw the same conclusion as I was toss-ing around in my head.

"I can't remember much," I told her. "The six of us—me and Hunter, Carrie Ann and Gunnar, T. J. and Lauren—walked into The Lost Mile together. Then Lauren got mad at T. J. and left before the rest of us. That's all."

"Think. Then what happened?"

"Nothing. We all watched her go, then we split up. T. J. went to catch up with her, but that was a while later, and he didn't find her. The rest of us walked out later, still watch-ing for Lantern Man, who never did show up. End of story."

I gulped before continuing. "Well, not exactly the end of the story. The medical examiner told me he thought some-one else might have been driving the car that night. I didn't really believe him. He'd been drinking and it seemed far-fetched. But I haven't been able to stop thinking, what if?"

"For cripes sakes, as Mom would say," Holly said with gathering excitement, since she was a sharp cookie. "And T. J. followed her!"

"I didn't remember about that until just a little while ago. It wasn't important at the time, since nobody ever con-sidered that anybody other than Lauren had been driving."

"And how do you know T. J. *didn't* find her?"

I paused. "I think he told me."

"When?"

"Back then, but later."

"Oh my gosh!" Holly and I stared at each other. We'd drawn the same conclusion. The pieces were beginning to fall into place. And they had nothing to do with Johnny Jay.

Thirty-five

Rain was coming down so hard I couldn't see out the windows, but I heard it pounding on the awning out front. We didn't have a single customer in the store at the moment.

"Okay," I said. "Let's pretend he catches up with Lauren and drives her home. He accidently strikes Wayne Jay with the car. But Wayne isn't dead, and he gets a good look at T. J., who realizes he's driving drunk and in big trouble. T. J. always had a lot of direction. He knew he wanted to go into dentistry from the time he could talk."

"And a charge of manslaughter would mess up his plans," Holly said, getting worked up and into the moment. "For COL! (*Crying Out Loud!*) It's possible! After that, he ran over Wayne again to finish him off, hit the tree, and left Lauren to take the rap for him, since at that point she was probably passed out. But why kill her now?"

My turn. "When he found out Lauren was coming back to town, he thought she might have remembered what really happened. Maybe she was coming back to confront him with the truth. So he killed her."

"But how did he find out she was back?" Holly wanted to know.

The answer to Holly's question came to me instantly. "I know the answer to that! Last time I was in the dental chair T. J. told me people tell him all kinds of personal information. Because he's a doctor they treat him like their personal therapists or clergyman."

Right then, I heard a voice directly behind me shout out, "You've nailed it!"

Holly squealed. I did, too.

There stood Patti, wearing a green rain poncho and looking like something that crawled out of the Blue Lagoon, dripping water everywhere.

"Will you please stop sneaking up on people," I said, relieved it was only creepy, crawly Patti. If she kept this up we'd have to rename her C. C. Patti instead of P. P. Patti.

"I heard everything," she said, "and I think we finally figured it out."

"*We* figured it out?" Holly said. "You weren't even here."

Patti ignored her. "We need more evidence. And a motive. If Lauren was dying, why would he kill her?"

"Maybe he didn't know she was dying?" I offered, since Patti must have missed part of my conversation with my sister. "Or thought she knew the truth? Right now, all we have are maybes and ifs."

Patti saw me pick up my phone and start punching in numbers. "What are you doing?"

"Canceling my dental appointment," I said.

Patti lunged and grabbed the phone out of my hands. "Hold on. You have an appointment?"

"Today. Give me my phone back."

"You're really seeing him?" Patti asked me.

I shook my head. "Not anymore. I'm canceling the appointment right now."

"No, wait." Patti peeled off the poncho and I could see electronics dangling from her neck, tied together into a plastic bag to keep them safe from the rain. Some were clipped to her belt, too. "This is the chance we've been waiting for."

I groaned. "This is the chance *you've* been waiting for. *Your* big scoop. You'd really sacrifice me for a job?"

"I'll be close by. Nothing's going to happen to you."

"We should call the police," Holly said. "Let them handle it."

I thought about that. "Johnny Jay is unofficially still running the police department. He'd rather string me up from a lightpost than listen to common sense."

"I'll talk to him," Holly said.

"He doesn't like you, either," Patti informed her. "Or me, now that I think about it. We'll have to handle this ourselves." Her eyes literally gleamed in anticipation. "This is my big chance. The big story that will get me a slot on the newspaper. I'll be a real reporter."

"I'm calling Hunter," I said.

Patti sneered. "Sure, have your boyfriend fix it for you."

Ignoring Patti, I punched Hunter's number into my cell phone and was rerouted to his voice mail. I left him a message to call me ASAP.

"He's doing K-9 training today," I said to Holly and Patti. "He must not have his cell phone with him. Or he turned it off." I'd watched him train before and vaguely remembered him removing everything from his pockets. When he was training dogs to attack, he wouldn't want to break anything. Just my luck.

Patti leaned in, conspiratorial, serious, professional. "We can do this. The three of us. We'll be your backup, Story."

"Not me," Holly croaked. "I have to watch the store."

Suddenly my sister was a responsible business owner. How nice.

"I haven't agreed to any of this," I reminded Patti.

"You'll be on the inside, in the dentist's chair, asking some tough questions and letting him know you're onto him," Patti said. "I'll be on the outside, close by, I'll be watching every move. We'll have video, audio, you name it, we'll have it all. Trust me."

"The last time I trusted you," I reminded her, "you ran away and left me in Norm's house to face the music alone."

Patti rolled her eyes impatiently. "But I saved you in the end when it counted, didn't I?" Patti didn't really expect an answer. I could tell she was thinking hard, working over the details.

I tried calling Hunter again. No answer.

Then I glanced at the time, which was running out. Whether I wanted to or not, I was in deep. And torn over what to do. My dental appointment really was the perfect opportunity to confront T. J. and possibly get the truth. And I *did* have backup support even if it was only Patti and my sister. What to do?

Patti dug through her arsenal and came up with a small electronic device. "We have to wire you. Well, it isn't a wire in the sense that I'll be able to listen in. It's a digital voice recorder," she explained. "Next best thing. Where's the duct tape?"

"Aisle two," my sister told her, going to get it herself.

"We'll tape it between your boobs," Patti said, studying my chest. "That should work. It's voice activated so you don't have to be concerned with turning it on and off. We'll have a permanent record of the conversation."

"So if I'm in trouble, who's going to help me again?"

"Your job is to make T. J. confess," Patti said. "He'll think he has you trapped so he'll open up and spill the whole story. If I see him make an aggressive move, I'll break down the door. "

"This is a really bad idea," I mentioned.

But then I thought of Carrie Ann, stuck in a jail cell

without an alibi, thinking she might have actually killed people during a blackout. Unlike Lauren, my cousin wasn't going to serve time for a crime she didn't commit. If this worked, she'd be free by the end of the day.

"It's bulgy," Holly said, checking out my wired-for-sound bra. "Won't he notice?"

"It'll work," Patti said. "Wish I could send you with a can of wasp spray but that would be a dead giveaway. Where's your pepper spray?"

"In my pocket."

"Now remember," Patti went on, "the first thing you talk about is him driving the car that night. Watch his reaction."

I nodded.

"And don't let him work on you, no matter what."

I gulped.

"Good. Let's go."

"One more thing," I said before I voluntarily walked the plank. "Ali is going to get me in the chair, then she's going to come over and help out here until I get back. Holly, don't breathe a word to her."

"'K," Holly said. "I can be cool."

My cool sister was biting her nails. She only did that when she was under extreme stress. It couldn't be a good sign.

Thirty-six

Patti left me alone at the door leading into the lion's den and went off to find the perfect place in back of the building to set up for surveillance. I took a deep breath and walked through the door.

Ali popped into the reception area, which was empty except for the two of us. "Hey," she said, looking surprised to see me. "You actually showed up! Good. I'm working on something in back. Have a seat."

So I plopped down in a chair and thought about what I would say to T. J. after I hit him with the driving question. Nothing much came to mind. But I'm a professional blurter. Something would come out of my mouth.

I had a few loose ends to wrap up in my mind, something not quite right regarding Carrie Ann and her lost-memory trail, so I used my waiting time wisely.

"Hey, Stu," I said into my cell phone, keeping my voice extra low. "When Carrie Ann was in the bar the afternoon

Lauren died, I forgot to ask you something. Was she with anyone?"

Stu didn't know for sure. He hadn't been paying attention. "Was T. J. there?"

He didn't think so, but talking about my dentist must have triggered a memory because he said he thought Ali had been sitting with Carrie Ann. Yes, now he remembered.

That sent a cold chill down my spine. I glanced around. Ali wasn't in sight, but I could hear her humming in the back.

"Did they leave together?"

He didn't know.

"Are you absolutely sure T. J. wasn't in the bar?"

Stu was almost sure, but not totally positive.

"One more thing," I said. "If someone has only one or two alcoholic drinks but still has a blackout, how could that have happened?"

"Drugs," Stu said. "They'd have to mix the alcohol with some kind of drug."

I hung up. And thought about all the different kinds of drugs in a dentist's office. I bet T. J. had lots and he knew how to use them. He could have spiked Carrie Ann's drink. That would explain her complete blackout.

What if he gave Carrie Ann drugs so he could set her up? Maybe he dumped her in The Lost Mile and left her unconscious while he met and killed Lauren and Hetty. That would explain Norm Cross's eye-witness report.

What if T. J. tried to give me something bad, too, like Patti had suggested?

Not good.

Ali had been in the bar with Carrie Ann. She would know all about drugs and how to use them, too. She'd worked here for years.

Were we after the wrong Schmidt?

Just then Ali came back into the reception area and led me into T. J.'s torture chamber. I sat down in the dental chair.

"Where's T. J.?" I asked, hoping I didn't sound as tense as I felt.

"He's finishing up with a patient in the other room." Ali attached a plastic bib around my neck. "I'll be right back with the tray, get things set, then head for the store."

I saw Patti go right past the window. I'm in this one, I wanted to yell to her, thinking she'd missed me. But a few seconds later, her face reappeared and she gave me a thumbs-up before ducking down. My cell phone, tucked in my lap for emotional support, was coated in a layer of palm sweat.

What should I say when T. J. came in? Should I just come right out and accuse him? Let him think I figured out what had really happened that night? Bluff? But what about Ali?

I wasn't sure of much, but I was absolutely positive my cavity would have to wait, because no way was either of them actually touching me until this was all worked out.

Ali came back in carrying a tray filled with instruments and set it down. "Let's make you more comfortable," she said, pushing a button that lowered me into a more relaxed position. Only I wasn't relaxed.

When she bent over to arrange T. J.'s dental equipment, I saw a heart-shaped locket around her neck, tucked inside her collar.

I groaned inwardly as my mind started working overtime.

The locket! I'd forgotten all about it after Gunnar had come into the bar with Carrie Ann's bad news. I'd left it behind, and Ali had taken it.

Right then I knew for sure. I'd made the wrong assumption. The locket hadn't belonged to Lauren. It was Ali's. She'd been the one driving Lauren's car.

"T. J. will be right in," Ali said before she left the room and closed the door softly behind her.

What was I supposed to say to T. J. now? Especially if

Ali had been the one driving the car that night? But I didn't have proof.

I had to get out of here and talk to Patti about this new development.

Patti popped up in the window again. I gave her a time-out sign with my hands. "Mission aborted," I mouthed slowly.

Then I heard Johnny Jay's voice from the front reception room. "Got a call," I heard him say. "Someone's lurking around outside the building."

"Hi, Chief," Ali said. "I didn't know you were back."

"Made it official a few hours ago. Mind if I check around out back?"

"Not at all," Ali's voice said.

Oh no! Some do-gooder thought Patti was trouble. Which she was, but mainly only to me.

I tried punching a warning into my cell phone, but I was flustered and ended up fumbling with the keys. I saw Johnny Jay's head as he ran past the window.

I considered bolting, since my backup had been exposed. In my panic, that seemed like the most reasonable course of action. Run like crazy. But if I wanted to be smart, I'd stay calm, not let on that anything was wrong.

There went Ali's head past the window, going in the same direction as Patti and Johnny Jay. I heard voices.

"What happened?" I asked Ali when she came back into the room.

"The Chief chased after somebody, but whoever it was got away. He's gone after them."

I yanked off the plastic bib. "I have an emergency back at the store," I said. "I'll have to reschedule."

"Relax," Ali said. "I'll handle whatever is going on at the store." She picked up a mask.

"What's that?"

"You'll feel better with a little nitrous oxide. This will be like a three-martini filling."

"Laughing gas?"

"Try it," Ali said, drawing the mask and tube down toward my face. "You'll like it."

"I have to go."

Then I noticed Ali's eyes didn't look right. They were kind of crazy and wild. And she kept coming at me. "You figured it out," she said. "I worried that you might after you showed up with the locket."

"It belongs to you?"

"So does T. J."

"You killed Lauren," I said, blocking Ali's effort to place the mask, hoping the concealed recorder was working properly, since I was out on the proverbial limb without a safety net. "You killed all of them. Wayne Jay and Hetty Cross and Lauren Kerrigan."

Ali tried to clamp the mask down on my face. She was strong and in a better position than I was. Fighting someone off from a prone position is a lot harder than it looks.

My cell phone went flying as we arm-wrestled over whether or not I would take the laughing gas.

"T. J.!" I yelled, hoping they weren't in it together. I was dead if they were.

"He's not here," Ali said, her voice ragged as we struggled. "It's just you and me. Like I wanted it." The woman was lying on me, pinning me like my sister sometimes did, her forearm across my throat, cutting off my airway while she shoved the mask down at me.

"Take it," she demanded.

I gave up fighting the mask and jabbed my index and middle finger into her mouth, aiming just under her tongue. By the gagging sound coming from her, I'd connected in the right spot. I also inhaled.

And felt a bit disoriented. So I grabbed her throat with both hands and squeezed.

That next inhale was a doozy.

I relaxed, dropping my hands and leaning back. "That's right," Ali said from far away. "Relax. Let it work."

My legs felt like concrete. Ali was still talking. "It was all a big accident," she said. "I was waiting for T. J. at the entrance to The Lost Mile. But Lauren came out and got into that old beater she always drove. Remember that one? It actually had bench seats."

Another inhale. Nice. I wanted to laugh.

"And she passed out in the driver's seat. All I wanted was to take her someplace and sober her up so we could have a talk. I never saw Wayne Jay until I hit him. But he saw me. I had to do what I did. You understand, don't you? No one would blame me."

Before the next inhale, which I was really trying to avoid in a helpless, feeble sort of way, I managed to get my hand on my trusty pepper spray. But it took all my willpower to blast Ali in the face. I started spraying. The mask fell away. Ali started making moaning, pained noises.

Through a nice, mellow haze, I rose on heavy legs and blasted her again.

My cell phone rang from the floor. I picked it up.

"Hi," I said, feeling like a million bucks.

"Are you okay?" Holly said.

"Just jiffy," I answered.

"Patti called and said she'd been compromised, whatever that means. What's that noise in the background?"

"My pal Ali." The nice place I'd been visiting began drifting slowly away.

"You sound weird. I got through to Hunter. He should be there soon."

"Okey-dokey," I said, not believing I'd actually said that. "No hurry."

Patti burst through the door and took in the situation.

"Ali?" she said.

"She's the murderer." I had to resist laughing.

Patti picked up the mask and gave me a look.

"She was trying to force me to take laughing gas."

"Looks like she succeeded," Patti said.

She grabbed the mask from me and shoved it on Ali's face. "We'll get the whole confession right now."

"Stop that," I said, with as much conviction as I could muster while still under the influence of the gas I'd inhaled. Caring was really, really hard.

Then there he was. My man, looking cute and sexy and really official.

I'm pretty sure the gas had something to do with what happened next, because Ali spewed out all the truth and nothing but the truth. Patti was right—we got the whole confession. That stuff was like truth serum. Here's what Ali told us:

- She found out Lauren was coming to town when she overheard one of the younger Kerrigans talking on his cell phone in the dental waiting room.

- Based on comments she'd overheard, Ali decided Lauren was coming back to expose her.

- So she started making plans, turned her attention to Carrie Ann, who was battling the bottle. She also bought a yellow wig that looked like Carrie Ann's hair.

- Then she called up Lauren, pretending she was Carrie Ann and had important information concerning the night Wayne Jay died.

- They planned to meet in The Lost Mile.

- Ali knew about Rita's gun because she'd been at the bar one night when Terry was talking about it. Guys and their guns! She borrowed it while Rita and Lauren were at the candle-making class, right after she saw Lauren in The Wild Clover.

- Lauren didn't stand a chance.

• And Hetty Cross was in the wrong place at the wrong time.

"She said she was coming back to make things right," Ali said in a whiny voice as Hunter looked on in disbelief. Apparently, he wasn't used to full confessions. And Patti and I hadn't clued him in about the gas. "That could only mean she remembered that I was driving that night."

"Or it could have meant she was coming back to make amends for what she thought she'd done," I said. "How could you kill a dying woman?"

"I didn't know about the cancer." Ali had a mellow look on her face from the gas. "Not that it would have mattered."

"Did you try to run me down?" I asked her, starting to feel clearheaded again.

Ali didn't even hesitate before she answered. "I did. Since everybody was focusing on Johnny Jay, why not implicate him even more."

"And what about Carrie Ann? What did you do to her?"

"I had slipped roofies in her beer and dumped her at her house. But not before giving her a makeover complete with a dirty face and leaves in her bed. Then I went to The Lost Mile wearing the wig."

"Insane," Patti said, scribbling in a notepad.

Right then, Johnny Jay burst in like he was saving the day. After a bunch of blustering and a few verbal shots at me, he hauled off the real killer.

Patti took off to work on her story.

Hunter and I ended up on the street outside the dental office. He still had that same expression of disbelief on his face.

"T. J. said Ali was with her sister," I said. "Girls' night out, he told us at the bar."

"According to her sister, she was."

"Ah, the bond between sisters." I knew exactly how strong they could be.

"I'm sure she'll be reversing her statement soon."

"She couldn't have known the whole story."

Hunter wrapped an arm around my shoulder as we walked down the street. "I owe you a dinner," he said. "You up for a steak?"

"You bet," I said, snuggling in.

Thirty-seven

"'Sup? (*What's Up?*)" Holly said, the next morning.

"What are you doing here so early?" I'd been rearranging the honey display at the front of the store when she arrived. Carrie Ann was checking out customers and preening in a small hand mirror she kept in her pocket, getting ready for the hot date she'd picked up while hanging around in jail.

"Not one of the inmates either," she informed me, spiking her short yellow hair.

"Who?" Patti wanted to know.

"None of your business," Carrie Ann said. "This one I'm keeping under wraps."

"Around here?" I said. "Fat chance. Besides, we all know it's Gunnar."

Carrie Ann smiled, but more to herself than to us. Maybe being in jail had brought them back together. I hoped so. They were meant for each other.

Stanley Peck came in and stayed to chat, talking bees and listening to gossip.

Milly arrived. "Here's a rough draft of the newsletter," she said. "Let me know if you find any typos. And you're going to see it anyway, so I want to tell you I did *not* figure out how to put honey in the morel mushroom recipe. Some things just don't go together."

"I have a few loose ends to wrap up," Patti said. "Before Joel and I turn in our story."

"Isn't it a bit late?" Holly said, since we all knew how quickly today's news became yesterday's news.

"Nope, this is a *weekly* newspaper," Patti reminded her, then looked down at a notebook. "I still can't believe what that crazy woman did. What a nutcase."

"I thought T. J. and Ali had tiffs all the time but always got back together?" Stanley Peck pointed out.

"That time was different," I said, referring to some of the juicy tidbits I'd heard from customers. "T. J. really liked Lauren and told Ali that. You know how passionate an eighteen-year-old can be."

Patti, still reading from her notes, said, "So she ran over Wayne Jay a second time to protect her identity and to frame Lauren. But I wonder why she picked Carrie Ann to be the murder suspect this time around."

"I don't understand that at all," Carrie Ann said. "I never did anything to her."

Patti piped up, "Ali must have thought you were an easy target."

"I am not."

"Well it worked, didn't it?" Patti pointed out. "But Johnny Jay was doing such a good job of convincing everybody he was the killer, Ali put her original plan on hold and even helped out in her own little way."

"By trying to run me down," I added. "And make it look like Johnny did it. I feel sorry for T. J. This can't be easy on him."

"How's Norm Cross doing?" Stanley asked.

"He'll be back home in a day or two."

Just then I saw Grams's car pull up outside. Mom got out of the passenger side.

"I'll be in back," I said to Holly. "Say I'm on vacation."

"You have to face the music eventually," my sister said.

But I wasn't hanging around to debate the subject with her. I flew into the back storage room and scooped up Dinky.

I made it out the back door and down the block before a squad car pulled over. Johnny Jay stepped out. "Fischer, you owe me a public apology," he said.

I kept walking, picking up speed, feeling trapped. My mother was hunting me. Johnny Jay was stalking me on the streets.

And . . .

There was Lori Spandle standing in front of my house, with both hands on her hips.

"I'm going to get some kind of official order," she said, "to make you clean up this place and remove those bees. And just so you know, your ex-husband is going to move back in if I can't sell this place by the end of the month."

Over my dead body, I could have said, but Lori might try to oblige me. That man wasn't welcome in my hometown. Ever. I'd burn the place down first. That idea had possibilities.

Right when I thought things couldn't get any worse, Hunter showed up and proved they wouldn't. I jumped in his SUV with Dinky in my arms and gave Ben a warm hello. Then I gave Hunter a hot hello and we blew out of town.

The Wild Clover
❧ May Newsletter ❧

Notes from the beeyard:

- The nectar flow has begun! Honeybees love dandelions.

- Watch those pesticides. They hurt good insects, too.

- If you spot a swarm of bees, call Queen Bee Honey. Story and Holly (grin) will remove them for you.

Here are a few simple breakfast honey concoctions:

- Honey cinnamon toast—mix together butter, honey, and cinnamon and spread over hot toast.

- Drizzle honey over a warm piece of coffee cake.

- Cut a grapefruit in half, cut around the pulp, top with honey, and place under the broiler until the honey caramelizes.

Chocolate Honey Cake

Nothing goes together better than chocolate and honey!

1½ cups flour
¼ cup unsweetened cocoa powder
1 teaspoon baking powder

½ teaspoon baking soda
½ teaspoon cinnamon
½ teaspoon ground ginger
1 egg
1 stick unsalted butter, softened
1 cup honey
½ cup buttermilk

Sift together the dry ingredients. In a separate bowl, beat egg, butter, honey, and buttermilk until smooth. Then add in the dry ingredients and mix well. Place in buttered pan and bake at 350 degrees for 30–35 minutes or until a toothpick comes out clean.

Honey Trail Mix Cookies

Take these hiking with you.

3 cups rolled oats
1 cup flour
1 teaspoon baking powder
1 teaspoon baking soda
¼ teaspoon salt
½ teaspoon cinnamon
½ teaspoon nutmeg
½ cup shortening
½ cup butter
⅓ cup honey
2 eggs
¼ cup toasted pecans
¼ cup toasted coconut
½ cup raisins

Mix together the dry ingredients and set aside. Cream together the shortening, butter, and honey. Add in the eggs, followed by the dry ingredients. Finally, mix in the pecans, coconut, and raisins. Bake on ungreased cookie sheets in a 375-degree oven for 8 minutes.

Notes from the garden:

- Try a tea garden this year. Plant chamomile, peppermint, lavender, lemon balm. Make your own tea and serve it with a spoonful of honey.

- Composting is fun and easy. Mix vegetable waste with chopped leaves or straw for the best fertilizer available.

Rhubarb Meringue Torte

Rhubarb is plentiful in Wisconsin during the month of May. Gather an armful and make the best rhubarb torte ever.

CRUST
2 cups flour
2 tablespoons sugar
¼ teaspoon salt
1 cup butter

FILLING
4 cups chopped rhubarb

CUSTARD
4 egg yolks
¾ cup milk
1 cup honey
2 tablespoons flour

MERINGUE
4 egg whites
1 cup sugar

Mix together the ingredients for the crust and press into bottom of 13×9 pan. Bake 20 minutes at 350 degrees. Remove from the oven and add rhubarb. Whisk together the custard ingredients and cook over medium heat until bubbly. Pour over top of the rhubarb. Bake for another 20 minutes and remove from oven. Beat whites on high, adding sugar 1 tablespoon at a time. Layer over top of the torte and bake for final 10 minutes.

Morel Mushroom Sauce

6 tablespoons melted butter
¾ cup green onions, minced
2 tablespoons garlic, minced
7–10 morels
1 teaspoon thyme
1 cup red wine
⅔ cup dry sherry
3 ½ cups beef broth (or chicken broth if serving with chicken)
½ pint heavy cream

Caramelize the green onions and garlic in the melted butter. Cook until golden brown (be careful not to burn) then add in the mushrooms, thyme, and red wine. Simmer until the mixture reduces by half. Then add in the broth and reduce again by half. Cool, puree, and add in the cream.

Serve with steak or chicken.

Common Bee-friendly Flowers

Spring

- Dandelion
- White clover
- Lilac
- Lavender
- California poppy
- Scented geranium
- Verbena

Summer

- Cosmos
- Coreopsis
- Purple coneflower
- Sunflower
- Russian sage

- Black-eyed Susan
- Pincushion flower

From the Garden

- Mint
- Pumpkin
- Squash
- Zucchini
- Oregano
- Rosemary
- Thyme

About the Author

Hannah Reed lives on a high ridge in southern Wisconsin in a community much like the one she writes about. She is busy writing the next book in the Queen Bee mystery series. Visit Hannah and explore Story's world at www.hannahreedbooks.com.

penguin.com

"Why are you even dealing with Johnny? He's a jerk, he's too emotionally involved, and if he isn't officially part of the investigation, why not blow him off?"

"It's a mess, that's why. Hetty was killed on county land, but Lauren's body was found on town property. We're forced to collaborate with the town official, and unfortunately that's Jay."

"Oh isn't *that* wonderful news."

I gave the man a well-deserved, parting hug for springing me from the town jail and headed into the store . . .

. . . only to find one of the twins bagging groceries and my mother behind the cash register. She had been trying to insinuate herself into my business, both my personal *and* my professional life, ever since I'd moved back to Moraine. Just let me turn my back for one minute, one time, and there she was, acting like she owned the place. Give that woman a foot in the door and she seizes control of the whole building. And as everyone knows, there can be only one queen bee.

The Wild Clover was my hive.

We stared at each other. "Hi," I said. My voice sounded weak.

"You weren't minding the store," she said, reading my thoughts, knowing perfectly well she wasn't welcome to intrude like this, but doing it anyway. None of the Fischer women could be called passive bystanders in the game of life. And my mother was a master player.

"Where on earth were you?" she asked. "I can understand taking a few hours, but . . ." Mom checked her watch.

"I'm here now," I said, before she could dive into a lecture about my poor business practices. "Thanks for helping. I'll be right back to take over."

I scurried for the back of the store.

Holly turned from straightening a shelf, saw me, and grinned. "FTF (*Face To Face*)," she said, too low for Mom

or any of the customers to hear. "I thought we'd be having all our future conversations through those jail phones.
Stanley was pretty upset about Johnny Jay arresting you."

"I'm not arrested anymore. What's Mom doing here?"

"Grams and Mom stopped in after church and decided
we needed major help, since you weren't around and business increased even more after they found Lauren's body.
I tried to stop them, I really did, but NFW (*No Freaking
Way*) were they leaving. It's kind of a miracle they didn't
hear about your latest brush with justice at church this
morning."

"Where's Grams now?" If Grams was in the vicinity,
she could pack up Mom and put me back behind the cash
register of my own store.

"She went home to whip up casseroles. One for us later,
one for Rita Kerrigan and another for Norm Cross."

In all the drama, I'd forgotten about Hetty's husband,
Norm, and how he must be coping with all this. I really
hoped the casserole was low-fat, because every time Norm
came into the store, he bought lots of bacon and sausages
and anything else that made major contributions to clogged
arteries. Real butter, whole milk, ice cream, beef liver.
And he weighed a ton.

If we had taken bets on which one would depart this
world first, my money would have ridden on Norm. But
then I hadn't figured tragic endings into the equation.

Speaking of bets. That reminded me of my cousin and
the bet we'd had that all of the seats at my candle-making
class would be filled.

"Where's Carrie Ann?" I asked, already feeling several
inches shorter, a condition that presented itself whenever I
had to deal with my mother on her terms. I felt like a visitor
in my own store. "Didn't she show up?"

"She's in the storage room, having a big talk with Gunnar."

"Gunnar's in the back with Carrie Ann?"

"No, they're on the phone."

"What are they talking about?"

Holly shrugged. "Probably the same old. Their kids and Carrie Ann's visitation rights."

"Who taught Mom how to use the cash register?" The golden rule popped into my head. Whoever watched over the money controlled the place.

"Really, Story," Holly said, "you don't have to be a brain surgeon to scan groceries these days. It's all computerized. And she's a fast learner."

"Can you get her out of here?"

"Maybe." Holly had a smug look on her face like she was at least one step ahead of me, maybe more. "But only if you never ask me to help with your bees ever again." She grinned slyly.

"Great. Cut me off at the knees when I'm already down. When I'm crawling to you for help."

"Promise."

"Fine. You win." I slammed into the storage room, before Holly could see the lie in my eyes.

Carrie Ann was draped in my office chair. She sat up straight when she saw me. "Gotta go," she said into the phone and hung up. Her eyes were red and swollen. She stood, then promptly fell into my open arms. I could smell fresh booze breath. "When they found Lauren's body," she said, backing away, wiping her eyes, "it hit me harder than I thought it would."

I shrugged and shook my head in a sad way. "I don't even know what to say to make you feel better. Except that drinking isn't the answer."

"How did you know?"

"Buy some breath mints. That will cover it up."

"Don't tell anybody. Please. I'm not going back down that horrible road."

"Everybody has relapses," I said, not really sure that was true. "I'll tell you what? You owe me since I won our bet, so you can pay me back by calling your sponsor."

Who happened to be my sort of boyfriend Hunter, who had a past of his own, but had straightened out and hadn't touched a drop for years and years.

"Thanks. You're sweet for understanding. I'll call him after work." Carrie Ann broke her grasp on me. "I don't know what got into me. Not that I wished her dead or anything, but I never liked Lauren Kerrigan from the very beginning." She wiped her eyes again.

That was a real understatement. Lauren and Carrie Ann had always sniped at each other. They didn't have complementary personalities and it didn't help that Lauren was always flirting with Gunnar even when she was with T. J.

"Gunnar was looking for you last night," I said.

"I know. He told me."

I didn't ask where she'd been, figuring it wasn't any of my business, and she didn't volunteer any more information.

By the time Carrie Ann and I returned to the front of the store, more customers had gathered and I saw Stanley in the middle of the group. He gave me an apologetic, helpless shrug, and by the time I realized why, it was too late to duck.

But in a place like Moraine, it was bound to happen sooner rather than later.

My mother, scowling when she turned to me, said, "Arrested? You were arrested? Oh dear God!"